Merry Christmas 1998 Pa!

AMERICA
The Search and the Secret

Illustrations
by
JIM MARSH

AMERICA
The Search and the Secret

A Novel by
James N. Sites

The Jesse Stuart Foundation
Ashland, Kentucky
1998

AMERICA: The Search and the Secret

Copyright © 1998 by James N. Sites

FIRST EDITION

All rights reserved. No part of this book may be reproduced or utilized in any form or by any means, electronic or mechanical, including photocopying, recording, or by an information storage or retrieval system, without permission in writing from the Publisher.

Library of Congress Cataloging-in-Publication Data

Sites, James N., 1924–
    America : the search and the secret / James N. Sites.
      p.   cm.
    ISBN 0-945084-71-4
    1. Depressions--Appalachian Region--Fiction. 2. Depressions--Ohio--Fiction.   I. Title.
PS3569.I847A8   1998
813' .54--dc21   98-19323
                                                                                     CIP

Book Design by
JIM MARSH and BRETT NANCE

Published By:
The Jesse Stuart Foundation
P.O. Box 391 Ashland, KY 41114
(606) 329-5232 or 5233

Dedication

This book is dedicated to Philip and Teresa and Walter and Erika and every other boy and girl growing up in this wildly challenging era of unprecedented change…so that you, too, might know a world that was. May it's values continue to shape you and your future!

Contents

Foreword

Chapter 1	*The Great Flood*	11
Chapter 2	*A Switch to Learning*	31
Chapter 3	*Down by the Riverside*	49
Chapter 4	*The Longest Winter*	63
Chapter 5	*Tomato Patch Perspectives*	81
Chapter 6	*Snake in the Bush*	103
Chapter 7	*Be Prepared!*	117
Chapter 8	*The Hills of Home*	135
Chapter 9	*Crime and Punishment*	155
Chapter 10	*The Circle Narrows*	169
Chapter 11	*Love Thy Neighbor!*	189
Chapter 12	*Crossing the River*	233

Afterword

The blessed believe and thus defeat the lie.
Too many swallow raw whatever comes by.
But a few search books, the arts and the sky.
Why? Because searching IS the reason why!

Foreword
The Search Begins

"The America you'll discover down there will be completely different from anything you've seen here."

Speaking was the schoolteacher mother of Philip Walter Sebring, otherwise known as Sonny. Tear-filled eyes belying her brave smile, she had gathered her three children together in their Pittsburgh home during the Great Depression to hear some unnerving news: In order to eat, the three were going to be "farmed out." This meant that they would shortly board a bus for "down there," where they would join their grandfather and aunt on a small farm on the north bank of the Ohio River, at the very edge of three major U.S. regions—Appalachia, the Midwest, and the South.

Thus was Sonny Sebring, a youngster with eight generations of America in his veins, launched on an action-filled, seven-year-long journey of discovery into his own country. Of necessity he went empty-handed—but not empty-headed. For his mother assigned him two daunting missions:

(1) To search out the real America.

(2) To find the ultimate secret of life—a secret that would also reveal the complete, four-dimensional person that he and others should strive to become.

Traveling with Sonny in this story from the heart of America, you'll survive flood and drought; get switched in school and baptized in the river; almost drown, burn up and die of stage-fright; wrestle with death; fall in love, and prepare for war.

You'll also meet indelible characters right out of our nation's grassroots, many of whom provide clues to Sonny's formidable searches and to their surprising conclusions.

Above all, you'll experience the real America and the ideas, ideals and values it stands for. For here it was that Sonny discovered the very foundations of the citadel of freedom that has long appealed so profoundly to the rest of mankind.

Why should this youngster's discoveries of that era be of interest to people today? Because, first, millions of Americans still live in this same spirit. Second, for those who remember, these events happened "only yesterday." And most important, because they deal in a real-life, appealing way with our roots as a people and a nation—deep-planted roots that, like those under a mighty Sequoia tree, continue to anchor and nourish this land and all who live in it.

Chapter 1

The Great Flood

The river cut right through everything, everywhere you looked. Sonny stood with Spot at the farthest edge of the ragged riverbank and looked out over the raging stream, his eyes filled with a clashing mixture of fear and wonder. A wind-whipped drizzle chilled his face and drove his hands deeper into the frayed pockets of his oversized jacket. His knees wobbled unsteadily on the soggy ledge, which he saw with alarm now lay little more than a hand's length above the murky, muddy, swirling water.

Above the slosh of wind and waves, he could hear a far-off voice calling him. He knew he should respond but, somehow, he just couldn't seem to get his feet to move. Nor his fixed gaze.

"It's awful. It's scary. It's...it's fantastic!" the boy murmured, completely entranced. He then added wistfully: "Oh, Spot, if Mom could only see this! We gotta write her all 'bout it...'Cause nothin'—abs'lutely nothin'—could be realer America than this." He hesitated a moment, then mumbled: "Er...ah...I mean...more real America!"

This sent Sonny's thoughts whirling back over the two-plus years since his mother had put him onto this discovery mission. And what a world of new things he had, indeed, discovered! Things about their small community of Shirlington and its surrounding farms and neighbors, their school and church and homelife, the sometimes strange local customs and the even stranger ways people talked. All of which made him feel that he was making considerable progress in this key area. But as for finding the ultimate secret of life, well.... The boy slowly shook his head. That mission, now, as often before, struck him as simply bewildering.

Spot reacted to these ruminations with an impatient low whine. He shook the rainwater off his wiry white fur that sported a big black spot on the back, and sidled up closer to his master's leg.

Sonny stroked his pal, brushed his own unruly brown hair back from gray-blue eyes and tried to see across to the far side of the river. No trees, no highway, no railway tracks met his gaze as in days gone by—only angry yellow, racing water reaching all the way over to the West Virginia hills. Porridge-thick with run-off from thousands of upstream fields, the rising Ohio River was putting on a frightening display of devastation. Rooted-up trees, fenceposts, planks and broken bits of furniture swept by, each chasing the other in a wild race to the distant Gulf of Mexico.

Far from shore a dark rooftop bobbed into view. Sonny winced. "Probably someone's once-happy home," he said sadly to the little dog who somehow managed to look even sadder.

Closer in, a weathered outhouse sped by, its halfmoon-graced door hanging on by one twisted hinge. This made the boy glance off to the right, at their own outhouse—which everyone called the John except Grampaw, who insisted on calling it the Jonathan. This normally reached placidly out over the riverbank. But now its long foundation posts were almost covered by water. Soon it will go, too, Sonny thought.

Looking beyond, he saw that the river had cut through the ravine at the edge of their two acres, surrounding and isolating their small white house on an ominously shrinking island. Grasping yellow fingers had crossed the road and were now reaching out through drainage ditches and the shallow areas of Sherlock's adjoining farm toward the mile-away hills. And still the cold rain fell, as it had for days on end. And the very earth shuddered as the massive, endless mountain of water rippled and roared and pounded down the wide valley.

The shuddering, the shaking, the trembling—this, Sonny decided, was the scariest part of the whole flood. The ground he stood on, the riverbank, their little farm had always seemed so firm, so secure. And now he wasn't at all sure of their solidity. Could they really stand up against the raw power of this mighty, unstoppable mass of muddy water? In answer, the earth's trembling reverberated along his nerves and right into his bones.

Was this the same peaceful stream into which he had leaped with joy after those long, hot days of hoeing corn last Summer? Where he had rummaged among the willows and through the piles of debris left by previous floods and gathered driftwood for the Winter? Where he had fished and skipped rocks and dreamed of the distant places the river reached, as the great towboats chugged by, their whistles hooting and paddlewheels churning? Of sailing downstream to Cairo and St. Louis and up the mighty Mississippi to St. Paul and Minneapolis? Or taking off onto the wide Missouri and crossing the Great Plains and the Dakotas to Montana and the towering Rockies? Or going all the way down to the fabled city of New Orleans and beyond and beyond to everywhere?

Puzzled as much as frightened, the 12-year-old boy tried to remember when the sun had last shone. It was late January and, instead of snow, they had seen just rain, rain, rain. Reverend Smith said the rain would go on for 40 days and nights, just like in biblical days. Many in their church's congregation, gathering in small knots in threatened homes, took up this cry and declared to everyone's mounting distress that the whole world was coming to an end. Responding more mildly to the situation, Grampaw stroked his long white moustache and allowed as how he hadn't seen such weather in all his 82 years. But Aunt Emma wrung her bony hands and worried loudly and endlessly over whether the rampaging waters would finally get their house. Or…heaven help us all!…sweep the whole lot down the river, as had happened to so many others over the past week.

Maybe what the preacher said was true, Sonny began to believe—that God was sending this terrible flood to punish a wicked world for all its sins, as He had done in Noah's time. Then, the alarmed congregation was assured, everyone was killed except for Noah and his family and the animals on the ark. The boy, his face crawling with worry wrinkles, shivered at the thought and burrowed deeper into his jacket.

This expressive reaction was hardly new. Sonny looked much like any other 12-year-old except for a highly mobile face and eyes edged with deep laugh lines—both of which mirrored almost everything he felt and thought. So he had long since given up trying to keep a poker face about things. It simply didn't work.

Spot jumped suddenly and barked, drawing Sonny's attention back to the river. Close inshore an entire haystack swirled into view, with a half-dozen water-logged chickens huddled in the shifting midsection and cackling in alarm over the horror that had befallen them. Sonny started involuntarily to leap to their rescue. But his feet slipped and he hit the wet ground with a loud "splatoo", almost falling into the torrent. A bolt of raw fear shot through his stomach. In his mind's eye, he saw himself flailing helplessly around in the onrushing current, grasping for something to hold onto, gasping for air, struggling to keep his head afloat.

As he rose unsteadily to his feet, he felt an invisible hand shove him sharply in the back, and now he really began sailing out into the flood. Almost immediately, however, he was gripped around the arms and hauled back...all to the tune of raucous laughter.

"Gotcha! Gotcha! Ha, ha, ha!"

It was his older and bigger brother Arnie, who had crept up behind Sonny as silently as a stalking Indian.

"Oh, my, look at that face. Scared to death! Oh, my...oh, ha, ha, ha!"

Sonny just gurgled in pain and perplexity. He was finding it hard to join in Arnie's merriment.

"Okay, sourpuss, then don't laugh," his brother went on. "But you'd better answer Aunt Emma's dinner call PDQ...or you'll soon be bawlin'."

And with that, Arnie whooped off toward the house, bending himself into a pretzel with still more loud laughter.

Getting a grip on his nerves, Sonny bent to pat Spot on the back—then jerked his head up as an odd movement in the water caught his eye. There, just below the river's surface and right under the riverbank, floated something peculiar—a dark, bulky mass. It came to a stop against a protruding tree, stirring up a swirling eddy. Sonny picked up a stick, reached out under the object and pulled—and screamed in terror! A huge hand, swollen and red and streaked with blue-black splotches, rose from the water and reached out directly toward him. He dropped the stick and tore out for the house, an equally terrified Spot shooting out in front of him. And right into the arms of someone who grabbed him in a grip as hard and strong as an eagle's.

It was Aunt Emma, her thin face and pale blue eyes twisted into one big grimace of concern, all oddly magnified by thick glasses under a strict frame of straight gray hair.

"In heaven's name, boy, you gone and lost all your senses?" she scolded. "There just ain't no call for you to be standin' out there like a lummox while I'm yellin' my lungs out for you to come to dinner. And look at your clothes. Soakin' wet!

Now you git into that house and change right now. Git!"

"But...but...but, Aunt Emma," Sonny exclaimed, almost breaking into tears. "There's something terrible out there. Maybe a man. Or a MONSTER! In the river...."

"For land sakes! There you go again. You're gonna simply day-dream your life away if you don't watch out."

"But it's true! It's awful but true. Come and you'll see it, too."

"Oh all right," she sighed and turned reluctantly. "Let's see what kind of nonsense you've found."

They retraced Sonny's flight path back to the riverbank, where he found his dropped stick and began poking around in the water again in the exact spot where the hand had appeared. But not a trace of the bulky object was to be seen. The body or whatever it was had broken free and disappeared down the river. Leaving Sonny looking foolish, indeed. But even more was he puzzled, for he knew darn well that something had been there.

"There, you see!" crowed Aunt Emma. "Your 'magination is off and runnin' and workin' overtime again. Now let's get goin'!"

But even as she berated him, she put her arm around the boy and hugged him hard as they marched off toward the house. She then came forth with her favorite "words of wisdom," which she constantly laid on everybody within earshot: "Life, Sonny-boy, it ain't no joke!"

• • •

The big question, as Sonny got it straight from Grampaw that night at the big round dinner table in their kitchen, was how soon the river would crest. Age-weakened eyes squinting in his long, leathery, work-worn face, he observed with shaky voice that the rising water, which was now pushing across their old potato patch toward the front lawn, would shortly get into the cistern and ruin their drinking water. Then, with another foot's rise, it would cover the pigpen and reach the house foundation.

Their house wasn't all that much to speak of. Wood-framed and set on cinderblocks, it had only three rooms on a single floor—kitchen, livingroom and bedroom. Plus an open frontporch and screened backporch. But along with the two badly farmed-out, scrubby acres it sat on, it was all the Sebrings had.

The family itself consisted of Grampaw, whose first name was Venton, Aunt Emma, Sonny, his 15-year-old brother, Arnie, and his 14-year-old sister, Teresa Erika, otherwise known as Sis. To Sonny no less than the others, the house was the finest place around; it was home—at least as long as it lasted.

The real problem they faced now, though, was that with another two-foot rise, the flooding river would cover the floor inside the house itself.

"Then where in tarnation do we go!" Grampaw demanded to know. "The hills will be the only place left above water. And I can tell you, boy," he said sternly, turning to Sonny, "that all that dadburned Boy Scout stuff you've packed up ain't a-gonna help a bit out there. We won't scarcely last a day...."

Well, Sonny himself thought the future looked pretty bleak, too. Yet, strangely enough, all he could think of at the moment were the words of that beautiful Psalm he had heard at their church last Sunday: "I will lift up mine eyes unto the hills, from whence cometh my help...."

The lines had a special meaning for the boy; in fact, they were involved in an amazing discovery he had made back in the hills one hot summer day while picking blackberries. He had come across a freshwater spring in a hollow (which everyone let him know in no uncertain terms was really a "holler") and, while drinking his fill, found himself looking up at a very big, very old beech tree. And there on the smooth bark, in three rows of letters a couple inches high, stood exactly these words:

I WILL LIFT UP
MINE EYES
UNTO THE HILLS.

Sonny almost choked in his drinking. God in heaven, could it be a message for him!

The letters must have been carved into the trunk when the tree was very young, for now they were huge and swollen and distorted, as though shaped by some vast forces pressing out from the very heart of the tree. So Sonny, completely awestruck as he ran his fingers over the words, concluded they must have been cut there by the Great Carver himself, just as He had emblazoned the Ten Commandments on the stone tablets for Moses. He was swept up in a wave of wonder, which shortly gave way to a pervading sense of uneasiness in the deep stillness of the woods. He beat it out of there plenty fast.

As his courage returned on the journey home, though, he vowed he would make this secluded and peaceful ravine his own private shrine. And visit it whenever he could.

Mr. Appleton, the big, gruff, easy-going but authoritative Justice of the Peace, whose land bordered on their west, put forward a more hopeful theory than Grampaw. Sonny picked this up while hiring himself out to haul firewood into the J.P. office that weekend. As the river spread out over more and more land, J.P. reasoned, its rise would slow and eventually stop.

Moisture-laden winds coming from the southwest were the real culprit, he said. They rose and cooled as they approached the high Appalachians and dumped rain all along the western slopes. And since man had cut away so much forest to create farming land and build cities, the rains became run-off and the run-off became a flood. But it couldn't go on much longer, he concluded, a bit hopefully. If the rains would stop, the flood would finally peak and start receding.

But all agreed that was one very big IF. And Sonny found himself flailing around in the rampaging river again that night wrestling with recurring nightmares. The main one involved that horrid hand he had seen in the river. Now blood-streaked and as hairy as a gorilla's, it kept getting bigger and bigger and reaching out for him. And no matter how hard he tried to get away, it finally grabbed him and dragged him under the churning water...all to the tune of some raucous laughter that sounded for all the world like Arnie's. He woke up screaming, with Aunt Emma hugging and shushing and reassuring him.

The next morning dawned with the same dark, glowering clouds in the heavens above and more cold gray rain pelting the earth below. Worse, they found that the water had risen beyond the stake Sonny had set out at its edge last night. Aunt Emma thereupon threw up her hands and proclaimed they were finished. Grampaw, however, fumbling around with the radiator—his word for radio—tuned in a news report that put a momentary halt to her dirge of doom. The announcer reported on the latest happenings in Washington, including a new public relief program being proposed by President Roosevelt. To which Grampaw retorted with a few well-chosen cuss-words to the effect that it was all a political trick to get votes and "we'll see nary a red cent of no such handouts." Then the announcer got to the real attention-getter:

Record high water levels and disastrous loss of life and property were being experienced all the way from the Monongehela and Allegheny to the Mississippi, with Cincinnati and Louisville particularly hard hit. He also mentioned, almost off-handedly, a different and very important fact: Upriver around Pittsburgh and Wheeling, the rain had stopped. Stopped!

It was startling news, moving Sonny to decide it was time to supplement his prayers with some serious wishing. And for this he turned to the wishbone he carried around in his overalls pocket—a bone that, with Aunt Emma's help, he had rescued from Arnie's grasp at a long-ago chicken dinner. He firmly believed now that if you rubbed it right where the two bone branches came together, most anything could happen.

He was careful not to wish for things, though. He felt that God or fate or whoever listened in on wishes would consider that greedy and self-serving. So he concentrated on happenings. Like getting Arnie to stop calling him bad names. Or having Sis learn to bake better biscuits. Or stopping Aunt Emma and Grampaw from quarreling so much. Or getting the teacher to ask questions he really knew the answers to on the next test. Or, like right now, having God roll back the Great Flood, as people were calling it.

Sad to say, Arnie roundly ridiculed Sonny's "stupid wishbone" and all his wishing. But not Aunt Emma. She had a whole string of superstitions she held were gospel true. So she spent a lot of time knocking on wood and throwing salt over her left shoulder and protecting mirrors against breakage and avoiding black cats. Not to mention having a dozen dazzling interpretations every morning for that night's dreams—most involving various forms of torture, starvation, disease, death and a hell hotter than any fire ever built on earth.

"Who-a there, boy!" broke in Grampaw, drawing Sonny back from his wishing. "We got work to do...."

Whether the news was better or not, he announced he was taking no chances on the flood's future. So he and Sonny drew several buckets of water up from the cistern and stored it in a barrel on the backporch. Their pigpen on the riverbank came next. Slipping and slogging around in the muck, they worked a rope around the front legs and back of Jack and Jill, their two bristle-haired young pigs, who screamed in outrage at the roughhouse treatment. The pigs were then dragged, kicking and screaming even more, to the last bit of higher ground near the house and tied to a tree.

But what, Sonny wondered, had happened to little Spot? The dog had simply disappeared. Since this had happened before, however, the boy wasn't all that worried. So he proceeded to tackle his morning chores, whistling windily while he worked. He carried wood into the kitchen to fuel their big, flat-topped iron stove and into the livingroom to keep the fireplace going. He sprinkled corn around the chicken-pen area that was still above water, stooping to stroke old Jerry, their rainbow-colored Rhode Island Red, as he strutted imperiously among their dozen hens.

And all the time, he kept his eyes open for Spot. Arnie solved the mystery toward noon when he came rowing home in a beat-up skiff he had salvaged from the flood. It was the first time Sonny had ever seen a look of sympathy on his big brother's handsome but frequently scowling face.

Avoiding work like a pestilence, Arnie had set out that morning with Spot and a couple of friends whom everyone called The Boys—and all of whom Aunt Emma lumped together as "a pack of loafers and ne'er-do-wells." Their objective: To explore the outer reaches of the flood. But at a point beyond Appletons' where the road again dipped beneath the water, a pickup truck had skidded on the wet asphalt and run over the little dog.

"Spot never knew what hit him," Arnie said.

Compounding the misery, The Boys had then decided to

get rid of the problem by throwing the crushed body into the racing river. Spot was truly gone.

And so was Sonny. He broke down into sobs of anguish over the loss of his faithful friend, with tears flooding down over his cheeks in rivulets of despair. He felt alone, empty, awful, that old feeling of homesickness tearing up to the surface again from deep inside.

Now, Sonny knew full well what most people firmly maintain: That Columbus "sailed the ocean blue" and discovered America in 1492. And that others claim that the Norwegian Vikings did it 500 years earlier. But for him, the true, factual, honest-to-goodness date was July 7, 1934. For that was the day he himself arrived in this Tom Sawyer-like setting along the Ohio and began his own explorations into the real America.

Sad to say, his first discovery was that Aunt Emma and Grampaw had no income, either. Still, they squeaked along and kept body and soul together through the crops they grew and odd-job earnings on neighboring farms. Staying alive here had certainly proven more manageable than in the big industrial city, where, when the great steel mills and machine shops along the Monongehela fell silent, they found themselves virtually helpless. Dad had been "suspended" from his job in the B&O Glenwood Yard and went west looking for work, any work. Mom's teaching job went from regular to part-time. The pantry went empty—the kids' stomachs, too.

Now, there was food on the table, at least in the summertime. Even so, it had taken Sonny eons to get over the shock of separation from Mom and Dad. As the months stretched out endlessly, he came to feel unwanted and rejected...despite all Aunt Emma tried to do to make up for his loss and create a good home. He desperately missed their old wildly mixed ethnic neighborhood—even the frequent fist-fights in back alleyways. He missed sledding down impassibly steep Almeda Street in the Winter snow and dodging the clanging streetcars on Second Avenue; playing ball on the dusty diamond on top of the hill and cheering for Dad and his B&O team; learning to write in big, circular letters at the nearby grade school; clutching his mother's hand as they struggled uphill to their little church.

But, above all, he missed sitting beside Mom and hearing her read those wondrous stories of pirates, explorers and trolls. Or recite "Little Boy Blue" and "Wynken, Blynken and Nod" and all those other beautiful poems she knew so well. And feeling the soft caresses that magically healed all those wounds inflicted by daily living. His one big consolation lay in her promise that, as soon as possible, she would come and take them all back home again.

It was Mom who gave him his nickname. When he was very small, Al Jolson was making a big splash with the song, Sonny Boy; Mom loved it and couldn't resist applying it to her own cheerful little son.

Meanwhile, only Spot seemed to understand how homesick his new playmate and master was, and he showered him with wet kisses and constant attention. But now Spot was gone, too. And Sonny's tears of grief threatened to match the interminable rains that drenched their land. After all, in a child's scale of values, a beloved animal can rank as high as any human. Maybe higher.

Sis decided it was time to lend a hand. Thin as an eel and wearing glasses almost as thick as Aunt Emma's, but with a bright and heart-warming smile always ready to lighten up her face, she had long since assumed the role of Sonny's guardian angel. So now, she tried to console him with a promise to get him another dog real soon.

Another dog! This brought forth even louder howls of anguish. Sonny blurted out that it would be just as well if they all followed Spot into the river and died together then and there.

Naturally, Sonny didn't really mean that. It was a relief valve letting off steam. It also helped to remember something Mom had said the last time he had seen her. There she stood alone on the bus station platform in Pittsburgh, forlornly saying goodbye to her three wailing children. He himself felt torn up inside over their coming separation, and Mom had said:

"Go on and cry all you want to, Sonny. It'll help. And so will time. When you're really feeling awful—when you're feeling there's nothing, nothing whatever left to live for, just wait awhile. Play for time. Time blunts all blows and softens all sorrows. Just don't do anything dumb on the spur of the moment. Give time an honest chance."

When Sonny thought of his mother now, though, it was mainly in terms of the two big jobs she had assigned him. Discovering what makes up the new America he was encountering had proven to be fun—serious fun. She had emphasized that he should look beyond such widely acclaimed all-American things as apple pie, baseball and 4th of July parades. So he had dug up a lot about their small town of some 200 people, who lived in modest white houses with green roofs...all strung out along a narrow, winding, pot-holed excuse for a road called Route 52. And had written Mom each week about his findings.

The big topic he was covering now was exactly what they were struggling against: The river. Its endless flow knifed through the wooded, softly rolling hills and added a measureless extra dimension to life here. In fact, Sonny got the impression that if the river were ever to dry up, so would everything else.

However, finding clues to the ultimate secret of life had proven a much tougher challenge. Solving this mystery, Mom explained, involved two practical, related objectives: Searching out THE way to live to get the most out of life, and developing an image or model of the complete person one should strive to become. She said this would be a much harder nut to crack, but that he shouldn't allow the difficulties to discourage him. "Keep searching! That's the key," she declared.

She also urged Sonny to ask a lot of questions but to keep his search "just between us." Thus, without tipping his hand about his reasons, he had asked so many "hows" and "whys" around the area that his teacher now called him Mister Whyhow. Which struck him as vaguely Chinese, which he was pretty sure he wasn't.

Sonny's questions ran up against one particularly impenetrable stone wall, and that was in the form of Grampaw. The crusty oldtimer shrugged off one and all, dismissing both them and Sonny with a curt: "One fool can ask more questions than ten wise men can answer."

Actually, this particular mission had come as a complete surprise to the youngster, though he didn't want to say so to Mom. He had never before thought there was any special mystery to a good life. You simply spent as little time as possible in school and as much time as possible having fun. Incredibly, though, here in the real America, he found that children were supposed to WORK. And that had turned his old assumptions upside down and left him wondering which way was really up.

Nevertheless, Sonny kept up his searching, trusting in Mom's word that the fog would clear away one day…and he would find the ultimate answer.

• • •

Scowling at the floodwaters, Grampaw wasn't quite as ready as others to throw in the towel to its ravages, and he let Sonny and everyone know his feelings in no uncertain terms. All day long he shuffled in and out on his gnarled cane, dragging along his grandson, scratching his craggy head and checking the skies and water level. Finally, he trumpeted his findings:

"It's leveling off!"

Aunt Emma went out to doublecheck and wound up delivering a blast: "Why, you doddering old dunderhead, you don't have the foggiest idea of what's goin' on no how!"

"O you wretched old witch," retorted Grampaw, "what the sam hill do you know about these things? Git back to your kitchen!"

This noisy clash of opinion made Sonny wince. But it was hardly unusual, he had long since discovered. Aunt Emma and Grampaw didn't seem to agree or cooperate on much of anything; they collided. Much like two ill-tempered goats meeting on a mountain trail and butting their heads together. Indeed, at the very first sight of the other, each charged spontaneously into hot combat. Yet Sonny got the distinct feeling that, somehow or other, they enjoyed it!

In any event, Sonny went out and checked the water level, too...and it turned out that this time Grampaw was right. This was confirmed the next day, then the next, as the flood crest held right at the house foundation. The soupy gray clouds began to break up and the rains stopped. One, two, three days went by—then slowly...oh, so slowly...the water began receding.

Hallelujah! everyone shouted in heart-felt relief. A rare smile even displaced Aunt Emma's normal look of acute distress. But there was little joy for Sonny—even when word came that Red Cross food packets were being passed out at Tim Woodworth's, the local combination grocery-hardware store and gas station a half-mile up the pike.

Despondent over Spot's death, sure he would never smile again, Sonny plodded along beside Grampaw, rowing over the old ravine and walking the rest of the way, and picked up their fat packet. They opened it eagerly and inside found flour, corn meal, lard, baking powder, sugar, salt, even a small slab of fatback bacon. Sonny could hardly believe his eyes:He wondered why in the world anyone would ever want to give away anything so valuable…free!

"Could be someone up there's watchin' out for us," Grampaw said with equal amazement. "Em can sure put it all to good use."

And she did. Sonny was sent to fetch a jug of buttermilk from Sherlock's dairy, and Aunt Emma whipped up the fluffiest bunch of biscuits he had ever eaten. Strips of bacon were boiled in with the last jar of last Summer's green bean crop, and they had a regular feast—first thanking the Lord for helping them survive the terrible flood.

Having been proven right about the Ohio River's turnaround, Grampaw ate with special relish; in fact, his slurping, shmosking sounds would have put pigs Jack and Jill to utter shame. By now he had less than a dozen remaining teeth, all told—and these were little more than tobacco-stained stumps. But he managed. Indeed, Sonny could only marvel at his technique when eating soup. Grampaw began a whistling inhaling sound about the time his spoon left the bowl; its contents seemed to be miraculously vacuumed into his mouth about a half-foot out. However closely he watched, Sonny could detect absolutely no contact between spoon and mouth. The long white moustache, meanwhile, didn't fare quite so well; it trapped a good deal of the passing food stream and thus required frequent cleaning by the back of Grampaw's hand.

Toward the conclusion of this cacophony, there came a whining and scratching at the kitchen door. Thinking without thinking that it must somehow be Spot, Sonny jumped straight up, almost knocking over his chair, darted over and threw the door open...and there beheld the wettest, skinniest, sorriest-looking animal he had ever seen. It was a small dog, so thin the ribs stuck painfully out under reddish brown fur, his protruding brown eyes pleading for help.

"Oh, you poor thing!" exclaimed Sonny, scooping him up and holding him tight against the chest...and getting soaked in the process. Yet, in that one gesture was formed a wondrously new and unbreakable bond.

"Get that mongrel out of here!" bellowed Grampaw. "No tellin' what germs he's got. Maybe even rabies."

That set off an explosion of voices, with everyone shouting at once.

"But we've got to help the poor critter," Aunt Emma finally cut in. "Can't we at least give him some food?"

And with that she produced some old rags, which Sonny used to dry the mutt, while she collected some scraps from the table. He ate ravenously. Next went down a bowlful of milk. Then, a bed was arranged on the backporch and the battered refugee from the flood, now looking much more shipshape, gave Sonny a sloppy kiss and sailed off to sleep.

"Can...can't we keep him...huh, Aunt Emma?" whispered Sonny hesitantly.

"Shush," she replied, glancing sideways at her father. "Let's give that other critter a chance to get use to the idea first."

Turning back, she added: "Watcha gonna call him?"

"Gee, I don't know...."

Then inspiration struck: "How 'bout what you might call any ol' dog that comes down the pike—or the river, either, for that matter. How 'bout Bowser?"

"Well, 'pon my word, that's sure not much of a name for a gift from God!"

"In that case, he can be knighted," Sis chimed in. "Then we can call him Sir Bowser."

Arnie scowled and growled: "You got the right word all right—benighted!"

Grampaw scowled fiercely and mumbled something to the effect that one and all looked "ready for the nuthouse."

Sonny for his part just smiled, for the first time in a long while...as he pondered the mysteries of a fate that had taken away a dearest treasure, then given in return this pitiful little creature in such need of help. If he embraced the newcomer too fondly, he asked himself, wouldn't that be cheating on his old pal Spot and his memories? And if he didn't, would God consider him ungrateful and take Bowser away, too? He trembled at the thought. He undressed for bed and finally resolved as he lay down to give Bowser the best of care...then see what came of it all.

At the same time, he chewed over in his mind the many exciting bits of information he had gathered from the Great Flood. Mom would hear all about it! And not only about the flood's destructive power...but also about the wonderful human drama he had witnessed of neighbor helping neighbor cope with the awful onslaught of natural disaster. He puzzled anew over whether any of it clarified his search for the ultimate secret of life. But boy-oh-boy! he thought, was he ever making progress in pinning down what the real America was all about!

Chapter 2
A Switch To Learning

As the floodwaters receded and the muddy river returned to its customary channel, Sonny turned his attention once more to school and its insistent study demands, although he would have far preferred to rummage through the inviting piles of driftwood debris left among the battered waterside willows.

He was now more than halfway through his third year (the seventh grade) at the Shirlington Grade School—which, not so strangely, seemed to interest him much more than his fellow students. The reason was the school's unique window on this special segment of America he was so busily exploring. Actually, he had long since discovered that schools were one tough place in this grassroots America—tough in terms of both study requirements and classroom discipline. No more easygoing teachers, drawing and handicraft classes, sing-alongs and fun and games...as he had known back in the big city.

No-sir-ree...here, you walked the mile to school through rain, snow or gloom of night and arrived on time. And with your home-work done. And you sang "My country 'tis of thee" and pledged allegiance in an upright and orderly manner. Then the teacher rapped the desk with his ever-present hickory stick and you really went to work.

Sonny kept digging for additional nuggets of information in his school experiences, assuming he still hadn't struck the main treasure-lode, both in terms of his search for the real America and the ultimate secret of life. And this was his frame of mind one mild day toward Spring when things had returned to near-normal in the once-flooded areas near home.

That morning Sonny and Sis packed their lunchpails and bundled their books together and started out for what they felt had all the makings of a really eventful day. They covered the mile into the center of town in good time, passing in turn Woodworth's general store at the hazardous double-L turn in Route 52, the white-steepled Methodist Church, and a long string of modest roadside houses in various states of disrepair. Then they arrived at the old, wooden, two-story schoolhouse, with its dull peeling paint showing it had once been red, just as the bell began tolling its final warning.

Arnie, they recalled, had surprised everyone that morning by leaving home earlier to meet with The Boys before classes began. Normally, he was the very last to get up and get moving—as were his buddies. These half-dozen like-minded characters spent all their available time at the local ballfield when the weather was good. And when it wasn't, they hung out in the Langley family's basement, where they played pingpong, ravished the family icebox and "shot the breeze"—mostly about their favorite subject, which, naturally enough, involved girls.

Arnie had somehow managed to make wiggling out of work into a fine art form, leaving Sonny holding the bag with double duty. Every time Grampaw put Arnie onto a job, he mysteriously disappeared—then miraculously reappeared at dinnertime. His one big interest in life was playing baseball.

"It's not like your brother's 'gainst work," the oldtimer allowed, much less disturbed than Sonny. "It's jist that he'd rather work on the ballfield."

Stomping noisily up the foot-worn stairs along with other

last-minute arrivals, Sis and Sonny hung their coats in the cloakroom and sank onto their seats just as the teacher, Max Doucette, entered the room. This was their action cue: They sprang to their feet, along with the score of other students. But this time the teacher, a tall unsmiling man with a gaunt face, a remarkably hooked nose and squinting eyes behind horn-rimmed glasses, was greeted with a wave of giggles. He stopped and looked at the students with surprise—which turned quickly to anger. He whirled around to his desk, drew out a short switch and waved it menacingly through the air. The giggling stopped. Right now! Sonny noted as he braced himself against the coming storm.

A sixth sense must have told the teacher what was afoot. He turned to the big blackboard that covered the front classroom wall and there beheld a rudely chalked caricature of a cross-eyed man with huge glasses and an enormous nose. The label underneath read simply "Teach."

More giggles were heard...but not for long. And not at all from the apprehensive Sonny. The switch again knifed the air as the teacher's voice boomed out: "Very funny."

After a dangerous pause, he added: "VERY FUNNY!"

Then came mirthless laughter: "Ha, ha, HA!"

"Now, whoever has done this humorous bit of artwork," he went on, "please step forward. Step forward and the rest of the class will not be held responsible for this...this...." Words seemed to fail him. "Nor have to suffer!"

Absolute silence greeted his remarks. No one moved. Sonny, growing increasingly uneasy over the teacher's ominous tone, stole a sidelong glance at Arnie, and saw he was struggling valiantly to suppress a smirk. So, Sonny thought, that's why he left home early!

The two sat in the same room, along with Sis, because of

a fluke. Since Arnie never did any homework, he had been forced to take the eighth grade over again. And now he sat in the same class as Sis. Sonny, meanwhile, had skipped a grade in the shift-over from Pittsburgh; he was now in the seventh. And the Shirlington Public School combined these two grades in one room, with two students sitting on a double bench behind a double desk, all lined up in six rows facing the front. Grades one through six were split between two other rooms in the building, while the fourth room was set aside for blacks, whom the school authorities called Negroes but everyone else in the community referred to as colored folk.

Once the pupils cleared the eighth grade, they were expected to move on to Cheswick High School—about four miles farther up Route 52 and beyond the bridge leading to Huntington, W.Va. And this was something all three Sebrings fully intended to do. Meanwhile, they found they saved money on the present arrangement (as though there was any to save in the first place) by using one set of books for all three. That is, Sis and Arnie teamed up on the texts in their grade, then passed the dog-eared results on to Sonny the following year.

But now Mr. Doucette's voice boomed again: "So the aspiring artist"—more half-choked snickers, more switching of the air—"will not come forward, eh?"

Another dangerous pause ensued while he erased the caricature: "All right, class, you can punish the culprit in your own way…for you yourselves will certainly be punished. All of you can forget about recess this morning. You'll have study-hall instead. While the other rooms are out in the yard playing and having fun, YOU STAY RIGHT HERE!"

Sonny breathed a sign of relief, for he was far from being disappointed at the sentence the teacher handed down. Arnie had once been caught red-handed firing spitballs at another pupil and had gotten a paddling right in front of everyone. "Teach" had not held back, either; that was obvious from the way Arnie's fists clenched and face flushed as the hard blows rained down. But no tears fell. And from the class' reaction, Sonny got the distinct impression that Arnie came out well ahead of Mr. Doucette in the encounter, at least in terms of crowd appeal.

"But we really haven't begun the school day properly, have we, class?" the teacher continued, getting down to business. He rapped on the desk and all the students clattered to their feet and began to sing, raggedly:

"My country, 'tis of thee,
Sweet land of Liberty—
Of thee I sing...."

And then came an equally ragged rendition of the Pledge of Allegiance.

Sonny didn't dare say so out loud, but he actually liked school—in spite of all the homework Mr. Doucette handed out, plus his tough classroom discipline. He liked learning about new things. And he was always on the lookout for good material that could be used in his letters to Mom explaining what the real America was like...and maybe even providing clues to his so-far-fruitless search for the ultimate secret of life.

He also liked to get together with his friends away from all the hard work around the house. And he even liked Mr. Doucette in a way, regardless of his community-wide reputation for being "one tough hombre." Sis shared his feelings in general, though with less enthusiasm, while Arnie considered them both hopelessly out of touch, if not out of their minds.

After that particularly rough paddling, Arnie had met with The Boys and their parents to see what could be done to make

Mr. Doucette ease up on discipline and punishment. But they got no support, least of all from Aunt Emma and Grampaw. The prevailing feeling was that if there was anyone at fault in such matters, it was "the little hoodlums" and not the teacher. Grampaw summed it all up by stating that in the classroom, the teacher's word was as much law as the captain's on a ship, and the students had to conform or else. And that Arnie had gotten exactly the "or else" he deserved.

Even so, Sonny looked up to his older brother as someone of real courage, who was always doing the kind of things he himself would have liked to do but never quite dared. Like the time Arnie decided the two of them should go exploring and find Rube Rolland's secret moonshine still.

• • •

Arnie said, sure, they could do it. In fact, he added with extra emphasis, they should do it. For no one had ever seen Rolland's moonshine operation. And Arnie said that he and Sonny owed it to their friends to confirm that the still did, indeed, exist.

The two had set out on the mile-long hike to the old hickory grove in the hills, sent by Aunt Emma to chase away the army of squirrels that collected there and to gather nuts for the coming Winter. Arnie's job was to clamber up the trees and shake down the nuts, branch by branch; Sonny's was to gather them up and fill their two burlap bags with as much as each could carry home. But now Arnie had come up with this tantalizing diversion.

Rolland's still, rumor had it, was another five miles or so back into the hills, in a sheltered hollow in deep woods and beyond all roads. It was so isolated, it was said that his old jalopy of a truck could get in only by driving up a dry creek bed. Arnie said the two of them could consider its discovery a great service to the community, much like Lewis and Clark's famous expedition to the Northwest. And Sonny, despite a flurry of misgivings, finally agreed to go along. So they dropped their bags at the foot of the biggest hickory and began beating their way northward through the trackless woods.

As they struggled up and down hillsides and over rocks and through dense undergrowth infested with briar patches, the going got steadily tougher. At last, they came to a barbed-wire fence, where Sonny tore a hole in the seat of his overalls as he crawled between the strands, which seemed unusually tight and close together. Exasperated, he turned to his brother. "Gee, I'm beat. Let's go back, Arnie."

But Arnie would have none of that. He looked fresh as ever and rarin' to go. "You're not a-gonna be a quitter, are ya?"

"But this is crazy. We're gettin' no where."

"Ah, but great discoveries don't come all that easy...."

He stopped in mid-sentence and held up his hand. His voice dropped to a whisper. "Hey, you smell that?"

Sonny sniffed around. Yes sir, he agreed, there was something in the air—a sour, pungent odor, almost like something dead and rotting.

"That's corn mash, sure as shootin'!" Arnie declared triumphantly.

He sniffed some more. "And it's comin' from that holler dead ahead. Let's go!"

Creeping along low to the ground, they slid down the steep hillside, then dropped onto their bellies behind a fallen oak. They heard voices. An acrid smell came up from below—a mix of wood burning and something funny cooking.

"Man, we've hit pay dirt!" Arnie exclaimed.

Just then a flock of crows sat down on the branches directly overhead, cawing loudly…for the world like a pack of sentries.

"Kee-ripes!" moaned Arnie, "who invited them buzzards."

Sonny was too excited to pay attention. Squirming around to get a better look through the trees, he rolled onto a dry stick which broke with a loud CRACK! This sent Arnie into a fit of grimaces and put the crows to flight with raucous squawking. Suddenly a deafening BOOM! broke over the boys' heads and echoed through the hills.

"Omygosh, they're shooting at us!" moaned Arnie. "We gotta get out of here."

But Sonny froze with fright, his heart in his throat, his stomach turning somersaults. Arnie tugged on his arm.

"Follow me. Keep low. Scram, man, scram!"

And Sonny did. Throwing all caution to the wind, the two charged out of that hollow lickety-split, like Jesse Owens at the Berlin Olympics—but making as much noise as a herd of stampeding buffalo.

B-A-L-O-O-M!

Another blast from a shotgun thundered behind, its pellets shredding the branches overhead. Its effect on the boys was like flooring a car's gas pedal. They took off and virtually vaulted over the barbed-wire barricade. They kept running and running, tearing both clothes and hide in the underbrush along the way…until they finally reached the hickory grove. There they collapsed in a sweating, huffing, groaning heap.

Nursing scratches and bruises and thankful to find himself still alive, Sonny made a solemn vow, much to Arnie's sneering displeasure: "No more great expeditions of discovery for me!"

• • •

The big challenge Mr. Doucette had scheduled for both

grades that morning was a combined spelling bee, to be held in place of the regular history and geography lessons. This spell-down had been announced—or, rather, threatened, as Arnie charged—well beforehand, to allow all the contestants to get ready. As though you could. Anyway, Sonny and Sis had tried to prepare by wading through the family's tattered, outdated dictionary whenever they could get some time away from their chores around the house.

Sonny felt unprepared, however. He tried to concentrate on how Mom would have handled such a spelling bee. Yet, he worried about going up against those big eighth graders—especially Tom Alleck, a red-haired, fast-talking kid who had inevitably been tagged with the nickname of "Smart" and whose eyes blinked nervously whenever he came under pressure. Sonny had placed first in the last spelling bee and, now, his "spies" told him that Smart was vowing to get even.

Sonny also wanted to do well to impress Virginia Lee Simms, the sharp-witted, serious beauty with the long dark braids who sat right across the aisle in his classroom. She, Sonny thought, was easily the loveliest creature God had ever created. But, alas, she had so far shown precious little interest in him. Worse, that red-headed rat of a Smart Alleck had lately been making goo-goo eyes at Jenny—giving Sonny all the more reason to want to clobber him.

When the awful time of trial came, Mr. Doucette lined the students up before the blackboard, like prisoners awaiting execution, and began firing words at them. Simple words came first, followed by progressively harder ones like "camaraderie" and "pneumonia." When a boy or girl gave the wrong spelling, it was back to the desk, with the next in line getting a crack at providing the correct version. The students began falling fast, including both Arnie and Sis—the first early on, the latter considerably later, almost in tears.

Finally, the teacher trumpeted the word "pharmaceutical"—and still more went down. Most tried to begin with an "f", while others used an "s" in place of the middle "c". At last only Smart Alleck, Jenny Lee and Sonny remained standing.

Now, it so happened that last Fall Sonny had accompanied Aunt Emma on a shopping trip across the river to Huntington, and they had stopped by a drug store to pick up some Epsom Salts, Bromo-Quinine pills and other dreaded medicines that he knew all too well from past bouts with colds and assorted illnesses. And there on the medicine counter stood a fancy sign which read "Pharmaceuticals." Sonny was intrigued by both its length and the mysteries it hinted at and he noted it carefully. So now in his mind, he saw the sign again in sharp clarity.

Smart tackled the word first and stumbled over the middle "c". He frowned, blinked furiously, then stammered out "s".

"Wrong!" bawled the teacher. "Next...."

With a victorious smile on her face, Jenny Lee leaped in and rattled off the correct letters, right up through the tricky "c". But then, to Sonny's surprise, she dropped the following "e".

"Wrong!" said the teacher. "Next...."

Sonny found himself in a quandary. He knew the spelling all right, but he wasn't about to outshine or embarrass Jenny Lee. So he took the one way out. He spelled the whole word correctly but then substituted "le" for the "al" when he got to the end.

"Wrong!" repeated the teacher, a quizzical look lighting up his squinting eyes...and the word fell like a hatchet on Sonny's ears. "Want to try again, Miss Simms?"

This time she did it right, and the room erupted with a spontaneous cheer. From everyone, that is, except for Smart, who had been dispatched back to his seat and now watched the proceedings with a dark scowl.

"The winner!" proclaimed Mr. Doucette, holding up the radiant girl's hand. "Congratulations...."

Jenny Lee preceded Sonny on the way back to their desks, and as they sat down she brushed her hand against his and threw him a dimpled smile. His stomach turned a funny flipflop. So she knew! He had lost, all right—but, suddenly, he felt he had really won. And the rest of the day he found himself silently singing:

"Sweet Jenny Lee—
From sunny Tennessee—
You'll love her when you see
Sweet Jenny Lee...."

When lunchbreak came, Sonny joined his best pal, Clay Wilkins, out on the school's grassy backyard that also doubled as a ballfield. There they sank onto a log under a huge oak while Sonny bit into the two pieces of cornbread Aunt Emma had packed, chased by a jar of buttermilk. He noticed that Clay had baloney on his sandwich—meat, of all things. Plus cookies and fruit!

"Spelling bee—smelling bee," grumbled Clay, who was a year older and correspondingly taller, with smile-crinkled eyes and an amazingly fast-talking mouth that always seemed to be stuffed with jokes. "And that drawing on the blackboard! Boy, the ol' windbag really blew his stack on that one."

He chomped into his lunch. "And speakin' of blowing, you really blew it today, too. Or is 'threw' the right word?"

Sonny grinned like a porpoise.

"Yeh, just like I thought," Clay went on. "I saw that smile on Jenny's face, too. Sonny, that girl has bewitched you. Not that I blame you. We oughta vote her the gal you'd like most to spend Summer with." He chomped some more. "Say, watcha gonna do after school's out next month?"

"Same's always," Sonny answered. "Got a fulltime job at home. Then I'll be working for J.P. and Farmer Denton and mowin' lawns—anything to make some money."

"Then watcha gonna buy?"

"Buy? Buy?" Sonny found it a strange word.

"Yeh, B...U...Y.... Buy! Like in a spelling bee."

"Why, nothin'. Nothin' at all. Everything goes to Aunt Emma for grub."

"But how 'bout those plane models we were gonna build?"

"Oh, those.... Just have to wait, I guess."

Clay's normal half-smile vanished. It soon returned.

"Hey, I know what we'll do. When I buy the model parts, I'll simply double the order. Then we'll both be able to build. We'll start with the Red Baron!"

Well, Sonny didn't care much for that solution...but allowed after a pause that he would go along with it as long as Clay agreed that both models would revert to his ownership when finished. Course, both also knew there would be mighty little left of the fragile balsam-and-tissue craft after they had survived their trial flights around the airfield across from Clay's home.

"But how 'bout your Summer, Clay?"

"Oh, it'll be the airport again. Repairing planes. My brother says I can work with him IF I stick to him like glue. Boy, that'll be fun! And someday, I'm gonna fly those babies myself!"

Clay's older brother was over 20 and as big as Grampaw. And in the way young people have of equating size with maturity, they both considered him no less experienced and wise. So Sonny viewed him as extending Clay a great honor—and even more so when his pal promised to take Sonny on a tour of the airport tower and hangars. And who knows, Sonny thought, maybe someday he, too, would fly!

• • •

BOOM! Boom! sounded the school bell, calling everyone back into the classroom to tackle the day's challenge Number Two.

The seventh grade was finishing readings in *McGuffey's Fifth Eclectic Reader*. And while no one quite knew what "eclectic" meant, it sounded so bad that none dared to find out. The assignment involved a recitation of poems from the book, with each pupil free to recite one of his own choosing. The one requirement: The choice had to be cleared with the teacher in advance, so as to avoid too much duplication.

Sonny really went to work on this one. Over the course of many evenings, as he and Sis sat around the big, round kitchen table doing their homework, he pored through the Reader, weighing several different favorites. Which should he choose? Then, remembering how his mother loved poetry, he wondered: Which would Mom choose?

Sis had been through the same process last year and had decided on "Forty Years Ago." Sonny liked that, too, but considered it altogether too sad. Besides, he had a hard time grasping such an eternity as 40 years, never imagining he could ever be in position to look back from such a far-off age. In fact, in 40 years, he argued, he would be over 50 years old— even older than Aunt Emma!

"The Village Blacksmith" came up for serious consideration next, but was also passed over. Even so, remembering how hard the family worked to hold down the grocery bill at Woodworth's, Sonny could only applaud the sentiment expressed in Longfellow's fine lines:

"His brow is wet with honest sweat,
He earns whate'er he can,
And looks the whole world in the face,
For he owes not any man."

And what a flood of memories—literally—were brought back by "The Rainy Day"!

So the winnowing-out process went on, with high marks going to Bret Harte's ironic "Fate" and to George Morris' beautiful "My Mother's Bible." The same for Caroline Norton's gripping tale of a legionnaire's death in a far-off desert land, "The Soldier of the Rhine."

Finally, it all came down to choosing between the inspiring "Abou Ben Adhem" and the funny "The Blind Men and the Elephant." Sonny leaned toward the former. He loved its image of "an angel writing in a book of gold" and of Abou's daring to ask to be considered as "one that loves his fellow-men." And how many times had he thrilled to those memorable concluding words:

"And, lo! Ben Adhem's name led all the rest!"

Sis maintained, however, that their fellow students would react better to something humorous—to something that also dealt with a more familiar object. Sonny at length agreed, and Saxe's poem about the elephant won out. So he went to work, reading it aloud several times and chalking its words indelibly on his mental blackboard.

Now, the second awful moment of trial that day was at hand. Sonny felt a wave of qualms at standing up and performing in front of the others. But he found it impossible to run, and there was no place to hide. So he concentrated on thinking about his peaceful shrine in the woods and rubbed his wishbone until it almost broke.

Finally, from a great distance he heard the teacher call out "Sonny Sebring." Blushing visibly, he staggered to his feet, lurched forward, faced the blur of students and began in a shaky voice:

"It was six men of Indostan,
To learning much inclined,
Who went to see an elephant
(Though all of them were blind),
That each by observation
Might satisfy his mind."

Steadying himself, Sonny went on to tell how each blind man, in meeting up with a different part of the beast, concluded in turn that an elephant was very like a wall, a spear, a snake, a tree, a fan. And as he warmed up to his reciting, he noted to his distress that Arnie was also warming up in the back row. Mr. Doucette now stood halfway back among the desks, facing Sonny and moving his ever-present switch in time with the poem's cadence, like a conductor leading an orchestra. But behind his back Arnie was making the weirdest and funniest faces Sonny had ever seen, as he lewdly illustrated in pantomime each part of the poem.

Stifling laughter, Sonny plodded on, finally coming to the next-to-last stanza where the sixth blind man seized upon the elephant's tail and pronounced him "very like a rope." At that point Arnie stuck his rump out into the aisle and twirled an imaginary attached rope around like a lasso. 'Round and 'round it went, rump and all. The sight proved too much for Sonny. He choked on his lines, gasped for air, then broke out in a loud, cackling laugh.

Shock spread over Mr. Doucette's face. He whirled around

and caught Arnie right in the middle of his cowboy act. He moved like lightning. His switch rent the air and came down squarely on Arnie's rump. That straightened him up plenty fast—just as the switch whistled again and came down across his shoulders.

"You...you...you...how dare you disrupt my class!" the teacher shouted, doubtlessly extra angry because of the unsolved mystery of that morning's caricature on the blackboard.

He seized Arnie by the collar and hustled him toward the door, almost bowling over the room's pot-bellied stove, its one and only source of heat.

"Out...out...OUT!" he barked, his face livid. "And don't come back until tomorrow."

Then, as Arnie stumbled down the stairs, the teacher bellowed after him: "And come prepared for a long talk!"

The class had dissolved into rank disorder during this highly welcomed interlude, with Sonny grimacing at Arnie's beating and shuffling around uncertainly up front. Mr. Doucette's return brought sudden stillness.

"Now, where were we?" he asked in a stern, somewhat breathless voice. "Ah, yes. Sonny, you had established that the elephant was like a rope, right?"

A flurry of giggles was heard—all halted in their tracks by one withering look.

Sonny pulled himself together and stumbled through the poem's conclusion:

"And so these men of Indostan
Disputed loud and long,
Each in his own opinion
Exceeding stiff and strong,
Though each was partly in the right,
And all were in the wrong!"

"Well done!" said Mr. Doucette. A relieved Sonny started to move toward his seat but was held at bay before the class.

"Now tell me what this poem is all about," the teacher went on, addressing him pointedly. "Just what kind of people do you think the author had in mind...as focusing on fragments and disputing loud and long, et cetera? And I mean what kind of people other than the six blind men."

Well, Sonny hadn't really thought about that sort of thing. But after scratching his head, he answered: "Couldn't he mean just about anybody? Like my Grampaw and Aunt Emma?"

More snickers rippled around the room, and even Mr. Doucette managed a small smile. Evidently the battling twosome had managed to achieve some note as just about the most quarrelsome people in the area.

"Yes, yes...but I was thinking about a special group...of, say, professional people or workers. How about it, class?"

"Preachers," someone said.

"Politicians," another piped up.

"Teachers!" bravely yelled one of The Boys from the back.

"Right...you're right on track! But tell me, has anyone read the paper lately? Or listened to the news over the radio?"

A rumble of sure, sure...yeah, yeah....

"Well, there you have the perfect example. It's reporters, journalists, news people. What do they give you in their news reporting? Fragments. Carefully selected fragments. And hardly anyone ever gives you the over-all picture. Or its significance. So when you read the papers or hear the daily news broadcasts, it's a wonder you get any understanding at all of what's really happening. Any at all!"

He took a deep breath, as though refueling for a long trip, and sped on: "Yet well-informed citizens are absolutely crucial to our form of government and way of life...."

The teacher gradually wound down and Sonny was excused. He almost collapsed onto his seat, sighing to himself with deep relief: "Ah, it's over!"

But it wasn't. Mr. Doucette came down the aisle with a serious look on his face and stopped right between Sonny and Jenny Lee. Once more the air was rent with a sharp whistling sound...and the switch cut like a knife across Sonny's shoulders.

"Wha...oof!" he exclaimed, recoiling in pain, a look of disbelief and consternation breaking over his face.

"That's for laughing out loud and disturbing the class when you should have been reciting," admonished the teacher. "Don't let it happen again!"

"It sure won't!" Sonny mumbled to himself.

"And that goes for every last one of you," Teach added, switching around and glowering at the whole room.

Sonny shook his stinging shoulders to make sure they were still intact, then his head. It had been a very hard day, he decided.

Even so, as he walked home and talked with Sis about Mr. Doucette and his tough approach to learning, Sonny felt he was really getting somewhere in reporting to Mom on the real America. As a teacher herself, she would certainly understand what had happened today. But would she approve? Sis maintained that she probably would. For Mr. Doucette had often assured them that nothing—NOTHING!—could be learned in a classroom without order. And as he further assured them in even stronger terms, he was darn well going to enforce that.

Sonny also wondered, could all this have something to do with the ultimate secret of life? Surely, a basic instinct told him, anything as basic and important as learning must somehow be connected with this mystery...and he resolved anew to track down the answer.

Chapter 3
Down By The Riverside

It didn't take Sonny long to find out that here in this special part of America, people made a big to-do over extra-momentous occasions, not only at school but even more so in church. In fact, he had found out early on that this backbone America was a place of deep religious convictions. No more remote ministers and impersonal church services, like back in his old Glenwood neighborhood.

Shirlington's white-steepled church not only towered over all the other buildings in town: It was the community center—a basic part of everyone's life from baptism at birth through revivals and Sunday picnics and marriages to solemn services at death. This came to include Sonny, as well, thanks mainly to a very devout Aunt Emma. Moreover, unlike brother Arnie, Sonny went along willingly to services, since he felt sure they would eventually provide clues—maybe even the final answer—to his search for the ultimate secret of life.

One special Sunday that Spring, the family got set for a church event that had all the trappings of a very red Red Letter Day. That morning, the sun rose like a big, round, crimson disk in a clear sky, getting things off to a good start. Grampaw, however, took a careful reading of his ever-creaking joints and forecast a change for the worse. Besides, he pointed out, the rising sun was too red even for a Red Letter Day...and he pronounced this a bad sign for farmer, sailor and Sebrings alike.

Sonny took this with a grain of salt. Weather worries were not for him that April morning, for it had long since been heralded as a big day...whatever the skies brought their way. And Reverend Smith was to be the center of it all. It was baptism time for new members of the Shirlington Church, including Sonny. And, having just turned 13, he was feeling pretty excited about it all.

Dressed up by Aunt Emma in old but shiny-clean clothes because of the watery event ahead, Sonny fidgeted impatiently through the Sunday School lesson and the short religious service, anxious to get on with the main show. Finally, at 11 o'clock, the congregation signed off with a rousing "Onward, Christian Soldiers!" and the preacher assembled the dozen "chosen ones" at the door, along with the 10-member choir.

Holding onto Aunt Emma's hand for support against the uncertainties to come, Sonny stepped out with the others into a sharpening wind and threatening skies. Ah, Grampaw knew! he conceded with admiration.

Reverend Smith, a quiet, scholarly, balding man whom Sonny found to be both likeable and approachable, got his flock into a line of two abreast outside the church, whose white and gleaming steeple and bell tower cut into the sky like a mother-of-pearl brooch. Not more than 25 feet wide and maybe twice that deep, it was the town's only church except for a make-shift structure a block away that housed the Holy Roller congregation. Sonny had never been inside that one, but he knew it well from its reputation for lusty singing. He had passed by once when the worshippers were belting out "The Battle Hymn of the Republic" and found it so moving he had to stop in open-mouthed admiration. And when they got to the "Glory, glory, hallelujah..." chorus, he waited breathlessly in fear the whole roof would fly off!

The Reverend, offering smiles and words of encouragement, now marched his flock off toward the river. The choir brought up the rear, gaily singing:

"We shall gather by the river, that flows past the throne of God...."

Sonny joined in, too...but ever so quietly. He found it a bit embarrassing to be parading so conspicuously through the small community and past his friends and neighbors.

Winding down a narrow trail past the riverbank, across the bottomland and through twisted willows that were just beginning to show bright new leaves, the little troop finally came to the edge of the river. Here, the ground was covered with gravel and rounded stones, thrown out of the channel by Army Engineers' dredging equipment. Everything was now wet and slippery. A light rain had set in, and it was hard for Sonny to figure out which was wetter—the river or their surroundings.

Undaunted, Reverend Smith began the baptism rites. As the crowd sang on, he waded out into the current, already muddied and speeded up by upstream rain, stopped with the water waist-high, turned back toward the shore and shuffled around to secure his footing. The first Chosen One struggled out into his waiting arms and was lowered, trembling with cold and uncertainty, under the rushing water. Others followed one by one. Sonny, assigned last position as the youngest, waited with chattering teeth beside an increasingly agitated Aunt Emma, shivering visibly inside the large towel she had brought along to dry him off.

Suddenly, the air was filled with the happy strains of one of Sonny's favorite hymns. Shrugging off the chill rain drops, the choir faced the rippling river and sang out lustily...

> "I looked over Jordan
> And what did I see
> Comin' fo' to carry me home?
> A band of angels
> Comin' after me—
> Comin' fo' to carry me home!"

Sonny heard Reverend Smith call out his name and started forward, spurred on as the words rolled out over the river:

> "Swing low, sweet chariot,
> Comin' fo' to carry me home...."

The chill water hit him with a shock and he leaned upstream, scrambling to keep his footing on the slippery stones. Reverend Smith, turning slightly blue from standing in the cold river so long, reached out a helping hand and managed a wan smile. He turned the boy around so that his back faced upstream, closed a sure hand over his nose and mouth and gently lowered him under the current, saying "I hereby baptize thee in the name of the Father, the Son and the Holy...."

Water roared in his ears and Sonny shook from head to foot as the cold stream swept up over his shoulders and face. Then he felt something awful happen. Tired and chilled to the bone, Reverend Smith lost his footing. His feet slipped right out from under him and he came crashing down on top of Sonny. Arms and legs flying, both sank to the bottom, muddy water filling Sonny's nose and mouth. For one seemingly endless, desperate moment, he thought he was going straight to the Promised Land.

The two thrashed around wildly as the current swept them along, each holding onto the other with an iron grip and struggling to get to his feet. On shore, the choir members and the other Chosen Ones, reacting with noisy dismay, stampeded into the river to help. Their shouts rang out:

"O my Lord!"

"Dear God, help us!"

"Sweet Jesus, save us all!"

And Aunt Emma, who couldn't swim a stroke, screamed in wild abandon, "Sonny, come back! Sonny, come back!" and plunged head-long into the swift current.

The more agile boy was the first to find his footing, all the while hanging onto the preacher for dear life. At the same moment, he felt a dozen helping hands grasping them and hauling them ashore. There, Sonny slumped onto the ground, coughing and snorting out water and gasping for air. And right alongside flopped Reverend Smith—disheveled, exhausted, a stricken look on his pale face.

But what in the world had happened to Aunt Emma?, Sonny wondered, looking around dazedly.

Ah, there she was! Water cascading off her frail form and eyeglasses dangling by one earpiece, she was being dragged shoreward by three men. She had sunk like a stone in her charge into the river, and now looked completely bedraggled. But she shouted for joy when she saw Sonny, and wildly embraced him as someone who had returned from the dead. And, indeed, that's exactly how he felt.

• • •

The baptism had been meant to be the final high point of the church season that began after Thanksgiving with prayer meetings and a great Revival Service. Even the most religious, Reverend Smith maintained, tended to backslide during the long Summer of hard work and assorted diversions…and had to be brought back into "the ways of the Lord." However, he recognized that he himself was no great shakes at firing up people. (Grampaw argued, in fact, that "he couldn't fire up a pile of kindlin' wood.") So he invited the young, handsome, spellbinding Reverend Johnson down from the Cheswick church to get things rolling. For Sonny it turned out to be a night to remember.

"You're no darn good, any one of you!" the new preacher thundered from the pulpit. Glaring at the congregation while his stunning words reverberated around the hall and up among the brown rafters reaching to the apex of the time-darkened ceiling, he added quietly, "…without Jesus."

"St. Paul has told you that, without love, you're nothing but tinkling cymbals and sounding brass. But brothers and sisters, I say you're worse—far worse. You are sinners of the worst sort.

"You're liars, thieves, bigots, adulterers...."

A rapt Sonny wasn't sure what those last two were, but they sure sounded evil. He shifted closer to Aunt Emma and Sis as the jarring words poured out from the pulpit-pounding, foot-stomping preacher.

"You covet everything your neighbor owns. You're selfish, greedy, grasping, conceited, self-righteous. You're sex-crazy and power-mad. You're a sorry lot! You're...not ...worth...a...tinker's dam...." His voice lowered to a barely audible whisper: "...without Jesus."

"O brothers and sisters," he implored with extended arms, "ask yourself before it's too late: What will you live for? A big house? Big cars and big cigars? Big parties and big sex? What will you devote your life to? To yourself? To your self-centered, self-seeking, self-inflated, self-indulgent self?

"O what a travesty such goals would be! A recipe for unmitigated disaster! For ruin! Not only for everyone around you but...yes, my friends...for YOU, too. For the sure result will be hollowness, emptiness, frustration, disappointment."

He stopped, looking just as disappointed in the whole flock, then came roaring back: "No, no, my friends, you've got to shove behind you your feverish concentration on self and live for something bigger and beyond yourself. But what will that be? Well, some of you will try to find that in your job. Others in learning, the arts, sports, public service, social work. All well and good...but with what results?"

He banged his fist on the podium, and Sonny ducked as though a gun had gone off. "MORE emptiness in your soul!"

he cried. "MORE personal despair! And all because you're trying to make it...without Jesus!"

His voice rose: "Without a firm faith in Almighty God! Without associating yourself with the greatest thing that's ever happened to mankind—AND WHICH CAN HAPPEN TO YOU, TOO!"

Hooray! Sonny felt like shouting. He had never heard such a spellbinder before...and he found himself truly spellbound.

"Jesus alone can lift you out of the gutter, the slime and the muck you've sunk into. Jesus alone can make you something more than the low, snarling, unfeeling, uncaring animals you really are...."

Well, Grampaw would certainly agree with all those bad names Preacher Johnson was tossing out, thought Sonny. The oldtimer wasn't about to go to church because he said it was filled with hypocrites—and he, for one, would do his worshipping at home and in his own way. Aunt Emma naturally didn't agree with these views at all, and they became the focus of many lively "discussions" between the two. Arnie himself steered clear of both church and subject. And when he felt absolutely compelled to attend a service, like at Christmas or Easter, he sat in the last row, as close as he could get to an escape route.

"Look around you!" shouted the preacher, leaving the pulpit and coming down the steps into the center aisle and waving his arms to the left and right. Sonny looked. So did Aunt Emma and Sis.

"Look at yourself! You're eaten up with pride...but what in heaven's name do you have to be so proud about? You've got gaping holes in your knowledge. Your experience is limited. Your vision myopic. Your attitudes biased. Your judgment warped. Your every action is filled with ERROR!"

Sonny leaned over toward Sis, who sat sandwiched in on

his right between him and Aunt Emma, and whispered, "Sound like anyone you know?"

"No," she turned and whispered back, "it sounds like ev'ryone I know!"

Now coming so close he was almost breathing right in Sonny's face, Preacher Johnson murmured: "Let's face the facts, my friends. Without Jesus, you're big babies in a world crying for grown-ups!"

He again waved his arms across the rapt congregation and said, "You...you're all proud of your good looks. But I can tell you here and now. You're going to lose them!"

"You men are proud of your strength. Forget it! You'll lose that, too!

"You women are proud of your fine hair, white teeth, and smooth skin. But I can assure you, ALL WILL BE LOST!"

The last words came in a scream that hit like a blunt club. It echoed around the hall and rattled the windows, and Sonny felt the audience reel.

The preacher then lifted his arms to Heaven and entreated softly: "But, friends, long after you've lost every battle and every possession, you'll still have one wonderful thing left: Jesus Christ! Jesus will never abandon you. Yea, though you lose every friend and everything on this earth, you'll still find Him by your side—your guide, your comfort, your salvation. Here is your one enduring friend and hope in this whole sorry mess of a world. Your ONE, dear friends. Your ONLY one!"

The preacher turned slowly and stood by the altar, his face dripping sweat and filled with compassion. "Yes, friends, there is hope. Even for the most wretched and most wicked among you. Even for the worst of you sinners. Turn to heaven! Let Jesus enter your life! BE SAVED!"

"Hallelujah!" the audience shouted in an explosion of relief.

"Amen, Brother Johnson!"

"Praise the Lord!"

"Be saved from your worst enemy," the Reverend went on. "Be saved from yourself!" His voice swelled: "Be saved from hellfire and eternal damnation! Look up to heaven! Look up and enter those pearly gates! Enter an eternity of joy and happiness! COME TO JESUS!"

The organ sounded and the choir boomed out, "When the roll is called up yonder, I'll be there!"

People began straggling toward the altar. Aunt Emma, chin trembling and tears swimming in her eyes, pulled on Sonny's arm. Sis was crying, too.

Sonny felt deeply moved but, try as he could, he couldn't seem to get carried away and lose himself in the moment as the others seemed to be doing. Hell sounded plenty horrible to him, and heaven sounded…well, heavenly. But somehow, he found it hard to work up either any real fear of the former or any burning desire for the latter, at least not right now. In fact, he had to admit that even with all its hardships and shortcomings, life here on earth seemed pretty nice after all.

Besides, before making such a momentous decision, he felt he had to check it out with Mom—secretly, of course. So he did, using his own special internal telepathic system. And the answer came back as fast as a pitched ball being blasted by a bat: Yes, absolutely…go to it!

"Come to Jesus! COME!" the preacher cried above the singing and the shouting.

Aunt Emma again tugged on his arm and Sonny shuffled off, with Sis in tow, making himself as small and unnoticed as possible. Once more he found it hard to make such a public display of what he considered deeply personal, private feelings. He knelt at the altar, closed his eyes…hard…and prayed silently. And the tumult faded away before the familiar, cherished words:

"Our Father which art in Heaven, Hallowed be Thy Name...."

• • •

As they walked home afterward, their way was lighted by a million stars in a cloudless sky. Filled with the inspiring events of the evening, they spoke little—just held hands.

So Sonny fell to thinking about the enormous events of the evening and the preacher's piercing words. He now knew beyond the slightest doubt that he had just been brought face-to-face with as basic a part of the real America as one could possibly find. Equally important, he felt that in his own search for spiritual fulfillment, he had also uncovered a firm clue to the ultimate secret of life—even though he couldn't define it as clearly yet as he would have wished.

He also wondered how all this might be connected to what Reverend Smith called the anchors of religious faith: Brotherly love and forgiveness. The ancient Greeks, he once said in a sermon that Sonny remembered so well, made a great hero out of the titan, Prometheus—who, according to legend, defied the Olympia gods and brought fire down from heaven to mankind. People then used it to escape from their wild animal state and become civilized.

But Jesus Christ, he declared, brought from our own loving God two far more precious gifts: Love of your fellowman to replace centuries of hatred and all the horrors that hatred causes, and forgiveness for even the most heinous sins.

How, though, were these great virtues related to the development of one's own spirit? And how was all this related to his search for the ultimate secret of life? When, in perplexity, he had written Mom about something similar once be-

fore, she had replied simply:
Keep searching!
And so he would.

Mom must have known he would run into this kind of religious involvement in these parts, he decided. She herself had grown up just 50 miles away, in eastern Kentucky. The cutting edge of the Bible Belt, she called it. Yet Reverend Smith maintained that Bible Belt morality had no boundaries—that all America outside the largest cities was one big Bible Belt. And since our cities were filled with people from the farms and small towns, even these were permeated by Bible Belt influences. All to the end, he said, of creating a great people and a great nation. Which, he also warned, would crumble into the dust bin of history if we were ever to lose that spiritual commitment. At the moment, though, Sis was saying something about her favorite hymn, forcing the boy's thoughts back to the momentous events of the evening.

Sure, Reverend Johnson had really fired folks up, but it wasn't only his words, Sonny felt. The music, the singing, the setting, the receptive audience itself—everything seemed to interact to create a giant blaze. Especially the music and lusty singing, which surrounded, submerged and excited you under rolling waves of sound.

Last Summer Sis had come home with an old recorder (which she also called a blocked flute) that one of her friends had dredged up from an attic. And Sonny had been discovering since the great joy of creating music—plus the wondrous effect music has on mood, especially when you feel down in the dumps. His singing sounded much like a frog croaking. But with his recorder, he found that even he could make music as well as anyone else. Eventually, that is, assuming he really worked at it. Indeed, his playing was opening for him a whole new world—the world of music. So he practiced whenever he could get a few minutes away from work and study, trying to echo the melodies on the scratchy old records played on their creaky old Victrola.

An even brighter day dawned when the church pianist came to his aid with her hymnal and the only sheet music in the area, and began teaching him the grammar of music. This, Sonny found to be as mysterious and intriguing as a foreign language. So he had listened with extra attention that night as the "Old Rugged Cross" and "Rock of Ages" and other glorious hymns filled the church.

After the others had gone to bed, Sonny slipped out of the house. He felt stirred to the depths of his soul and filled with a strange lightness of spirit. He sat on a log on the riverbank, buttoned his jacket against the night's cold and thought of what Reverend Smith had told him once about what it's like to have God in your life.

"You know how scared youngsters are when they're alone and pass a graveyard at night?" he had said. "Well, imagine you get your father to come along and can reach up and take his hand. Suddenly, you're no longer scared. Gravestones and goblins just fade away. And that's how it is with Jesus. Just reach up and take His hand...and, suddenly, your whole life changes."

Just reach up and take His hand.

Sonny nodded in the darkness and decided he would remember that. He looked out over the silvery-dark river, then around at his garden, now lying bare and empty in the late Autumn night, and began singing to himself his favorite hymn, "In the Garden":

"I come to the garden alone
while the dew is still on the roses...."

He trembled involuntarily as he came to the chorus:

"And He walks with me, and He talks with me,
And He tells me I am His own;
And the joy we share, as we tarry there
None other has ever known."

A twisted nearby locust tree caught his gaze…and immediately dissolved in his thoughts into that great beech tree in the ravine in the hills, with its ancient message urging him to lift his eyes. He did. And as he stared long and intently at the stars above, he beheld them for the first time as glittering windows to heaven. He shivered at the solitude and his aloneness in the night, at his smallness alongside the enormity of the universe above, at his ignorance in face of so many mysteries of life. Then suddenly he felt as though the stars began to blur and merge into a burst of light. It lasted only a moment, but it left him sweating and overwhelmed with wonder.

What was it? Had he caught a glimpse of another world? Of heaven? Had he seen a sign of God? Had he been touched by the Holy Spirit?

No answers came, and Sonny almost fled into the house. He undressed hurriedly and lay in bed, profoundly shaken by the experience. His thoughts whirled around aimlessly for a moment, then settled on the image of his far-away mother and her shining eyes and sweet smile—a vision that gradually merged into the picture of Jesus he knew so well from above the church altar, with His level, reassuring gaze. Then, like a burst of that same brilliant light he had seen in the night, he sensed he heard as a glorious personal gift those very last words Jesus spoke to His disciples as He ascended into heaven:

"I am with you always, even unto the end of the world."

Chapter 4
The Longest Winter

An unusual combination of rough events the following Winter painted a vivid picture, for Sonny, of the real America, Depression-era style.

The Great Flood was one culprit; it had left the earth completely soaked and delayed Spring planting. Then, that Summer brought what Reverend Smith said was another terrible punishment for man's wickedness: A searing drought, accompanied by clouds of insects. Dust from farms all across mid-America filled the sky and darkened the sun, even at noon. The result was burned-up crops and much less canning, scrawny pigs, slimmed-down chickens and fewer eggs.

Against the background of this turmoil and growing need, the stage was also set for another of the daily "postal express" races between Aunt Emma and Grampaw. And today promised to be a close one, with Aunt Emma determined to beat Grampaw to the mailbox this time for sure.

Sonny saw the whole thing from a strategic position near the kitchen window, where he was peeling potatoes. On the floor beside him stretched Bowser, long since fattened up and filled out in the year since the Great Flood, his soft brown eyes following his master's every move. Sonny whispered his assessment of the contest in Bowser's floppy ear—that age, not cunning, would make the big difference.

Aunt Emma had been hovering close by the same window, acting as though she were setting the table for lunch but concentrating mainly on the view west along Route 52 for the first sign of the mailman's dusty Model A. Grampaw, meanwhile, had taken up his customary fair-weather position in the sagging wicker rocker on the front porch—it being a mild day in March—and likewise had his eyes peeled westward. His tall, angular frame looked relaxed, but Sonny knew this was misleading; his jaws chomped a bit harder on his tobacco chaw and his white moustache fairly bristled with alertness beneath his long, thin nose.

At last, a cloud of dust appeared down the road as the mail car left the Appletons. This kicked off a hectic scrambling. Aunt Emma bolted out the kitchen door just as Grampaw lurched out of his rocker, his cane hammering noisily down the front steps. He covered about half the 20 yards to the mailbox in record time. But, suddenly, a white blur shot by. It was his daughter. It was no contest.

Not that the victory did Aunt Emma that much good. Sonny saw that the latest Sears catalog was the only item she was able to gather that day. And she was fuming as a result. No hoped-for, longed-for letter from Dad. This triggered a tirade:

"Your father's an ornery, cussed, good-for-nothin'! He doesn't give a hoot in a holler for any of us. Here, we're down to skin and bones…and he doesn't send a penny! I can tell you what he's doin'—he's out spendin' all his money on fancy clothes and eatin' in fine rest'rants…."

Her voice shook as she rolled on, wringing her hands and squinting her eyes—with one going up and the other down. Arnie maintained at such times that she thus became the spitting image of Maggie in the comic strip, "Bringing Up Father." But Sonny didn't find it funny at all.

"And that lazy mother of yourn! You think she cares? Hah! Even a skunk loves its own children—but not her. Why, she went and ABANDONED you young'ns—dropped you like so many pieces of old junk. And here, I'm workin' my fingers to the bone...day in and day out...so's SHE can have it good!"

She caught her breath, then released it in an agonized wail: "Oh, what in heaven's name are we gonna do!"

Turning her distraught face directly toward Sonny, she cried, "Now, here's what YOU gotta do. You sit right down there and write your father. Write and tell him we're starvin'. We're starvin' and we gotta have money!"

Her voice rose several notches and picked up volume as she again caught her breath and cried out:

"WE'RE STARVIN' AND WE GOTTA HAVE MONEY!"

Grampaw, during all this, had shifted to his other rocker in the livingroom and was now sawing back and forth, moaning over and over in a voice that would wring tears out of a rock: "Hard times a-comin'. Hard times a-comin...."

"Shut up, you old croak!" Aunt Emma cut in. "Hard times are HERE! Right here right now. And you better straighten yourself up this very minute...or else. Or else you go straight to the po' house."

"O you hellion!" he shot back. "You...you've made my life a misery on earth...."

Sonny knew that threat about the poorhouse well. In his own case, he had often been warned of the horrors of the orphanage...if he himself didn't soon "straighten up". Now, though, he saw that Grampaw had become so mad he was choking on his chawing tobacco. He gurgled, spit the whole wad a-sizzling into the fireplace, and blurted out:

"I sw'an I think you've been sent by Satan to torment me

and ruin my last days on earth. Go back where you came from, you old witch. Back to the devil!"

Sonny reacted to all this with singular calm. How many times had he heard it all before! And it all seemed so pointless. He had come to love Aunt Emma in spite of her shortcomings. Or at least he loved her good side. But he also loved his mother and father, and nothing was going to make him change. Besides, the Bible stated that you MUST honor your parents. So that was that.

Also, he was finally coming to understand what Mom meant when she wrote that she would love to come for a visit but that "no house is big enough for two women." She had warned him and Arnie and Sis when they left home not to take Aunt Emma's tirades too seriously. It was to be considered her way of letting off steam, as from an overheated boiler. Besides, Mom said, life was simply too precious to ruin with a lot of bickering and silly grudges.

Yet, despite this advance warning, he knew all too well from his first encounter with them that Aunt Emma's scathing words could be devastating. And they would be today, too, if he had been listening closely. But as the storm gathered ferocity, he concentrated all his thinking power on not even being present—at least not in spirit. By coincidence, the whistle on the tea kettle on the stove went off at just that moment, projecting Sonny onto the deck of the gleaming white passenger side-wheeler, the Betty Frances (ballyhooed by its owners as "The Royalty of the River"), just as she was about to dock in her homeport of Pittsburgh. People in the same kind of fancy clothes he was given to understand his father wore, were laughing and dancing on the afterdeck, while the great steam calliope gaily boomed out, "My Bonnie Lies over the Ocean." Soon, he knew, he would be able to rush ashore and back into the loving arms of his mother.

• • •

Finishing off the last potato brought Sonny back to reality. He mumbled something about gathering wood for the stove and escaped with Bowser into the fresh, clear air. Drawing a deep breath, he looked searchingly up at the sunny sky and prayed:

"Please, God, help Aunt Emma and Grampaw. God help us all!"

Then he remembered Aunt Emma's worries and added reluctantly: "And please have Dad send some money…soon."

Sonny had made it a rule never to ask God for favors in his prayers, any more than in his wishing. It just didn't seem fitting in such a relationship. And didn't Mr. Appleton always say that God helps those who help themselves? And turns His back on loafers and lazy louts? Still, things looked pretty desperate now—so he decided an exception might be in order.

All this led him to reflect on how the five of them had come to this point of pressing need. As he had found out during the past three years, it was hard to get through every Winter, but this time things required even tougher measures.

Right before Thanksgiving, their pig, Jill, was sold off to Farmer Denton to become a breeding sow, and then Jack met what Sonny thought was a downright appalling fate. With Denton helping, Grampaw first delivered a knockout blow to the head with his sledgehammer. Next, the poor critter was strung up by the hind hocks and, right before the boy's stunned eyes, had his throat cut and blood drained out and guts removed; he was then skinned and cut up into slabs of meat. The bigger pieces were packed in salt so they wouldn't spoil. The fatter scraps were rendered to make lard, and the leaner pieces ground up for sausage. And while Sonny gagged on the first bites of his old farmyard companion, the meat tasted so good he decided to swallow hard and shove the whole episode into the back of his mind.

In spite of Jack's all-out contributions, though, the family entered the current Winter with lower reserves of all foods, and now there was nothing left except for a half-dozen chickens. To make matters even worse, a chemical company upstream had dumped poisonous wastes into the river and killed all the fish—a sad fact attested to by the smelly carcasses lining the shore. So there was no use looking to the river for help. Topping it all off, their grocery bill at Woodworth's had recently climbed above $40 and owner Tim was now saying he simply couldn't afford to give them more credit without going broke himself.

Grampaw came to the rescue by making a deal with Farmer Denton in which he bartered a day's work during the coming planting season for a bag of potatoes. So they found themselves having fried potatoes for breakfast, potato soup for lunch and mashed potatoes for supper…until Sonny felt he was beginning to look like a potato, eyes and all—a much-shrunken one, at that.

In fact, the well-fed Mr. Woodworth allowed on Sonny's last visit to his store: "Hey, you're looking a little peaked lately."

Well, holy Ohio! Sonny felt like saying, if you hadn't eaten for as long as I have, you'd look pretty darn peaked, too!

Certainly, they were all getting leaner. And Aunt Emma, Sis and Grampaw could hardly afford to lose more weight. Arnie for his part seemed to be managing better, merrily mooching off The Boys and their families whenever possible. But he also contributed in an unexpected way one day when he came home lugging three thoroughly shot-up rabbits—the fruits of a hunting foray by his gang. The game went immediately to good use, turning that day's soup into a stew with real meat in it...plus some stray buckshot.

After their thin meal of potatoes one evening, a still-hungry Grampaw leaned back from the table and said, "Well, guess Jerry's time has come. We gotta hang on to the hens to get eggs for new chicks...so that means ol' Jerry goes next."

This produced a gasp from Sis, a chuckle from Arnie and a wail from Sonny. Aunt Emma responded to the alarm:

"No sirree! The hens are ready to set, and you ain't a-gonna get no chicks without Jerry."

"Okay, so we'll wait till he's done his job and then we'll get him."

This sent Sonny scrambling out the door to check the ground around the back of the house, where they grew smaller crops. It still felt too wet to spade. But if the south wind could hold for another couple days, he figured, he would be able to dig up the soil, plant vegetables like lettuce, carrots, onions, beans and peas, get in an early harvest, and maybe save Jerry from the axe. He had come to love the big, swaggering rooster and his day-breaking crowing—though, of course, not in the same way as Bowser. He simply liked animals and felt that all living things should be accorded respect; still, he wasn't quite so sure about the more loathsome varieties like wasps, spiders and the big green worms that feasted on their tomato plants.

Reddy he liked, too. This was the redbird Sis had found as a chick when they first arrived in these parts. He was helplessly fluttering on the ground, apparently fallen from his nest.

They built a big screened cage for him in the kitchen, and now each dawn was heralded not only by Jerry's lusty crowing but also by Reddy's gusty warbling. Then, when the weather was just right, this unlikely duet would be joined by a chorus of countless crickets, the croaking of frogs, the hooting of a distant owl, the grunting of their pigs, the mooing of Sherlock's cows. And across the river would occasionally cut in the low rumble of a long freight train, its whistle wailing and echoing mournfully down the valley.

To one appreciative listener named Sonny, it all harmonized into a mighty melody of America.

Those fantastic smells of the countryside were nothing to sneeze at, either, Sonny had discovered. He loved the sweet scents of apple blossoms that came with the Spring and of wild flowers on a rocky hillside; of newly tilled earth and wet hay; of fresh-washed clothes drying in a flapping breeze; of molasses being boiled down from sorghum-cane squeezings. There were also nose-wrinkling smells: Pungent odors of fresh manure being spread on a field; their nearby pigpen; dust swirling up under a wagon on a back road.

Best of all, though, was coming home after a hard day's work to that glorious smell of wood smoke leaking out from their castiron stove, coupled with the thousand heavenly odors of country cooking. Sadly enough, though, this was fast becoming a distant memory of late.

But Aunt Emma was now calling—in a different tone this time, Sonny noted happily. She hugged him, pushed his hair out of his eyes, kissed his cheek and said:

"Sonny, you've heard me say this before and now I gotta say it again: Life, it ain't no joke. You gotta go to Woodworth's and get some victuals. We're plumb out of ev'rything—absolutely ev'rything. And you're the only one who stands a chance of wringin' some food out of Tim."

She reached out a scrap of paper listing the things needed. Sonny recoiled from it as though from a live bomb and started to protest...then hushed up and took it with great reluctance.

So he hitched up his faded blue overalls and trudged along the pot-holed road the long half-mile to the store, steeling himself with each step for the gruesome, embarrassing task ahead. He fretted especially over arguing his case for help in front of the town's elderly checker-players who usually hung out at Woodworth's. He had played each of them at one time or another, often winning. And now he could see them rubbing their hands over the chance to watch the "little upstart" get his comeuppance.

At Woodworth's store, Sonny's fears were confirmed by one glance through the window. Two players were hunched like stone statues over the checkerboard at a corner table. And looking on was the very man who had fired the shotgun at Arnie and Sonny during their exploring back in the hills. It was moonshiner Rube Rolland himself—his swollen red eyes, drooling mouth and sagging jaws showing that he was the best customer of that mysterious still of his. Sonny braced himself for their kidding.

But then, lo and behold, he got the kind of reception he was completely unprepared for. A big smile lit up Mr. Woodworth who, with his white hair and ample midriff, looked like Santa Claus himself. And never more so than today.

"Hi, Sonny! Haven't seen you here'bouts lately. Where you been keeping yourself? Oh, I know, you've been 'fraid I would beat you at checkers!"

Then, noting the boy's troubled face—in addition to his peaked look—he turned serious, too. He added quietly so that the others wouldn't hear:

"Look, Sonny, I know you folks can't be managin' so well lately. And I've found I can extend a bit more credit. So let me see that paper you're waddin' up in your hand there, and we'll see what we can do."

Sonnys mouth flopped open, but he found himself too tongue-tied to respond. Meanwhile, Mr. Woodworth busied himself getting flour and meal and the other scribbled-down essentials weighed and packaged. He then continued with a friendly nod:

"Remember what a fine job you did on my lawn last Summer? Well, it'll soon be time to tackle it again. And, my boy, here's some real news: Your pay's gonna get raised—to 20 cents an hour!"

Sonny's eyes widened. For who, he thought, would be happiest to hear that news? Aunt Emma!

Mr. Woodworth paused while he dug into a box, then added off-handedly as he rolled something across the counter: "Incident'ly, you just might like a Tootsie Roll."

Well, the experience was almost too much for Sonny. Though loaded down, he left Woodworth's feeling he was walking on air. Especially since he had that rarest of all treats in his pocket: a piece of real factory-made, store-bought candy! He would have run all the way home if it hadn't been for the heavy bag he was delivering.

The next day being Saturday and a free day from school, Sonny began spading behind the house for the new garden, working on the better-drained area first. It was heavy going, but he put in extra effort on behalf of saving Jerry. Down his foot shoved the spade; down he bent to lift the soil and turn it over; down he stooped to bust up the clods.

Down, lift, turn and bust....

Down, lift, turn and bust.

And so it went all day long, from 7:a.m. that morning till a noon lunch-break, then from 1:00 till 6:00 that evening. Finally, completely done in at day's end, he dragged himself into bed right after dinner.

Next morning he awoke to find every muscle in his body howling with pain, with his back aching so much he could hardly move. He lay there looking at the ceiling, debating whether to even try to get up. But the chickenhouse just then erupted with a loud crowing, and there right before his mind's eye intruded the picture of his old pal, Jerry. And wasn't that a plea for help in his beady eyes? So Sonny made a few tentative moves, recoiled in agony, then struggled painfully to his feet. Aunt Emma came running with a bottle of Sloan's Liniment and rubbed it hard along his wracked spine. Finally, smelling like a hospital, he wolfed down a couple biscuits and went at it again under threatening skies. Down, lift, turn and bust! Down, lift, turn and bust! And by that evening, the job that normally took three days was finished.

Everyone except the ever-absent Arnie joined in to rake the newly tilled soil and set the seeds in neat rows a foot or so apart. Just in time, too, for the off-and-on sprinkles finally turned to rain. And a relieved Sonny collapsed in a sweating heap on a stool on the porch.

Two weeks went by and the food situation went from bad to desperate again. All agreed they simply could not ask Tim Woodworth for more credit. And while the first green sprouts were now shooting out of the ground Sonny had dug up, they reckoned it would take another month of decent weather to reap any help there.

Meanwhile, Grampaw hobbled around all over the area, trying to scrape up some work for himself and Sonny. But everywhere he went he got the same message: "Sorry, Vent, it's just too early in the season."

Sonny knew in his heart there was another and truer reason: That they considered Grampaw, despite all his spryness, too old—and himself, despite all his willingness, too young.

March 20th finally dawned. It was a day Sonny would normally have rejoiced in since it was his birthday—this time his 14th. Yet, with the cupboard bare, Aunt Emma announced that there could be no cake and no dinner-party, only good wishes. And then came a miracle, in the form of a cardboard box from Mom. It had taken a beating in the mail, and the postman delivered it with its contents almost spilling out. But what contents! Oranges and nuts and hardtack and something Sonny had never seen outside a store window before: A box of chocolates! And topping everything off was an official Boy Scout knife for himself, a pad-and-pencil set for Sis and a baseball cap for Arnie. Sonny was so overwhelmed he just sat and stared as the others lit into the goodies.

Mom's miracle held off the accounting a bit longer, but as the lean days returned, all eyes other than Sonny's came once more to fall on Jerry. Eggs had now been accumulated for two setting hens, with the expectation that in three weeks, a score of chicks would be hatched out, replenishing the depleted flock for the future. And, as Grampaw pointed out, one of these newcomers could well become the new Jerry. So Sonny found himself pleading his pal's case to deaf ears. The case was closed.

As Jerry's magnificent head was stretched out on the chopping block that Sunday, with Arnie holding him by his feet and Grampaw wielding the axe, Sonny fled down to the river and ran far up-stream to escape the murderous sight. The atrocity being perpetrated by his family struck him as worse than the French Revolution with its bloody guillotine.

Later at dinner, while everyone else ate the tough old bird with gusto, he refused to touch a bite. He found that no one minded at all. Arnie summed up their views:

"Okay, knothead, go hungry. And thanks for leaving more

for the rest of us."

Sure, Sonny felt hungry enough. But he withstood the pangs in his stomach better than the others because he was also filled with something he felt was more important: The two key missions Mom had set him on. The Winter and Spring were providing mountains of material for his letters about the real America he was experiencing. And as for the ultimate secret of life, well, he had something in mind that he thought would clarify that, too.

The next Saturday's race to the mailbox brought a triumphant Aunt Emma stomping back into the kitchen waving a letter from Dad. With both Sonny and defeated racer Grampaw looking on hopefully, she shredded the envelope...and out popped two $10 bills. A fortune! They were saved!

Sonny read the letter hungrily. Dad wrote that he had hitchhiked to Detroit and landed a job on the DT&I Railway. However, he had soon been laid off as the carrier's freight traffic dried up; only high-seniority railroaders were still hanging on. He had then landed a job in the Plymouth Assembly Plant but had also lost that after a couple weeks; cars simply weren't selling. Through the inside help of a fellow Legionnaire, he had now wound up as a salesman in a men's clothing store, working two evenings a week and Saturdays. And while he didn't know how long this would last, either, he said he would do his darndest to send them enough to live on.

Tears filled Sonny's eyes as he finished. And at least one was for the departed Jerry, a victim of very bad timing. His imagination told him that Dad was going through an agony as tough as theirs—just as Mom was. According to her own letter which had accompanied her birthday package, she was continuing to work part-time as a substitute teacher and was somehow managing to make ends meet. He knew they were both trying hard to help. So he winced with pain at Aunt Emma's reaction to the gigantic-looking ten-dollar bills.

"I jist don't understand it," she said. "What does he mean, sendin' so little! Didn't you tell him we're goin' through pure hell here? And might not make it at all?"

But then, an amazing thing happened. Instead of launching her usual barrage of complaints, she broke down crying. Dumbfounded, Sonny reached over and took her worn hand.

"Oh, Aunt Emma...Aunt Emma, what's wrong?"

"He shouldn't have done it," she sobbed. "He lied to me. I got took...taken in. Oh, why'd he do it? Why did I do it!"

"He, who! Who, Aunt Emma?"

"No matter," she sobbed. "It just don't matter."

She hugged the boy and stroked his hair: "It just ain't workin' out, Sonny. It just ain't a-workin' out!"

Well, by now Sonny also felt things weren't working out. But he still wanted to know who it was his aunt was talking about, so he persisted...and got no where. His questions were brushed aside, and the mystery was left hanging in mid-air.

Grampaw, in the meantime, had gone back to sawing away in his rocker, chawing extra hard and mumbling a new refrain in tune with his creaking chair:

"Old and gray and in the way. And no place, no place, no place to stay...."

For Sonny the two heart-rending dirges proved almost more than he could take. He thought of Mom and how she would come one day—oh, may it be soon!—and take him away from such carrying-on. He felt on the point of bawling...when all of a sudden he sensed the surrounding voices blending into crowd noises. He saw himself standing with Bowser at the river's edge, swinging a big stick and hitting stones far out into the water. Suddenly and miraculously, the scene shifted...and there he crouched at homeplate, sporting the uniform of the Pittsburgh Pirates and waving a far bigger bat in a vast, noisy ballpark. The bases, he saw, were loaded. The pitcher eyed the catcher, wound up and hurled the ball toward him. Sonny swung with all his might. There was an explosive crack. The crowd roared...and the ball sailed over the bleachers and out of the park.

• • •

Sonny felt it was okay to run away like this—in effect, to retreat from reality—when that reality became unbearable. But he was also smart enough to know that such a cop-out did nothing whatever to solve the basic problem causing all the trouble. Nor was he sure there was a solution. But one day he decided to see if anything could be done. So, shaking with hesitation, he went to see Reverend Smith. He dared to do so because he felt the two had something special in common as a result of that rough dunking they had gone through in the river during his baptism.

At the church office he was greeted warmly and asked to have a seat across the big desk from the minister. However, having come this far, he now found himself fidgeting around in his chair a lot and commenting on the weather.

"You know, Sonny," the Reverend said helpfully, trying to draw him out, "now that you're a full-fledged member of our church, you can feel free to come in here any time and discuss anything that might be bothering you. Like right now."

"Yeah...yes...yes sir." he began shakily, "I wish I knew...I wish you could tell me, Reverend, why do some people complain all the time and...and accuse others of terrible things? And what...er, I mean, can anything be done about it?"

Reverend Smith smiled slightly, as though he already knew

what Sonny was getting at.

"Well, I must tell you that I myself gave up complaining long ago," he said. "Why? Because no one cared to listen, in the first place. And even when some rare bird did listen, I found he came to feel there was something wrong not with what I complained about, but with me! And as for accusers—well, haven't you noticed that people will go to almost any lengths to blame fate or circumstances or others for their misfortunes or failures in life—but NEVER themselves? Or they'll blame others for precisely those short-comings they themselves have?"

"Yessiree!" Sonny sang out, thinking of the many times he and Arnie had sawed wood with the big crosscut saw. Arnie was always harping, for benefit of the nearby Grampaw, about Sonny not pulling his weight on the saw. When, in fact, it was Arnie himself who was always dilly-dallying on the other end and laying down on the job. Grampaw, though, wasn't taken in at all, as Arnie repeatedly found out to his sorrow.

The Reverend shifted his glasses and peered at Sonny. "But all this doesn't answer your basic question, does it?"

"Huh-uh...."

"All right, then let's look at it this way. Chronic complainers and accusers have some real problems with themselves. Sometimes you find they've suffered a lot...or had something bad happen to them. This warps their whole response to life the same way our church piano would play if you busted its sounding board. As a result, they just can't seem to harmonize with others anymore. They see only the bad around them, not the good. And they see other people as threats, not friends."

Sonny nodded vigorously in recognition. It sounded much like Grampaw's own admonition: "If you can't say nothin' good 'bout no one, then don't say nothin'."

"So is there...What's the answer?"

"Well, you can't do much to cure such people of what ails them, but you can show them understanding and compassion. There's no use responding to their attacks with criticism or counterattacks—that only makes them feel more threatened."

The Reverend leaned back and placed his hand on the Bible. "Love is the answer," he said emphatically. "Love, Sonny."

"Now, you'll note there's nothing revolutionary about this kind of prescription. You've heard me say before that brotherly love—plus the spirit of forgiveness—is the essence of Christianity, the very foundation of our faith. And, believe me, it works! The sad thing, though, is that all too few really practice it."

Well, Sonny could agree with that, all right. For proof, all he felt you had to do was open your eyes and look around.

"And by love, I don't mean the sticky or soupy stuff that comes with a lot of mushy words," the reverend continued, shaking his head emphatically. "You find that's generally more grasping than giving. I mean being considerate and helpful and extending the kind of tenderness to people in need that you would give, say, to the victim of an auto accident. That kind of love is the one way to draw the really troubled out of the deep hole they've dug themselves into."

He stopped abruptly, as though wrestling with a contrary thought: "At the same time, though, Sonny, you've got to be on your guard against crooks."

"Gangsters, you mean?"

"Sure, those, of course...but I was really thinking of the less obvious kind: Those with crooked thinking. People who get pleasure out of others' misfortune. The parasites who lay back and sponge off others—who demand and demand. And the more you do for them, the more they demand you do. Helping that kind isn't love; it's sheer stupidity!"

The Reverend stood up, came around the desk, put his

hand on Sonny's shoulder and said earnestly: "Yet, in the case of Em...er, I mean the person you had in mind...or I should say the matter you brought up...I know of but one approach that can help:

"Love is the only answer."

"Gee," Sonny mumbled, once again at a loss for words. It was pretty heavy stuff for a youngster, but he got the picture. He murmured thanks several times and turned homeward, repeating over and over again Reverend Smith's last sentence and reveling in what he had just heard.

How complicated people are! he thought to himself. And how complicated his search for the ultimate secret of life seemed to have become. Yes, Reverend Smith had offered a straight-forward answer—love of one's fellowman—that was easy to understand but, oh, how hard to apply! Just look at mankind's murderous history of wars upon wars, plunder and rape, torture and inquisitions, slavery and other forms of inhuman treatment of other humans. Or even the trickery filling people's daily dealings with one another.

Yet, as Reverend Smith had often said, it's exactly these horrors that prove that a totally different approach to life is needed, and that the brotherhood of man must become THE answer. The big remaining question he posed, of course, is whether people are really capable of abandoning their morbid concentration on self, on power and personal gain, and making such a turn-about. And, if so, shouldn't that start right here in their community? Right in one's own home?

More pointedly for Sonny was the question of whether love of one's fellowman was the ultimate answer to his own search. He vowed to continue seeking to unravel this apparently impenetrable riddle, confident that even if he failed, he could count on his mother to provide the solution.

Chapter 5
Tomato Patch Perspectives

"Sure, it's a gamble, but this year, me boy, we're really gonna score—make no mistake about it."

It was Mr. Appleton talking as they set out tomato plants that Spring in the quarter-mile-long rows of fresh-tilled earth that stretched dark and rich between their two houses. And when his boss of the moment talked, Sonny listened. Not just because the Justice of the Peace, or J.P. as he was universally called, was as tall as Grampaw and twice as thick and looked like a moving mountain alongside his small helper. But also because everyone in the community had long since found that in his quiet and gruff but friendly way, he made sense.

Because of this, Sonny also hoped that J.P., if prodded along properly, might contribute to his twin searches for the real America and the ultimate secret of life. He didn't like to admit it but he was feeling mighty frustrated about Mom's second assignment—even to the point of losing sleep wrestling with the riddle. He would wake up after a couple hours in bed, his thoughts whirling around and around in his head, as aimlessly as a dog chasing his own tail. Sure, Reverend Smith had helped…but Sonny finally had to face the hard fact that he really didn't know enough to come up with a solid answer all by himself. Yet, he felt sure that his big boss did.

"Yessiree," J.P. went on, huffing and puffing from all the

bending, "we're getting in these plants...the earliest ever. And given even a little luck...with the weather...we'll have ripe tomatoes...on the market...before anyone...in this whole region. And that, me boy, means we SCORE!"

As Sonny served up one tray of plants after another, he was captivated by the way J.P. managed their planting with little more than one hand. His left hand had been badly mangled by a piece of shrapnel in the World War, and only the thumb and little finger remained. He had been an Infantry Captain then. After the war, he worked in Washington for several years, both as an aide for a Congressional committee and downtown in a government office. Now, he was commander of the local American Legion post and was looked up to as the area's authority on defense and veterans affairs, as well as politics generally and just about anything else.

At the moment, though, Sonny found himself working over J.P.'s elementary economics lesson. Even though he had found it one tough subject, he had seen with his own eyes how prices fell during the Summer as more and more tomatoes came onto the market in Huntington. Last year he had accompanied J.P. on several of those five-mile runs to market, and he had watched with alarm as the price for a peck basket of their hard-grown beauties, which sold initially for around $2.50, went down and down until they were being virtually given away for 30 to 40 cents. This was little more than the basket itself cost.

"A sure way to go bankrupt," J.P. called it.

"Yet, like it or not," he added, "that kind of rough competition is also part and parcel of the real America. You take your chances. And sometimes you win. Sometimes BIG. Other times you lose your shirt."

Course, Sonny got the same pay regardless—$1.25 for a

10-hour day, running from 7:a.m. till 6:p.m., with an hour off for lunch. So, as Smart Alleck had assured him, he needn't have been that concerned about his boss' profit problems. Even so, by now he had become so involved in their yearly project that he felt no less responsible than J.P. himself for its success or failure. And he enjoyed or suffered through the outcome in equal measure.

Preparing for this day, in January J.P. had planted seeds from last year's finest tomatoes in his homemade greenhouse. Now, in April, they were thick and sturdy plants, eager to get on with their mission. Then, yesterday, Farmer Denton, whose sizeable pig farm was just north of the Appletons, had come over with his big brown mare and plowed and harrowed the land and made these arrow-straight rows they were now working on.

Afterward, Denton had gone on over to the Sebrings' own small field and done the same, and Sonny could only marvel at this vivid demonstration of the superiority of horsepower. In one hour, this one horse and farmer had plowed ten times the ground it had taken Sonny two days to spade behind the house! The deal was that Sonny and Grampaw would each give Denton, in exchange, a couple days' work during the Summer—mainly hoeing corn for his ravenous pigs.

Tomorrow, Grampaw planned to get the Sebrings' own corn and potatoes in the ground. But no tomatoes. Not now, anyway. They would wait a couple more weeks before setting these out, to reduce the risk of their being killed by frost.

And this was the gamble J.P. was now taking. As he bent over, up and down, up and down, setting the plants some two feet apart, he talked at length to his captive audience of one about people and current events.

About the Depression, he allowed that "America's gonna

come out of these bad times stronger than ever—mark my word!"

About Washington and government in general, he said you'd be safest to regard politicians, with rare exceptions, as "one big bunch of conceited, conniving, calculating, self-seeking, power-hungry bandits. People who make a big noise about serving the public interest while looking out strictly for Ol' Yours Truly."

"But, Mr. Appleton," Sonny protested, remembering his studies about the great men of America's past, "our public leaders—aren't they somethin' pretty special?"

"Leaders, my eye!" he snorted. "Politicians don't lead anyone anywhere. They follow. Go all the way back four hundred years before Christ, to the great Greek philosopher, Plato, and read his book, The Republic...and you'll find there the formula that politicians have followed ever since: They simply grease up to people. They take polls to find out what voters want to get from government, then out-do each other in promising to give it to them. Through big handouts of the taxpayers' money. Of OUR money! Then they have the nerve to call this political science and public opinion research. Why, it's nothin' but legalized robbery!"

Getting so angry he seemed to forget all about planting tomatoes, J.P. said, "No, me boy, most of today's crop aren't interested in rallyin' people behind sensible solutions to public problems—only in doing whatever it takes to get reelected. Getting reelected. Staying in office. That's the whole game. And us poor voters lose ev'ry deal!"

A couple more plants barely made it into the ground...before J.P. again straightened up with another blast:

"Above all, me boy, beware of political bleeding hearts. They'll have you weepin' and wailin' over the poor and downtrodden. And how we taxpayers simply got to help. But have you ever heard of one of them contributing a red cent of his own money to help? No, you haven't...and the moon'll turn blue 'fore you do!"

Sonny wrestled with this eye-opening lesson in government while his boss caught his breath, then felt what he considered a brilliant idea breaking through.

"But what if...Mr. Appleton. What if every time Congress proposed a big new welfare or jobs bill or other...ah...handout, the members took a cut in their own pay? Say, one per cent or so. You know, as a way of showin' concern—their own personal concern."

Well, Sonny never got to finish explaining his brilliant idea, for his big boss broke out in a roar of laughter that could be heard all the way to Kentucky.

"Oh, my...oh, my!" he shouted between laughs, his whole body shaking from head to foot...while Sonny stood utterly speechless at the reaction his idea had triggered. Had he said something right? Or wrong?

"Me boy, you oughta get the Medal of Honor for that one! You've saved the Republic! With that law in place, I guarantee you'll see government spending nosedive. The bureaucracy will shrink. Taxes will be cut. And you'll never see another federal budget deficit again as long as we live!"

Wiping tears from his eyes with the back of his hand, J.P. gradually stopped chuckling and got back to normal. "Me boy, I've noticed you ask a lot of questions. But let me pose a tough one for you. What's worse than vote-scrounging politicians?"

"Handout-scrounging voters?"

"Oho, you're catching on fast! Actually, you've put your finger on the greedy, built-in combination that could undo our democracy. But I was really thinking of the politicians' abominable offspring—government bureaucracy. Bureaucrats! People who dole out the handouts and 'minister the regulations—people who specialize in telling you what you can and cannot do. So you want some government help? More security? Controls over business and union abuses? Sounds great. Right? But watch out…there's a joker in the deck! For you'll pay for each of these fine-sounding moves with your freedom—with more and more government control over your life. And sometimes with your life itself, as you've seen in Communist Russia. The fact is, the bigger government gets, the smaller people become. Until they're reduced to handout-scrounging slugs and bureaucrat-manipulated puppets. Is this what God intended when He created man in His own image? What a farce! I tell you, me boy, the welfare state is breeding a whole new race of pygmies!"

"No more 'giants in the earth' like out West?"

"'Fraid not. Those giants sprang from the prairies, out of extreme conditions of hardship and struggle. We'll not see their likes again."

J.P. shook his head sadly. "Worst of all is the effect of all this on people's spirit. In welfare nations, 'The State' becomes the new God, and squeezing the most out of government becomes the new national sport. Yet, the more the state does for people, the less they do for themselves. Meanwhile, the real producers of society are taxed and controlled to the point that they lose all incentive to produce. Soon, then, you find there are more people riding in the wagon that there are people pulling. And that, me boy, is a sure-fire recipe for national ruin! So government action that looked in the beginning like a good thing, maybe needed to correct some real problems, finally becomes a noose around the people's neck."

J.P. waved his hand across his forehead as though to chase

away some bad thoughts and said, "But, for goodness sake, let's talk about something of more interest to you. F'rinstance, have you ever thought of life as a great adventure?"

"You mean like Buck Rogers and space travel? Or Jules Verne's *Twenty Thousand Leagues under the Sea*?"

"No, I mean everyday life, like right here 'round Shirlington. Not everyone seems to know it, but everyday life can be a great adventure, too. Not to mention planning for the future. And what would you say if I told you that schooling and learning gen'rally is the greatest part of that adventure?"

"You're kiddin'!" Sonny blurted out.

"Not at all! It's absolutely true. For instance, imagine yourself a sea-roving Viking...or Columbus, Hudson, Drake or Magellan...exploring exciting new worlds. But this time it's not new lands you're discovering but new realms of knowledge. Why, it's fantastic how you can extend your horizons! You can dig deeper and deeper into one subject or continually open up whole new universes of thought. Fantastic, me boy—and exciting!"

He stopped and looked at Sonny as if to see if his words were sinking in. They were...and how! Sonny was listening as intently as the first time he had heard the Story of Creation.

"But it's important to remember, me boy: It's not how much knowledge you accumulate that counts; it's how you use that knowledge. And that depends squarely on character—on the kind of person you are."

J.P. stopped, apparently reflecting on his comments. "Do you know what the ancient Greeks said about character? No? Well, they believed that character equals fate—that a person's character inevitably determines what happens to him in life."

He squinted hard at his small helper, who stared straight back like a blank question mark. A wide smile finally broke over the squire's craggy face. He nodded and continued:

"Course, you have to learn to think, too. Think! And make sound decisions. And not just clutter up your brain with a lot of trivia. That's like storing a lot of useless junk in your attic.

"With many people—maybe most—the more information they get, the less understanding they have. They simply become confused. You've also got to beware of rattlin' empty wagons among the educated. Learning's got to backed by solid experience in its practical application before it can qualify as wisdom.

"You can't just accept the prevailing opinion about things, either. In fact, the easy answer people spout off is generally the wrong answer. Wrong! Which means you should always take a close look at the opposing side. Why, even the devil reads the bible."

"Wha...howzat?" Sonny exclaimed.

"Yep, that's how he got to be so clever at undermining the righteous. What I'm saying is, if you're going to beat an enemy, you darn well better get to know him first."

J.P., panting, bent to more planting, while huffing and puffing like a steam locomotive.

"Now, you're probably thinking that knowledge is just something you absorb and use on the job or for jawboning around the fireplace. But there's another effect that's far more important...and that's what wide reading and intensive study does for you as an individual. It adds extra depth, me boy—an extra dimension to your personality. It brings you farther and farther away from your caveman origins. You grow. You begin to become a truly developed...a civilized...human being."

J.P. rose and caught his breath. Then came another stream of comments:

"Now, you noticed I used the word 'intensive' in referring to study. That's because real character-building can come about only through the hardest personal effort. In fact, like those giants we mentioned, EFFORT is second only to hardship and struggle as a character builder. And I can assure you, me boy, that the superficial stuff that passes for most education nowadays isn't gonna do anything for anybody. It's like white-washing that rickety old outhouse over there. Sure, it'll look better on the outside...but, underneath, it's still the same old outhouse."

And with that he waved a big hand toward Grampaw's weather-worn Jonathan.

"But, Mr. Appleton," Sonny ventured, hoping to draw J.P. into giving some firm answers to his quest for the ultimate secret of life, "our preacher says you can look to religion to do a lot of that for a person. If learnin' can work such wonders, where does religion fit in?"

"Ah, there you have one BIG question! Now, me boy, you're getting to the very heart of our existence."

J.P. pulled himself erect and squinted off toward the far horizon where the green hills met the blue sky in a long jagged line. Sonny had never seen him looking so thoughtful.

"You know, we've been talking about the head, not the heart. And not about the soul or spirit. Fact is, all of us long for a meaning to existence. We long to feel our lives have a real purpose. We long to believe that everything we've done ...and become...doesn't simply end with death. And there's only one thing that can provide that meaning and that's an abiding faith in the Great Spirit that created us."

He extended his arms toward the sky and his deep voice boomed across the fields. "Faith, Sonny! Faith gives you an inner security, an outward grace. It lifts your spirit and makes you one with the gods. It does things for the soul that no amount of learning will ever accomplish."

Then came more bending, more moaning, more digging, more groaning.

"But think, me boy!" J.P. added with sudden enthusiasm, his rugged features lighting up like the eastern sky at sunrise. "Think if you had BOTH!. Both learning and faith. Think what THAT would do for you!"

A shout from Constable Flint sent J.P. off to answer a phone call, leaving Sonny working happily over the answer to his question. He felt that, somehow, he had just been handed a golden key to life's greatest mystery...and to his future.

Yet, he still wondered if this was the final answer he

had been seeking so industriously. It sounded close, certainly, leaving Sonny feeling pretty good about the whole conversation.

Returning limping and holding his back with both hands, J.P. grunted loudly, "Oh, my back is killing me!"

Well, Sonny felt the same but didn't consider it appropriate for such a young "whipper-snapper," as Grampaw called boys, to appear to be complaining in such an august presence.

J.P. looked around at their handiwork—they were on the sixth and final row—and said:

"By golly, Sonny, I'm not sure my back's gonna make it. Maybe we'd better put the rest off till tomorrow."

He winced and added: "But, then, we can't just fold up now, can we? Maybe we might try a little poem my daddy taught me about a thousand years ago."

And bending again to the task, he recited in between some rending sighs and moans:

"When a job is first begun,
Never leave it till it's done;
Be it great or be it small,
Do it well or not at all!"

J.P. then turned to Sonny and said, "Okay, me boy, let's try it together."

And they did: "When a job is first begun..."

"Now try it alone."

And Sonny did: "When a job is first begun..."

"Me boy, you've got it! Now it's yours as much as mine. But can you tell me what it really means?"

"Never give up...NEVER!"

"Yep...and strive for excellence in everything you do—for the highest quality in everything you produce. Do that, me boy, and you'll really stand out." His face turned serious. "And speaking of standing out, now that you're winding up your first year of high school, I'm sure you're giving some thought as to what you want to do when you grow up. And become. Any conclusions?"

Sonny chewed the question over for a while, then said he had not yet decided on much of anything. Oddly enough, he went on, he had found almost everything interesting. He had grown to love farming and the sheer magic of growing and creating things from the land. At the same time, when he heard Mr. Doucette talk at school, he thought teaching might be nice. The same when he heard Reverend Smith or Preacher Johnson in church. And that time he had his tonsils removed— —nasty as the experience was—he concluded it would be fantastic to be a doctor. Then there were all those Civil Service announcements he had noticed in J.P.'s office—especially those tantalizing descriptions of Ranger positions in the National Parks. Or why not study engineering and build great dams and highways and Empire State Buildings?

He paused and caught his wind: "Then, when I read the newspaper, I think, gee, wouldn't it be great to be a news reporter. That must be the life!"

J.P. made a wry face at that comment and mumbled something about some people "always being observers and critics and never doers." He looked off in the distance again and added, "I really can't say much 'bout your becoming a member of the press, me boy, but I sure got something to say 'bout the power of the press. And power elsewhere. And that's BEWARE!"

The last word rent the air and hit Sonny so hard he dropped a whole tray of tomato plants. This was followed by a long string of "gee whizzes" as he scrambled to repair the damage.

He finally gurgled out, "Watcha mean?"

"Just this: Power's like a virulent acid that corrodes and consumes the container that tries to hold it. Or person. Whether he's a politician or business, labor, religious or press leader...or whatever. An insufferable arrogance, or plain fat-headedness, seems to overwhelm those with power. They proceed to lose whatever common sense they might have had once. And who pays the bill for their resulting madness? You guessed it...we, the people!

"You know, me boy, the great genius of our democracy lies in its proven ability to counterbalance and control concentrations of power. So far, that is. But look at what's happening today. Power's becoming more and more concentrated. In Big Government, Big Business, Big Labor, Big Publishing—creating more and more danger for individual freedoms. Plus ever greater need to fight to protect them.

"In this respect the press is both part of the problem and its cure. A free society couldn't exist without a free press exposing fraud and corruption in high places. But who's gonna expose corruption among those exposing corruption? Press people today have such power over public opinion—and votes—that government leaders of all stripes grovel at their feet. It's disgusting!"

J.P. looked as though he was about to throw up. He swallowed hard and continued: "That's not half of the problem, though. Add in the broadcasters, moviemakers, advertisers and other means of communicating...and you find that every day we're being bombarded with as many impressions as artillery laying down a barrage on a battlefield. And that, me boy, I know a bit about!" He raised his battered hand for extra emphasis. "'Cept in this case, the battle's for your mind—for your attitudes and buying decisions for everything from alphabet soup to zippers. AND your votes!"

Filled with wonder at the strange new world J.P. was describing, Sonny asked, "Gee, is there any real defense against this kind of...er...bombardment?"

"Yep, you wake up...and wise up. Too many people, I fear, swallow raw whatever comes by, just as long as it's labeled 'new' or is being pushed by some famous face. They're simply unaware they're being manipulated and jerked around like puppets on a string.

"So never stop asking about a communicator's methods and motives. What kind of axe is he grinding? Why is he pushing a particular attitude or viewpoint? Who gains and loses from the result—and how will that affect you and the over-all public? Then make up your own mind if it's good or bad. And forget what others think. Chances are, they're not thinking at all!"

A glazed look came over Sonny's face. Gosh, he thought, if a guy can learn such things out here in the tomato patch, why go to school? J.P.'s remarks also reminded him of Hans Christian Andersen's pointed fairy tale about "The Emperor's New Clothing." It finally took the unclouded, uncontaminated vision of a child to cut through the make-believe and see that the parading emperor was, indeed, wearing no clothes at all!

His big boss dug some more in the rich black soil and switched back to their talk about Sonny's future. "Actually, me boy, it isn't so important to decide anything about a career right now...but it is important to begin thinking about where you're going in life. What will you do with this one life you're given? What kind of person do you want to become? What will it take to get there?"

He then pulled off one of his noted conversational U-turns: "You know, we all harp too much about achieving goals. Fact is, it's the striving and the struggle to reach our goals that is the real reward. What I mean is, once you've arrived, you look back and find to your utter surprise that getting there was the most fun. So, instead of harpin' and bellyachin' about all the effort it takes to get somewhere, enjoy it!"

Sonny just stared with open mouth. Was this upside-down viewpoint somehow connected to his search for the ultimate secret of life?

J.P. bent and planted and grunted some more and added, "Everything, me boy, depends of what you expect of yourself in life. If you got low expectations, you're sure as shootin' gonna wind up low on life's totem pole. In fact, this may be the one advantage that kids of wealthier and better-educated parents have: They automatically absorb the higher expectations of their folks.

"Course, all this is also related to the matter of respect. Getting other people's respect, not to mention admiration—this is probably the greatest single motivating force in human nature. Folks'll do almost anything to get other people to think well of them, to look up to them."

Next came another sharp U-turn that left Sonny straining to hold on: "But then, sad to say, they find themselves marching to other people's tunes, not their own. And who wants to live like that!"

Sonny went to fetch another tray of tomato plants. He came back looking crestfallen. "You know, Mr. Appleton, it's really dumb for me to talk about a career and all those fancy jobs. It's day-dreamin'. They all require college. And that takes an awful lot of money. And you know how things are at home on that score. And…and…."

"Nonsense!" J.P. interjected. "You mustn't let that discourage you, me boy. You're an American. And that means that even when you've got nothing, you've got everything. Potentially, that is. There's a whole continent full of opportunities out there just waiting for you to tap. And here you sit with the greatest possession of them all—freedom. Freedom, me boy! That means you can prepare yourself and go out and grab a-hold of any of those opportunities you choose. Believe me, it can be done."

They finally reached the end of the last row, and J.P. let out a loud howl as he straightened up. He then turned back to his helper, wheezing with back pain as he talked:

"I tell you, me boy, you can become whatever you set your mind to. You got smarts—you have a way of catching the essence of things in midair. You don't rattle on 'bout things either. Which is a good sign, 'cause people learn through their ears and eyes, NOT their mouth. You're not afraid to work hard. You've got an open, honest face...so people don't feel you're out to trick or deceive them. And under those mild manners, something tells me you've inherited the same streak of will power—or plain old bull-headedness—as the rest of you Sebrings. And all that, me boy, makes for a combination that can't be beat!"

With that J.P. hobbled off holding his back. And now Sonny really had something to chew on. His boss' remarks had awakened some dormant questions that he had preferred to let rest under the surface, on the assumption he had another three years of high school to go before needing to come up with answers. But there they were again: What did he want to do in life? What did he want to try to become? Should he just leave everything to fate, chance, Lady Luck...or the "confluence of the stars," as Aunt Emma put it. Or should he grab hold of things and try to create the future he wanted? But then, again, what DID he want?

So the questions went, 'round and 'round in circles, like Bowser chasing his own tail. Till Sonny felt like yelling.

The overriding fact was that the Depression had made the Sebrings about as poor as you could get and still get by without becoming a burden on others or the state. And they would rather die than do that. But like every other American they knew, they considered themselves as good as anyone around. So Sonny had long felt that all it really took to make something out of himself was the means; he would provide the effort.

Yet J.P. was now saying something radically different: That if you set your mind and will on your course and try hard enough, the means would follow.

Sonny was also becoming aware, however, that nothing whatever was going to happen unless and until he came up with a vision—a concrete idea—of what he wanted to do with himself in the years ahead. And that wasn't proving easy at all.

• • •

As he plodded homeward nursing his own sore muscles, Sonny felt the air turning colder. Looking nervously at the brave green plants bowing before the stiffening wind, then up at the pale-blue, cloud-streaked sky, he said a prayer for his favorite boss. Then, to be doubly sure, he rubbed his wishbone and crossed his fingers.

After a couple of uncertain days, as luck would have it, the weather turned amazingly warm, with temperatures reaching into the 80s. And the tomato plants really took root. The next weekend Sonny spread a thin circle of nitrate fertilizer around each.

"Six inches away, me boy—no less," J.P. cautioned. "Get too close and you'll burn them alive!"

Midway in this chore, Sonny was hailed by his boss from

the small Justice of the Peace building adjoining his big white house. He went running over, only to meet up with a worried look on J.P.'s face. His words came short and fast:

"It's your brother Arnie. The police have picked him up in Gallipolis. Thumbing a ride...apparently trying to get to Pittsburgh. I'm sending my deputy up there to bring him back. You run home and tell Vent. Nothing to worry about, tell him. We'll have Arnie home pronto."

He turned and disappeared...and so did Sonny. He ran as fast as his legs could carry him. Home, he burst through the kitchen door and blurted out the news. And Aunt Emma's reaction stopped him cold:

"Hell's bells, why didn't they just let him go on! That no 'count loafer ain't no use to no one 'cept his mother. That's where he belongs!"

Constable Flint drove up to the house that evening in his supercharged Chevvy, and Arnie emerged from the right-front seat with a triumphant look. He had become a celebrity! Even Grampaw was impressed by his daring.

"You almost made it, boy!" he said, clapping Arnie on the back.

"O Arnie, you could have been killed," Sis wailed.

Sonny felt a sudden sense of resentment that his brother had not taken him along. Then they both might have realized his old dream of seeing Mom again. So he commented sourly: "Runnin' away from work again, weren't you?"

"Aw, waddayu know about my feelin's, you little runt," snarled Arnie. "Here they're workin' your tail off and pocketin' all you earn and you don't have sense enough to know you're being taken to the cleaners. Wise up, knothead!"

"Well, I sure don't want to become like you."

"Okay, then become like Aunt Emma. Me...I'll take Mom

any day!"

Aunt Emma went off like a rocket and almost hit the ceiling on that one. And Grampaw, putting in his two bits from his creaking rocker, groaned, "O what an awful sight, to see two brothers fall out and fight."

A measure of peace finally settled in as Arnie sailed off to see The Boys and bask in his new-found notoriety. Sonny patted Bowser and joined Sis at their homework while Aunt Emma shuffled off into the livingroom and cranked up the old Victrola. Soon, the air was filled with the scratchy melody of Grampaw's favorite record:

> "The house is falling down, the roof is falling in.
> The leak lets in the sunshine and the rain.
> And the only friend I have now is that little dog of mine
> And that little old log cabin in the lane...."

The Summer wind that everyone had briefly enjoyed gave way the next week to a chill blast that blew in all the way from Canada. J.P.'s worst fears seemed about to be realized. Everyone's eyes became glued to the thermometer. The tomatoes squeaked through one cold night. Then another. But an even worse forecast was made for the third.

J.P. decided to act. He broke out big bundles of paper bags he had stashed away for just this kind of crisis and, all that afternoon, he and Sonny worked in tandem, setting them down over the plants and piling dirt around the base to seal out the cold.

That night frost hit and Sonny didn't sleep much. When morning came, he looked out and saw the cold earth covered with a film of white frost. Oh, they're finished! he moaned to himself. Yet, when the sun warmed things up and they took off the paper bags, they found the plants still green and upright and very much alive. J.P.'s gamble had panned out!

As the weeks went by, Sonny helped J.P. cut saplings among the willow groves along the river and staked the tomatoes. He pulled off suckers, tied up the vines and hoed and hoed…until there wasn't a weed in sight. Yellow blossoms appeared, followed by tiny green globes. The vines grew higher on the stakes…requiring more pruning, more tying, more hoeing. And by late June, huge tomatoes were everywhere, many already beginning to turn red.

In another week, Sonny joined J.P. in picking the first of the crop. They packed up some 20 baskets and drove off in the boss' rattling pickup to Huntington. At the marketplace right off the bridge over the Ohio, they backed into an empty stall, let down the tailgate and opened for business. People came and stared in disbelief. Fresh tomatoes this early? And they sold out in no time at all—for a record $2.75 per basket!

The same thing happened the following week, except that then they came with 40 baskets. And a week later, with tomatoes busting out all over their patch, they came with 60 baskets.

Course, their good fortune couldn't last, and the price duly sank as others' tomatoes flooded the market. But J.P. was as happy as a kid.

"By golly, Sonny, we did it!" he exclaimed when they got home from their last trip. "We beat the odds!"

"Yeah, guess we were pretty lucky."

"Luck, my foot!" rejoined J.P. "I'll admit we can use all the luck we can lay our hands on. But I gotta tell you, I find that the harder and smarter we work, the luckier we get."

He gave his small helper a pat on the shoulder and added: "But it wouldn't have gone without you, me boy. And for that you deserve a reward…."

Sonny's eyes got about as big as their biggest tomatoes as J.P. drew a wallet out of his pocket and pulled out a $20 bill. He put it in an envelope and wrote "For Sonny" on it and handed it over with a bow, like in a formal presentation ceremony.

"Now, this is no gift, me boy. It's a bonus. Something you've earned. And thanks, Sonny…thanks for all the help!"

This time Sonny really beat it home, overflowing with confidence that his work with J.P. was providing great input for his searches for both the real America and the ultimate secret of life. There, he proudly handed his big bonus over to Aunt Emma. She laughed and kissed him and said, "O Sonny, now we can get you some nice clothes for high school!" He had never seen her so happy.

And that made Sonny happy, too. Many times he had heard people say that it is better to give than receive. Yet Arnie derided that as sheer trickery on others' part—a ploy aimed at getting you to give more while they gave less. Nevertheless, Sonny found he got a good feeling in turning over his earnings, the big reward coming in the praise he got for helping support their home. It made him feel mature, responsible. Indeed, Aunt Emma said that with Grampaw ailing, he had actually become "head of the household." Pretty heady stuff!

Not that he wouldn't have liked to get more of the good things he saw his friends showing off. Like smarter clothes for school to replace his baggy corduroy pants, oversized pullover with the patched elbows, and blue shirt with its frayed collar—all hand-me-downs from Arnie. They didn't do much to impress Jenny Lee!

Aunt Emma shrugged off such longing, claiming it's "pure p'ison" to envy others.

"'Bove all," she said, "don't let others pressure you to follow the herd—to conform to their ways and their dictates.

And never, never take another's dare. It's a sure way to get into trouble—BIG trouble."

How right she was came out later. Billy Buckner, one of the nicest boys in the next class, was goaded by some older boys into trying to walk along the parapet of a building in downtown Huntington. He lost his balance and fell to the sidewalk six floors below, to his death.

Sonny also thought about the toys and games he liked so much, including airplane kits and stamps for his scrawny collection. Yet, these were things one dreamed about. Mom had sent a little red rubber firetruck with him when he had come from Pittsburgh, and this remained his one and only plaything. Except, of course, for the rubber-band-propelled tanks that he and Arnie made from old thread spools, the screw-off bottle tops they spun around their kitchen-table racetrack in the evening…and the hoops they rolled around the yard with bailing-wire guides.

Despite all the drawbacks, however, Sonny had long since decided that he wouldn't trade the present giving arrangement for all the getting on earth. For nothing—absolutely nothing he could conceive of—could beat the great joy he felt when his contributions brought a warm smile to Aunt Emma's troubled face. And he would continue to do anything to bring that about.

Chapter 6
Snake in the Bush

In tracking down information for his reports to Mom on the real America, Sonny had come to consider himself a news reporter. Unfortunately, an unpaid reporter. Yet it was fun. And, as he asked himself, even when the need for money was the most pressing, wasn't that what counted? Well, he knew what Aunt Emma would answer to that one!

Now, however, he felt he had raked over and around Shirlington so thoroughly for news that he wasn't sure anything was left. So, like any other reporter, he decided he had to develop some new information sources. And there, right before his eyes as he looked northward one day, he perceived anew the rolling hills with their deep hollers. All of which suddenly struck him as an endless realm of discovery possibilities. So he got set for a new journey there…just as Aunt Emma announced that the canning season had arrived AND she needed "input".

Actually, by mid-Summer, the crops from the Sebrings' garden, coupled with the wild-growing bounty of nature itself, were making the long, tough Winter of want a receding memory. Sonny found that the fields and hills around the small farm could be foraged for berries, nuts, greens, persimmons and many other edibles. Yet, the biggest prize of all was also one of the most delicious—blackberries—

whose thorny vines grew thickest along the lower hillsides and back in the ravines. And it was here he found himself one bright—very bright—day in late July.

The blackberries were sweet and juicy and as big as his thumb, and Sonny was shoving almost as many into his mouth as into the two galvanized iron buckets he and Grampaw had brought along. It was the high season for berry picking, and the day was getting hotter by the minute. Beads of sweat crept out from under his floppy straw hat and ran over his forehead and bare shoulders and down beneath the soggy galluses of his worn overalls. There was a lot of wind-blown dust in the air; his eyes smarted, his skin crawled and he itched all over.

He could see that Grampaw was feeling the heat, too— even though he had only recently shed his long-handled underwear, which he considered virtually an extra layer of skin. He also wore overalls but with a difference: His ever-present plug of tobacco lay in one pocket and, tied to a belt-loop by a leather thong in the other, dangled his trusty pearl-handled jack-knife, worn and stained by years of hard use.

With Bowser barking and cutting up alongside, they had started out right after sunrise that morning, hoping to get their quota of berries picked before the sun reached its zenith and the scorching noontime heat hit. And as they trooped off, Aunt Emma let loose a loud laugh:

"My land, what a pair you two make! Just like Mutt and Jeff. With those silly hats and old overalls, you could go right into the comics."

Sonny looked up at Grampaw and smiled. And for the first time since they had come to live together, the old gent smiled back. He put his hand on Sonny's shoulder, and off to the hills they marched.

Fog lay thick and gray along the river. Yet, as they covered the dusty mile of dirt road and narrow meadow paths to the first rise of ground before the hills, it thinned out...and they could see the sun beginning to break through. By 7:30 they entered a valley that cut straight back across the ridges. And there, right ahead and off to the left, as Sonny knew from last year's berry-picking, lay a lush berry patch where they could begin the long, tough job of filling their buckets.

But blocking the way was a barbed-wire fence that marked the boundary of Farmer Sherlock's pastureland. Oh-oh, thought Sonny, now comes the big challenge: How would they get Grampaw across?

"Nuttin' to it," he announced with considerable bravado.

Well, Sonny knew better. They first tried the easy approach, with Sonny stepping on a middle strand of wire and pulling up the next higher one. But despite all the creaking effort he could muster, Grampaw just couldn't bend so far and still get his long legs to move him forward properly.

"Dadburn it all!" he exclaimed. "Let's stop this nonsense and take the long way 'round."

"But, Grampaw, think of all the time we'll lose! Can't we try once more? How 'bout goin' right over the top? See how loose this top wire is. I can press it down and...."

"Yeah, and raise hob with my underside!"

So Sonny suggested they place their two straw hats together on the top wire, and Grampaw agreed that this looked likely to provide the needed protection. The operation then got underway.

Sonny first helped Grampaw lift one stiff leg up...up...up, almost high enough to get it over the fence. But not quite. Grampaw flailed his arms and fell back into Sonny's grasp.

"Damn and tarnation!" he bellowed in frustration, his

voice echoing like gunshots against the hills in the morning stillness.

They hauled away once more and, halting inch by inch, finally eased the right leg over. And there Grampaw now stood, straddling the fence and resting on the straw hats like a reluctant cowboy on a skinny steer.

"Oh, what a pretty pickle you got me in now," he groaned.

Bowser, keeping tab on all this hard maneuvering, merrily circled the panting pair, yapping encouragement. He then moved in to help. He sank his teeth into a leg of Grampaw's overalls and pulled mightily.

"Leggo, you dadgum mongrel!" Grampaw barked, shaking his leg and sending Bowser screeching for cover.

Sonny next strained to get the other leg across but Grampaw weaved and tilted precariously, and it became obvious that he would wind up in a heap on the other side if they continued with that approach. So Sonny crawled through the fence and pulled on Grampaw from the far side. The left leg came up and almost cleared...but caught on a couple barbs at the last second. Suddenly, it pulled free with a SNAP! Grampaw came zipping over like a rock out of a slingshot and landed squarely on Sonny.

"Damn and tarnation!" he howled again, almost stampeding Sherlock's far-off cows.

"Who-o-o-of!" came Sonny's response as the two hit the ground with a thud, Grampaw on top.

Now, Sonny could have been pretty thoroughly flattened by this accident except for one thing: He landed smack-dab on a big pile of cow dung. Which, luckily, cushioned his fall. However, as Grampaw was quick to point out, he didn't smell particularly appetizing afterward.

The two finally picked themselves up, brushed both dung and morning dew off their clothes, and set off once again, only slightly the worse for all the wear.

"Do me a favor, boy," said Grampaw, looking fierce as an eagle, "let's take the round-'bout way home, okay?"

As they arrived at the dense berry patch and began to pick away, Sonny thought of how these hills had become a beloved area for exploration and conquest—second only to the river itself. As he pointed out to his berry-picking partner (who, strangely enough, seemed to know the area well anyway), right ahead huge rocks had broken off the face of a cliff ages ago and piled up into a maze of twisted caves. He had spent much time there penetrating their mysteries.

And off to the right, at the end of Sherlock's farmed land, was an abandoned apple orchard. He had clambered up every one of those aging trees at one time or another to shake down the apples. As proof, his collarbone was still slightly askew; a limb had once broken under him, sending him crashing to the ground and knocking the bone right out of its socket with a painful PING! He was considerably more careful after that.

Worm-eaten the apples were, but not so much that Aunt Emma couldn't salvage enough to make an apple pie that melted right in your mouth. Plus apple jelly for the Winter. And, as Sonny thought happily, it would soon be time for another raid on that very orchard.

A little to the left, as Grampaw also knew well, was a sassafras tree. Here they came each Spring to dig up some roots, which were then boiled to make a delicious tea. Grampaw called this the finest of all Spring tonics; he imbued it with mysterious health-giving qualities. Maybe, Sonny thought, that was why he was still going so strong in his 80s!

Up on top of a hill to the right was the hickory grove where Sonny had come with Arnie that lively Fall day to gather nuts as well as reconnoiter Rube Rolland's still. Persimmon trees grew all through the area, their delicious soft fruit ripe for the plucking after the first frost. Walnut trees were nearby, too. And once frost hit, he would knock off the stained husks and gather up a load of them, as well.

Both hickory nuts and walnuts had hard, tough shells, but some determined hammering and picking would yield nuts a-plenty for baking and even an occasional platter of fudge, Aunt Emma and their sugar budget willing.

But most important of all the hills' secrets lay at the end of that nearby ravine with the big beech tree and its mysterious carved-out Biblical message. This was a spring where cool, clear water bubbled up into a stone basin from deep inside the earth. They had put this to good use this very day. And now, since their sightings of the sun told them it was nearing noon, they decided to top off their buckets and visit the spring for one last long drink before heading home.

Bowser had something to say about this plan, though. Sonny got so busy wiping away sweat and scratching chigger bites with one hand while picking berries off the thorny bushes with the other, that he neither saw nor heard the danger lurking in the shadows. But Bowser did, and he set up a furious barking.

"You gotta stop that consarned dog from all that dadburned barkin'," growled Grampaw.

"Hush, Bowser!" Sonny said, trying to sound strict.

And with that he reached deep into the bush to pick an especially big clump of berries. There was a rustling sound. A dark rattlesnake's head darted forward like an arrow. Piercing teeth sank into Sonny's outstretched hand.

"Ow...ow...OW!" he howled, reeling back and almost falling. "Grampaw, it's a snake. I bin bit!"

He looked down at his painfully smarting hand. And there on the back, right between the thumb and first finger, appeared two jagged, ominously red tooth marks.

"O Grampaw, what'll we do. I bin poisoned! I'm a goner!"

Propelled by Sonny's cries of desperation, Grampaw

lurched to the boy's side and pulled him farther from the bushes, where Bowser was now hopping and barking at the snake in full cry. He grasped Sonny's wrist above the bite with one long hand and squeezed hard. With the other, he whipped out his jackknife.

"This is gonna hurt, boy," he said urgently in a gruff voice. "Better turn your head...."

Working the blade out without releasing his tourniquet-like grip on the wrist, he cut into Sonny's hand right across the tooth-marks—first one way, then the other. It burned like fire and Sonny cried out and jerked his hand. But Grampaw held on tight. Blood ran. He bent over and sucked hard on the wound, spitting blood and corruption out in a windy blast. He did it again...and again. He then pulled his soiled old sweat rag out of his rear pocket and placed it over the cuts. He spoke softly, hurriedly:

"Here, boy, press this down...hard...and hold it there."

Rummaging around and locating a big stick, Grampaw turned back to the bushes, where Bowser was still breathing fire and dancing all around the rattler. Crash, bam, bang! went the club. Until Bowser quieted down and Grampaw tersely announced, out of breath:

"Good riddance! There's one son-a-gun who ain't a-gonna bother no one no more."

Looking at Sonny with real concern showing in his piercing eyes, he went on, "How you feel, boy?"

Well, Sonny didn't feel well at all. His head was spinning like a top and his stomach seemed to be tied in knots.

"Water, boy, you need water—lots of it!" Grampaw grunted.

So, helping Sonny along, he half dragged the stricken boy over the rough ground back to the spring. Here, Sonny dipped his head into the cool, refreshing water—and drank deeply. They washed the wound and bandage and, at Grampaw's urging, Sonny drank still more water.

He felt awful. Then came a horrible thought stalking into his whirling head: "Dear Jesus, I could be layin' here dyin'! Lyin' like a chopped log. Dying! And only 14!"

He rolled onto his side...and found himself looking up at his big beech tree. He read, cleared his eyes, and re-read the gnarled letters:

I WILL LIFT UP
MINE EYES
UNTO THE HILLS

The message imparted a strange feeling of lightness, of peace. He moaned softly. Well, maybe he was dying. He swallowed hard and gritted his teeth.

He thought of Mom and how she would mourn his death. And of how he would never come to finish his search for the real America or find the ultimate secret of life. He thought, too, of Aunt Emma and Sis and their sorrow. Then a strangely comforting thought also crept in—as to how much Arnie would regret how he had treated his little brother. Finally, getting more practical, he thought of Grampaw and the impossibly long trip he would have to get home and back to get help to carry out his body—then home again.

Suddenly, like a lamp being lit, the rest of that beautiful biblical passage broke into his thoughts: "I will lift up mine eyes unto the hills from whence cometh my help."

FROM WHENCE COMETH MY HELP!

Help from the hills! From this spring! From this water!

He rolled back to the spring and drank and drank and drank ...until he couldn't hold another drop. All to Grampaw's noisy approval.

He began to feel a bit better.

"Think there's any poison left?" he asked shakily.

"Nope, I reckon we got it all."

"Think there's any danger of infection from the knife-cut?"

That brought a laugh: "Nah, that tobacco I chaw would kill just 'bout any germ that ever lived."

Sonny nodded toward the big beech and asked: "Ever see that carving before, Grampaw?"

"Yup."

"Oh?" replied a surprised Sonny. "Then maybe you also know how it got there?"

"Yup, I do. It was cut there by brother Ben...back when we were boys."

"But that must have been sixty-seventy years ago!"

"Yup. Back in the last century. Ben was always quotin' that passage from the Bible."

"Well, darn if that don't beat all!" Sonny exclaimed in exasperation. "I thought I was the only one who knew about this spot...."

"Boy, that's the trouble with you young'ns these days: You don't give us old folks credit for knowing nothin'! You don't listen to a word we say. So then you gotta go out and rediscover everything all over again. And make all the same old mistakes we did. Bah!"

"But, but...I mean...I thought...but...."

A baffled Sonny sputtered into silence, his speaking motor temporarily needing recharging. He was beginning to wonder if most of the mysteries of life might well have a rational explanation, after all—maybe even a simple one.

Like the ultimate secret of life. But how on earth could one develop the required knowledge and insight to solve them? How on earth?

Sonny tried out his shaky legs. He got to his feet and gave Bowser a lingering hug. Then he tried the same with Grampaw, who brusquely shook it off as a completely unnecessary and embarrassing show of affection. They then turned homeward with relief...plus the day's pickings.

Aunt Emma almost broke down when she heard what had happened. She bandaged up the hand with a wet borax acid compress "to draw out the p'ison," got him out of his smelly over-alls and sent him down to the river to wash off the last traces of the cow manure he had picked up. Then, over Grampaw's heated protests against "sp'ilin' the boy," she confined Sonny to the house for the rest of the day.

She next proceeded to bake a big blackberry cobbler. And as Sonny ate first one, then two absolutely delicious pieces, she and Sis busied themselves preparing the first batch of food of the canning season.

As the washed berries were brought to a slow boil, Ball jars and lids and rubber sealers were covered with boiling water. Then, once the berries had reached a fine finish, they were ladled into the drained jars. A half-dozen quarts were thus sealed and stashed away for use during the coming Winter. In the days ahead, Sonny knew, more berries would be picked and canned and made into jams and jellies. Tomatoes, green beans, corn and cucumber-pickles would follow until, finally, over a hundred jars would be so set aside. All hard, demanding work in a steamy kitchen—which, thanks mainly to Aunt Emma, would keep them all going during the cold days of Winter when the only thing growing would be their appetites.

While all this heated activity was going on in the kitchen, Grampaw had retired to his rocker on the frontporch, where he appeared to be dozing after their strenuous berry-picking tour. Actually, he was playing 'possum while engaging in his favorite pastime: Counting the cars passing by. Last Sunday he had come in for dinner and proudly announced that he had counted 137 cars, 28 trucks and 2 buses that day. Sonny wasn't quite sure what the significance of all this was...but, as he argued with a scoffing Aunt Emma, if it was important to Grampaw, well, it just had to be important.

Today, in any event, something important did seem to be happening out front. One of the cars being tallied actually stopped, and someone called out a few words to the old-timer relaxing in his rocker. From his kitchen perch, Sonny saw that it was a big black sedan with a whole slew of people inside...and it was loaded to the axles with scruffy suitcases and cartons tied to the top and rear-end.

Grampaw, his hearing getting worse by the day, obviously didn't hear a word being shouted to him. So he got up and lumbered down the front steps and across the road to the car. He leaned in the window and, suddenly, Sonny saw a very fat, dark-haired woman running her arms over him. And, of all things, Grampaw seemed to be enjoying it!

Aunt Emma then stepped over and blocked the view.

"Land o' mercy!" she cried out. "It's a whole carload of gypsies!"

She dropped everything and went high-tailing it out the kitchen door and across the front yard. As she drew near, the fat one shoved Grampaw unceremoniously aside. The car engine roared, the wheels spun on the roadside gravel, and off the sedan zoomed. But not before an angry...and alert...Aunt Emma got the license number.

Well, it took only a second or two before Grampaw let out a blood-curdling yell. His wallet was gone! Along with the seven dollars he had scrounged up by hard work that Summer and salvaged from Aunt Emma's eager hands.

"'Pon my word, if that don't beat all!" exclaimed Aunt Emma.

Since Sonny was ailing, she dispatched Sis to J.P. to report the robbery, then turned on Grampaw with her sharp tongue whipping around in that distraught Maggie face:

"My, oh my, did they ever take you for a ride!"

"Why, I didn't budge an inch."

"Not that, you silly old fogey! I mean they took you to the cleaners. They seen you was an easy mark—ripe for the pluckin'...and they cleaned you out."

"But dadburn it all," he said, "they asked the way to Ashland and...and I just tried to help out...."

"Bah, you've just proven again there ain't no fool like an old fool."

Grampaw thereupon r'ared back and in his most solemn Bible-quoting style, declared, "He who calleth his brother a fool is in danger of hell fire!"

"Well, praise be I'm no brother of yourn."

"No, you're worse! You're my daughter—a witch daughter!"

Constable Flint just then drove into the yard and broke up the proceedings.

"We nailed the rascals good!" he shouted from the car.

Draping his lanky frame against the cinderblock wall leading up to the porch, he told that J.P. had alerted the police in South Point and Ironton, and that the big black sedan had been spotted and stopped while turning onto the bridge leading over to Ashland, Kentucky. More to the point, as the highway patrolman pulled the car over, he caught a glimpse of something being thrown into the roadside bushes. It turned out to be Grampaw's wallet—a thoroughly emptied wallet.

"Caught red-handed, the pocket-pickin' polecats!" the constable chuckled.

Anyway, the wallet and its precious seven dollars were now on their way back to their rightful owner. And the pickpockets were being treated to a night in jail. "To teach 'em to steer clear of these parts," as Flint put it.

By this time, Sonny was polishing off his fourth piece of cobbler, with his teeth turning several shades of blackberry blue. Nothing had ever tasted so delicious! Yet, somehow, it wasn't sitting well in his stomach. His face was also turning somewhat blue. Suddenly he doubled over as cramps convulsed his belly...and he rushed outside to throw up.

Hobbling back, he found Aunt Emma waiting for him with a glass of water into which she was stirring a spoonful of baking soda—the old reliable all-purpose household remedy that was used for everything from baking and cleaning to itches and tooth brushing. And down it went. But Sonny didn't know whether the upset was due to the snakebite or to all the berries and cobbler he had eaten.

In any case, off to bed Sonny went—a temporary victim of life with nature, a nature that he had learned once more could be at once bountiful and dangerous.

But he felt it had been a banner day in his own special way, too. For he had gathered in still more solid stuff about the real America. And Mom would shortly be reading all about it....

Chapter 7
Be Prepared

Nature got involved in another tricky situation for Sonny the following Winter, setting the stage by ushering in some record-breaking bone-chilling weather. In fact, it was so cold one Friday evening in early February that Sonny could see the river's edges were frozen over and, looking off in the distance, that great blocks of ice were sweeping down the river in midstream, banging into each other and piling up in jagged clumps far from shore.

He was on his way to a Boy Scout meeting, for which he had been drilling hard, since he was up for his test to become a First Class Scout. He felt a little uneasy about that, even though he found scouting really interesting. One big reason was that it was deeply involved in another major discovery he had made about America: It was a most neighborly, gregarious place. Sometimes too much so!

People, he noted, were joining all kinds of organizations—religious, farm, business, labor, fraternal, veterans groups, you name it. Some organizations did real good for the community. But it seemed that most, as Grampaw remarked dryly, "hold meetin's just for the sake of meetin'." But now the sharp wind forced him to focus on the weather. He pulled Arnie's old jacket tighter around his neck and broke into a trot to keep warm.

Glancing off to the river on his right, he thought to himself that this is how it must have been for Eliza in "Uncle Tom's Cabin" as she fled over the Ohio with little Harry in her arms. He had thrilled to that drama when a traveling stage group put it on last year in a tent show on the town square. And now he was on his way to the same area for the scout meeting.

Harold Hammer, their scoutmaster ("forget the Mister— just call me Hammer"), had gotten the town council's okay to use an old, one-room wooden building in the square for Troop One's meetings. Some said it was an old slave quarters; others that it was once a tobacco smokehouse, and Aunt Emma was convinced it was "ha'nted". In any case, it had a big fireplace and he now looked forward to thawing out before it.

Sure enough, Sonny found the fire blazing brightly and crackling merrily on arrival, and the old shack was beginning to heat up despite the numerous air leaks around the two small windows and door. A dozen of his pals were already on hand, beating themselves noisily to keep warm.

Smart Alleck, who had apparently appointed himself firetender for the evening, laid another log on...and the fire leaped still higher. He had an ornery expression on his face, which reflected itself precisely in what he had to say:

"That s.o.b. Hammer's gonna get what's comin' to him tonight. I'm gonna burn his tail!"

Smart was riled up because Hammer, as their highschool coach, had just booted ("excused" was the word he used) Alleck off the school's tumbling team. The reason: He was too "disruptive." A description which all the other team members, including Sonny, considered an understatement. They also now laughed off Smart's current threat as the harmless bleating of a sorehead.

Sonny himself loved tumbling. He was now in his second year of highschool and got a chance to show off backflips, frontflips and all kinds of team acrobatics in the gym before each basketball game. All aimed primarily at impressing Jenny Lee Simms with his prowess. Besides, he felt tumbling had to be one of the finest of all physical conditioners, keeping him in good shape as he grew taller, almost by the day.

"All hands on deck!" Hammer shouted as he barged into the shack. Young, heavy-set, fair-haired, his eyes sparkling with enthusiasm, the coach/Physical Ed teacher/scoutmaster called the troop to order in a no-nonsense, military style. This was an outgrowth of Army Reserve training in college. And now, the troop felt, he was out to show them what a great general he would make.

"All right, Hoot Owls, let's see the Scout salute…smart and sharp—and pull in that belly and stick out that chest!"

Sonny raised his hand in the three-finger salute along with the others.

"And the Pledge of Allegiance…."

They faced the flag near the fireplace and loudly intoned the Pledge.

"Now, let's hear the Scout Oath…."

And the boys proclaimed the Oath in a shrill, discordant, uncoordinated blast.

"Oh, that was awful!" Hammer growled, a look of horror filling his face. "Let's do it again…right this time!" And they did:

> "On my honor I will do my best
> To do my duty to God and my country
> and to obey the Scout Law;
> To help other people at all times;
> To keep myself physically strong,
> mentally awake and morally straight."

It sounded a lot better the second time. Sonny, meanwhile, went on repeating to himself the last two lines, which he had come to like as summing up volumes of personal guidance. And now he also found himself wondering if they might have something to do with his search for the ultimate secret of life.

"Okay, be seated!" Hammer sounded off.

The boys scrambled to their places on two scarred benches, one on each side of the fireplace—which Smart, his hair gleaming as red as the fire, again stoked up with another log. The scoutmaster seated himself on a rickety chair in the middle and began shuffling through some papers in a battered briefcase. Like the scouts, he wore everyday clothes—in his case, dungarees and a blue shirt under a heavy sweater. As Sonny had happily found out on first joining the group, no one, and least of all him, could afford an official uniform. Yet, each of the boys had managed to obtain a scout hat and neckerchief and what Sonny considered the most precious prize of all, the *Boy Scout Handbook*. So they viewed themselves as equally equipped as any scout troop in the country.

The drill tonight, Hammer announced, would include the admission of two new scouts, the promotion of two others from Tenderfoot to Second Class, Sonny's exam for moving up to First Class Scout, an exchange of ideas on community services they might undertake—such as cleaning up the debris along Route 52—and planning for a Springtime visit to Lock 28 on the Ohio, a couple miles east of Shirlington. Sonny rubbed his hands at that one; he had always wanted to see how the great towboats and their long strings of barges were stepped up to a higher river level when going upstream—and vice versa. And now all of them would have that chance.

Bang! The door flew open and in burst Sonny's friend, Clay, red-faced from the cold wind and long walk from his home near the lock. Clay's arrival meant the night would be fun; Sonny knew he could count on him to sound off later on with the latest jokes from Amos 'n' Andy and that fast-quipping new star, Bob Hope.

"Shut the door, you idiot!" came an agonized cry as the chill blast hit the troop. And Smart threw another log on the roaring fire, casting a sidelong glance at Hammer as he did so. Which led Sonny to wonder if his threat should be taken seriously.

Rapping for order, Hammer called for a show of hands of those who were actually reading their *Handbook* assignment.

"ACTUALLY, Hoot Owls!"

Well, one hand shot up plenty fast and that belonged to Sonny, an avid reader of just about anything he could lay his hands on. His *Boy Scout Handbook* hadn't just been read; it had been devoured. Sonny reveled in its sections on handicrafts and rope-work, on nature lore, hiking and camping and cooking outdoors, on first aid and personal hygiene.

He had found much practical information there for use in everyday life, too. Like the suggestion to drink a glass of water each morning 15 minutes before eating. Everyone in the area seemed to be plagued by constipation (Aunt Emma said it was because of the hot biscuits and fresh-baked bread they ate)—but not Sonny, at least not in the year since he had started the pre-breakfast water ritual. And it sure beat taking Aunt Emma's foul Epsom Salts or castor oil!

Then, there were the *Handbook*'s drawings of various exercises. Hammer had singled out one as the most important to physical health—sit-ups. A dozen times each morning of sitting up and touching your toes would, he said, give you a hard, flat stomach, strong back and well-tuned internal organs. Sonny was giving this a try, too…to the daily accompaniment of some very loud and merry derision from Arnie.

Now, though, Hammer was drawing something on the shack's cracked blackboard. It showed two boys in a race. One had two mammoth iron balls chained to his ankles—one labeled "tobacco", the other "alcohol". Well, it took no genius to see who was going to win that race! Even so, he asked the troop:

"Okay, Hoot Owls, who's gonna win this race?"

"The guy with the ball and chains!" Clay cracked.

"Oh?"

"Yep. Those balls are actually balloons filled with helium. He's gonna soar right over the other guy and...."

A collective roar was followed by a chorus of boos and hisses.

"Well, that's creative thinking for you," Hammer said with a chuckle. "So how 'bout the rest of you being a little creative, too?"

He thereupon asked everyone to reproduce the drawing, each in his own way, and bring it to the next scout meeting. That way, he concluded, "You just might remember it and steer clear of drinking and smoking."

"Does that include cornsilk and Indian cigars?" someone asked.

Scowling at the interruption, he charged on. "Don't—repeat, do NOT—depend on doctors to keep you well. That's your job, not theirs! And you do it by keeping in top physical condition—by eating right and living right." He paused to collect his thoughts. "And one other thing, men: Be on guard against drugs and medicines of all kinds that aren't absolutely necessary for survival. Take too much of such things and...wham!...you're dead!"

Well, thought Sonny, that sure sounds like J.P.'s "boomerang theory": Overdo anything good and it automatically becomes bad. And as for doctors, he tried to remember the one time he had seen one since coming to this special part of America. Ah, yes, it was the time Aunt Emma decided he had to have his tonsils removed. And what made him remember was the acrid smell of the ether he had been given—which, sad to say, still hung on.

"By golly, it's plenty hot here!" the scoutmaster abruptly added, mopping his brow and moving back to his chair.

"Yeah, but it's still plenty cold back here," one of the boys yelled from the far end of the benches. And Smart, watching the scoutmaster like an attacking hawk, threw another log on the fire.

Hammer then proceeded with the night's drill:

"First, let's hear your favorite Motto."

"Be prepared," came in a mumble.

"C'mon, guys, act like you mean it."

"BE PREPARED!!!"

He turned around and spotted Sonny: "Okay, now comes your turn."

Sonny stood up, and was promptly greeted by a low-loud whisper from Clay, who had already reached the exalted status of Star Scout: "He'll never make it!"

"All right, Sonny," said the scoutmaster. "You know the Scout Law?"

Yep, he allowed he did...and proceeded to rattle off the dozen "commandments": "A scout is trustworthy, loyal and helpful...friendly, courteous and kind...obedient, cheerful and thrifty...brave, clean and...and...reverent."

"Ah, yes...mighty big words, aren't they?" Hammer commented. "Know what they mean?"

"Yeah, I think so..." Actually, since Sonny was now a member of the church and tried to live like one—though not in the sticky, goody-goody way Reverend Smith had cautioned against—he found no difficulty in agreeing with the elements of the Scout Law. He thought they made good sense and took them seriously as practical guides to everyday behavior. And couldn't they also serve as a guidepost to the ultimate secret of life? Sonny chalked this up as another good question for his next meeting with Mom.

"Okay, so I won't ask you to define them," Hammer went on. "The main point is that they add up to a way of life—a darn good way—a way of being fair and square...and civil and decent...and helpful to others."

"And if you guys aren't already that," he added, glaring around the room, "you're gonna have to answer to ME!"

"But now, tell us, Sonny, how you rank the Duties of a Scout. Which come first in importance?"

Sonny found himself sweating, and it wasn't because of the scoutmaster's grilling. Behind him, the fire by now was really roaring. He decided Hammer had understated the matter: It was DARN hot.

"Well, a scout's first duty is to God. Then to his country. Then to others. And, finally, to himself."

"And why is duty to yourself put last?"

"Gosh, I'm really not sure. Because the others involve more people, I s'pose...."

"Well, I'll tell you why. It's simply because people don't need any reminder about watching out for Ol' Yours Truly. They do that instinctively. But it takes hard training on our part...and real effort on your part...to begin thinking of others and putting others' welfare first. And that's the kind of training you're getting right now."

"Give him more—he's still resistin'!" cut in Clay.

Hammer smiled: "Here's a question for all you Owls. If you look at both the Scout Law and a Scout's Duties, what do all their requirements really add up to? Want to take a first crack at answering, Sonny?"

Was it smoke he smelled? Sonny wondered. But, of course, it would be from the burning firewood. He coughed and responded:

"Why, I guess you'd say they're all meant to make us better people—better citizens."

"That's right, but I was thinking of something even more basic."

Clay piped up: "Yessir, here's one. Preacher Johnson says people are basically animals at heart—actually, wild beasts. And living in line with the Scout Law...plus, of course, the Bible...is our only hope of becomin' real human beings."

"And giving up our dog-eat-dog ways," chimed in another.

"In favor of live and let live," added Sonny.

"No, no, that's too easy an approach—too passive!" Hammer cut in. "You gotta be more action-oriented. The key is summed up in that good old phrase, 'I am my brother's keeper'. But let's round out the picture. What's our troop's Mascot?"

"The Hoot Owl!"

"And what people are not Hoot Owls?"

"Others!"

"And what's our troop's Motto?"

"Let's give a hoot!"

"A hoooot for whooooo?"

"Others!"

"And what should a good scout be doing every single day of his life?"

"A Good Turn!"

"A Good Turn for who?"

"Others!"

"And what's the Golden Rule?"

The answer sounded pretty ragged but the main elements came across: "Do unto others as you would have others do unto you!"

"And what's the Rule's key word?"

"Do!"

Hammer abruptly threw up his hands, as though imploring heaven for help, and bellowed: "Doggone it...can't you birds ever get it right! Try again...."

"Others!"

"I can't hear you...."

"OTHERS!" The old shack shook with the boomed-out answer.

Clay whispered in Sonny's ear, "Sounds great, but our ol' pal, Moonshiner Rolland, has another version: Do in others before they have a chance to do in you!"

"Yeah, and that's exactly the kind of moonshine you'd expect from a moonshiner!" Sonny shot back. This was one area where he felt he needed few pointers. If there was one human fault Sonny had come to despise above all else, it was people lording it over others or taking advantage of others.

"Okay, Hoot Owls, now you've got the big picture," the scoutmaster went on, warming up to his subject. "All these rules of scouting are meant to do one big thing, and that's pull people out of their shell of a total concentration on themselves...and make them more considerate of others. From focus on self to a focus on others—that's the ticket. That's the only way we can live together, work together, build together."

He abruptly shifted ground, both in subject matter and to get away from the roaring fire. "Now, having said all this, let me give you birds a word of warning. One day you'll find yourself out in the cold, cold job world...competing for positions, promotions, raises. And you're gonna run into some real skunks—people who won't be playing by the same Boy Scout rulebook as you are."

Hammer's mouth and eyes—his whole face—twisted with disgust and he almost choked on the next words. "Now, I'm not talking about your everyday garden-variety type of skunk either. I'm talking about dirty, low-down, contemptible, mean, vicious skunks. If they think you're a rival for an opening they want, they'll interpret your being fair and square and considerate of others as a sign of weakness. They'll see this as an open invitation to knife you in the back, bash in your head and steamroll you in their frenzy to get ahead."

This set off a clamor, punctuated by a plaintive voice from the back: "So after you've been cut up, clobbered and flattened, what's left?"

"Your principles, numbskull!" yelled Clay.

"Not far off track," Hammer came back to Sonny's surprise. He visibly wound up to make his real point: "No gain I can think of is worth abandoning your ideals. Or your self-respect. Hang onto those with your very life! You'll get just as far ahead without using gutter tactics. But BE PREPARED! Keep your guard up...and your mitts ready. And remember always the Golden Rule of Self-Defense."

His eyes swept over the troop: "Does anyone know that one?"

"Naw...nope...no...never heard of it!" came the answer.

"Well, you'd better learn it by heart, gang...or else you're gonna run into a peck of trouble in life. It's simply this: If you don't take care of your own hide, you'll soon find yourself unable to help anyone else take care of his."

Sonny nodded, looked around...and now, to his alarm, smelled a more acrid smoke than before. From somewhere deep inside, he heard an old and familiar but suddenly urgent call: Lift up your eyes! He did...and thought he saw wisps of white among the dark rafters overhead. Was that the smoke he smelled? From the shack's own timbers? He shifted uneasily just as he noticed Smart pull a small blazing stick out of the fire and sneak up behind Hammer. Over he bent, reaching out to put the stick in Hammer's pants cuff. Sonny coughed violently and yelled, "Let's get away from this darn fire. It's too hot!"

Everyone did, including Hammer...who thus barely escaped "having his tail burned." Smart blinked furiously and started to say something to Sonny when....

WHOOOOMB!

Sonny felt the explosive boom first, then saw its triggering cause over his shoulder in its rawest form. The whole super-heated wall around the fireplace burst into roaring flame. Fire shot upward and out toward them with a deafening blast. A dozen boys recoiled simultaneously in terror and stampeded toward the door. But since this opened inward, they piled up against it in panic and kept it closed...producing even worse panic. Equally terrified, Sonny joined the others in screaming at the top of his lungs and adding to the pandemonium.

"Away from the door!" the scoutmaster shouted above the din.

To no avail....

He lurched to the side and lunged against the pile-up in a classic football blocking style, clearing a hole in the line. And there stood the door! Sonny jerked it open so hard it almost came off the hinges...and a dozen fire-propelled boys rocketed out of that burning building. In the nick of time, too. For the flames spread instantly through the tinder-dry shack right up to the door wall. Soon it was one huge, fierce inferno.

Outside, Sonny looked around wildly, saw Clay...and threw his arms around his friend and gulped in the clear cold air. "M...my...my God, Clay, we almost didn't make it!"

"Y...yeah, tonight, for sure, God's got to be watchin' out for fools and idiots."

The smile had gone from Clay's face. This was no joke. He then caught a glimpse of Smart slinking off toward the back and tore into him. "Darn if you didn't outsmart yourself this time, Smart. You almost burned Hammer's tail, all right. Plus everyone else's, including your own. Too bad you didn't stay in there!"

Smart's chin trembled and tears suddenly gushed from his eyes. He looked so miserable that Sonny clapped him on the shoulder. He wanted to say something reassuring but stopped in mid-sentence. It would surely have been a lie. For Smart was truly a louse.

The boys huddled together and stared in dismay at what could have been, and almost was, their funeral pyre. Sonny shivered, and not just from the cold. What if he had been burned alive! He thought again of Mom and Aunt Emma and their grief on hearing the news. But equally disturbing was the thought that something, or someone, had forced him to move away from the fireplace...and saved him. Was it a sixth sense? Or instinct? Or had God Himself intervened?

But that made no sense at all, he decided. For why would the mighty Creator of the universe—the Lord of billions—pay any attention whatever to any one person...and one so insignificant as him? And if God had acted to spare him, why? For what possible purpose?

Sonny wrestled in awe with such thoughts as he watched the shack burn. Flames reached one of the oil lamps, which exploded with a splitting C-CRACK! spewing out kerosene and converting the whole building into one giant fireball. It lit up the entire community, bringing the nearest neighbors yelling out into the square.

"Darn if the scouts haven't set fire to the town's shack!" one yelled in disgust.

"Water!" hollered another. "Let's get a bucket brigade going..."

"Too late!" Hammer shouted back, looking plenty embarrassed. The wind was luckily blowing fire, smoke and sparks toward the river. "Nothing we can do now but let it burn out."

And it was too late, Sonny noted. Roof, walls, supporting timbers—everything—were now ablaze, with fire pouring out the window and door openings. It was both horrible and gripping, as though they had accidentally opened a gate to the fiery furnace of hell itself.

"Biggest show in town!" one of the onlookers cracked.

"Even beats the Fourth of July!" yelled another.

And since the boys now found themselves surprisingly very much alive, they began to smile—finally letting loose with some shaky laughter.

Sonny found himself no less embarrassed than Hammer at the weird turn of events. He wondered, could the troop survive the disaster...and... the town's ridicule? Well, they at least had survived, and wasn't that the first essential for rebuilding?

One thoughtful neighbor came out with blankets and threw one over Sonny's trembling shoulders. He nodded in thanks, thinking, "Boy, Arnie's gonna see red when he finds his jacket's gone."

The blazing roof abruptly caved in, sending flames and a great shower of sparks skyward. Sonny jumped back in alarm, seized by a terrible thought: What if the whole world went up in flames like that? It could happen, Mr. Appleton had told him. And power-mad monsters like Hitler and Stalin were just the kind of people who might well do it.

"It's fine to be a good scout," he had declared, waving his shrapnel-shattered hand to give the point extra emphasis, "but in a world filled with tyrants, commissars, warmongers and gangsters of every kind and description, you darn well better do like Teddy Roosevelt and carry a very Big Stick."

Sonny stirred himself, looked down and saw that, somehow, he had come through all this commotion still clutching his *Boy Scout Handbook*. He went over to his scoutmaster, held it up, and said:

"Look, Hammer, we did save something. We can use this to get going again."

"Yeah," the scoutmaster sighed, his face lit up by the fire's red glare, "and next time, I can tell you, we're gonna be a lot better prepared."

He looked at Sonny and added with a warm smile. "Oh, incidentally, you passed," he said. "You're no longer just an everyday ordinary garden-variety good scout; you're now a First Class Scout!"

As the show finally broke up and all the spectators disbanded, Sonny trudged homeward, clutching his thin blanket against the fierce cold and feeling mighty glad to be alive. Now he had a story for Mom! One that would really grab her attention. Not that this particular fire was so much a part of the real America. But the Scout movement was, like nothing else—both boy and girl varieties. In fact, Scouting looked to Sonny like the very essence of the real America. It was an unbeatable formula for people living together in harmony.

Scouting also singularly encompassed the heartfelt love of country that Sonny had found so strong in this Tri-State area of Ohio, Kentucky and West Virginia. Here, America wasn't just a place; it was a magic word, all wrapped up with everything people held near and dear. It was a word people spoke with a touch of reverence. America here meant that people had the chance to become all that their vision and abilities allowed. There was missionary zeal in the word, too. As J.P. put it during one of their talk sessions:

"People from throughout the world have contributed to the making of America. Now America's gonna contribute to the remaking of the world."

But what about Scouting and individual aspirations? Did the field and its teachings also hold clues to the ultimate secret of life? Sonny stopped at that one, completely unsure of the answer. He thought he had come close to solving the riddle several times but, then, it always seemed to slip away from his grasp.

Actually, he had lately found this second big exploration assignment increasingly intriguing. Ever since J.P.'s talk about combining the pursuit of learning with religious faith, he had been working over a long row of questions, mainly at night before drifting off to sleep. For instance, he wondered, could the ultimate secret of life, however one finally defined it, also lead to riches? And if it did, would that make any real difference in a person's happiness? Or would wealth even work against this larger life goal?

Sonny remembered well the time that, in total ignorance of the consequences, he had fed their chickens too much corn. Matching his ignorance, they, in turn, ate and ate and ate. Until their craws almost burst. The result: Two dead young roosters. And while this led to an unexpected meal of fried chicken, it also brought a tongue-lashing that still stung.

So now he wondered how much in material goods and sensual satisfactions a person could rake in to himself without becoming like one of those roosters...or exploding like an over-inflated balloon. Can the human personality, pumped up too taut by having it too good, really withstand affluence?

A related question then crept into his thinking: What about fame? Would living according to the ultimate secret also bring public acclaim? And would the human personality be able to withstand that, too? Or, as J.P. had said about politicians and kindred stuffshirts, would the public spotlight have the same disastrous effect on a person as using a magnifying glass to focus the sun's rays on a fragile piece of tinder?

Sonny's own brief flirtation with the limelight was a warning signal. He recalled how much he had enjoyed his studies and the excitement of exploring new universes of knowledge. But then, when good grades started rolling in and teachers began to praise him, his head began to swell ominously. He began to think he was somebody!

"Better get off that high horse 'fore you fall flat on your face," Arnie had snapped in his old, inimitable manner. And who could know this better than a sometimes sports star? One who had often heard heartening cheers turn suddenly to jarring jeers?

So Sonny began to walk more humbly and keep a low profile. Not only to moderate others' resentment and potential enmity but also to avoid a crackdown by what he saw as a very fickle fate.

This very subject had come up at a recent bible study session at church, where Paster Smith posed a surprise question: "Why do you think religion is important?" He got all kinds of answers, among them:

"So's you can be good and do good."

"So you can get into heaven."

"So you can have one real friend in a friendless world."

"So you can get some inspiration into your humdrum life."

"So you can get God's help in facing trials and tribulations."

Someone then threw in a curve: "So you can get help in putting up with your relatives and in-laws!"

"Okay...now, try one more," the minister continued. "And that's so people can keep perspective. We poor humans find it almost impossible to handle wealth, status, power, public acclaim. It's intoxicating! And the more you drink of this witch's brew, the drunker you get. Modesty and humility go out the window. You begin to think you've moved beyond mere mortals...when, in reality, you've become only a crooked caricature of a mortal. No matter how many nations you conquer or how many people you command or how many possessions you accumulate, you remain as fragile and vulnerable in time and space as our tiny Planet Earth is in the vast, unpredictable universe. We need to believe in something far greater than ourselves—something with infinite power over our lives and fortunes. Which is what the Old Testament's lowly Job found when he talked with the mighty Voice out of the Whirlwind. Only then can we begin to relate realistically to others, to our surroundings, to God and, by no means least, to ourselves."

Paster Smith went on to say that much of this was marvelously summed up by that great Scotch poet, Robert Burns, when he wrote...

"Oh wad some Power the giftie gie us
to see ourselves as others see us!
It wad frae monie a blunder free us,
and foolish notion."

Sonny considered this subject intimately related to one other thing, too, and that was his own searches. He was finding them both instructive and real fun....

Chapter 8
The Hills of Home

Just as Sonny had looked to the hills earlier to provide newsworthy material for reports to his mother on the real America, now he decided he had been seriously neglecting perhaps the most important news source of all. So he turned 180 degrees around and looked southward...at the wide, gleaming river that rippled its way downstream just 100 yards away—when it wasn't flooding, that is.

Hadn't Mark Twain captured much of what America was all about in his writings on his early days of working on the Mississippi?

Yet, there was one thing he felt he needed to sharpen his vision and give his own river-roving reporting some "inside" character, and that was a real river veteran. And who could perform that role better than his Dad, who had also told tall tales of sailing these inland waters when he was young? But Sonny knew this couldn't be, since his father was too far away. Then, as though by a miracle, it happened....

Dad's coming!

The news rang through the house with the power of a hundred church bells. Sonny could hardly contain his excitement.

It was all in the letter that Aunt Emma came up with in her latest race to the mailbox. The Plymouth plant in Detroit, where Dad was now a foreman on the final assembly line, was shutting down for a model change-over. He would arrive in late August and would try to stay for several weeks.

A busy half-year had passed since what local citizens called the Big Scout Fire. Sonny had turned 15 and was getting set for his junior year at Cheswick High School. There, his classwork was going smoothly. At least enough so that he felt Dad wouldn't get after him as he would with Arnie.

Grampaw grunted at the news and allowed as how it would be mighty nice to see his son Bob, one of eight children, again. Sis sparkled at the thought of being with her all-time idol once more. Aunt Emma relished the prospect of getting another live audience for her complaints. And Arnie, apprehensive over the coming accounting, looked unusually troubled.

"Now you're gonna get it," Aunt Emma told him with no little pleasure. "When your Pa sees how you've been behavin', he's gonna snatch you bald-headed. First, you're gonna get it from him—then he's gonna get it from me."

"Aw, go fly a kite, you old bat," Arnie muttered, just loud enough for the nearby Sonny and Sis to hear.

"Hey, hey...what's that you say!"

"I said it'll sure be great to see Dad again, won't it?"

So the day finally came when the big Greyhound bus stopped outside and Dad came striding across the road, lugging his suit case as handily as a lunch-pail. Bedlam broke loose as three bawling kids and one howling dog besieged him. Even Grampaw's eyes moistened; he hadn't seen his boy since Bob had come home from France as a war hero, got married to that pretty, soft-spoken school teacher from Kentucky, and left for Pittsburgh.

Aunt Emma was distinctly more distant, barely nodding a polite welcome.

Sonny found it all a little overwhelming and was glad when the uproar finally settled down and they went inside for dinner. He could see at a glance that his brother Arnie was truly a "chip off the old block." Dad had wavy brown hair and the same blue eyes as his father. He was solidly built. He moved with the easy grace and compressed energy of an athlete, and he acted with a certain swashbuckling, devil-may-care attitude. Sonny decided the others might be right in saying that he himself, being slimmer and more reserved, took after Mom.

There was a lot of catching-up to do, and the children listened open-mouthed as Dad recounted the happenings in the years since they had parted. It was the height of the crop season and the table fairly groaned with the output of Sonny's gardening. Aunt Emma fixed fried chicken and biscuits, roastin'ears, green beans, sweet potatoes and a big bowl of sliced tomatoes, cucumbers and onions. Dad praised it all lavishly while Sonny beamed with pleasure. Then came a revelation: Uncle Joe, who lived in Huntington and worked on the river, had talked with the big mate on his towboat and gotten a job for Dad as a deckhand. He would be going to work in 10 days.

Aunt Emma, who had been listening to all this with gathering impatience and assorted "harrumphs!", audibly relaxed at the prospect of Dad working and, hopefully, laying her hands on some real money. But she didn't relax so much that she was going to miss out on a chance to have it out with the brother she labelled "the shiftless one."

"Uh, Bob, about your young'ns," she began in a rising tone of voice, her tongue starting to flutter like a flag flapping in a stiff breeze, "I just cain't stand it no more. Each day I work till I drop. I...I...."

Oh, oh...here we go again! thought Sonny as he saw the Maggie face coming on and braced himself for a big blow-up. Aunt Emma looked all too ready to make some fresh soup from old bones.

Amazingly, Dad reacted completely different from Grampaw. He got up from his seat at the table, went around and took Aunt Emma's worn hand in his and stroked her lined cheek.

"Em, Em," he called softly. "Remember when you were a girl like Teresa Erika? And all the fun we had when you were learning to cook? And I was your human guinea pig?"

His sister almost blushed.

"Well, no one knows better than me how hard you work ...or all you've done for me and the kids. Or appreciates it more. You know that. But, Em, things are gonna be better now. Believe me. We're gonna work things out. And in ways you'll really like."

With that he pressed a wad of greenbacks into her hand and kissed her on the forehead. Aunt Emma's troubled face broke into a smile that reached from ear to ear.

Oh, if only Reverend Smith could see this! thought Sonny. Didn't he say love was THE answer?

There was more smiling after dinner when Sis broke out her banged-up second-hand guitar (seventh-hand would be a more fitting description) and started picking out some well-known tunes. Arnie tuned up a mouth organ which he had learned to play from one of The Boys. And Sonny himself got out his recorder which he was now playing fairly well—allowing, of course, for a missed note here and there.

They all seated themselves on the frontporch steps and played and sang lustily, just as virtually everyone they knew did in these parts. No matter how bad things were, people managed to make musical instruments, whether it was only a washboard or even a saw, and lift their spirits through music. So they dedicated to Dad songs like "I've Been Workin' on the Railroad" and "I'm a Yankee Doodle Dandy." Sis wasn't quite Kate Smith and Dad wasn't quite Bing Crosby—Aunt Emma's favorite singers—but they harmonized surprisingly well on "When the Moon Comes over the Mountain" and "Let Me Call You Sweetheart."

Then came cowboy tunes and Stephen Foster's soulful songs from the Old South. And when they got to "My Old Kentucky Home," Dad let the others sing on while he sat there looking out at the hills with a wistful look in his eyes. Sonny knew. They all felt Mom's presence.

Sis next came up with the surprise of the evening—a special song she and Sonny had written for just this occasion. A song Sonny hoped would capture some of the spirit of the real America. Its name: "Melody of America." The tune, she announced, had been borrowed from an old song about Montana. So, overriding catcalls from Arnie, they launched into their work:

> "Let's sing this melody about America,
> The greatest gift of God man's ever won.
> The glory of the West, America's the best:
> My heart goes out to you when day is done."

Well, the first stanza sounded a bit flat, and Sonny decided to forget about being a songwriter. But then everyone began to get the hang of the melody and the second stanza came off better.

> "Steamboat's comin' hootin' down the river,
> The freight train's whistle wails across the vale;

Crickets are a-chirpin', the rooster's crow is rung:
It's the finest melody I've ever sung."

The singers now hit full stride, and the final stanza came off with a rousing ring:

"Let's sing this melody about America,
Of workin', prayin' people proud and free;
A land for dreamin' dreams, the country of our birth,
The last, best hope of man upon this earth!"

Some boisterous cheering erupted, and everyone joined in singing "Melody" all over again. Dad pronounced it the perfect ending for their songfest. It all reminded Sonny again of the wondrous mood—that magic web of good feeling—that music can weave.

Jaws sagging from all the singing, the family then got back to planning out Dad's visit. Before he took off for his riverboat job, it was agreed, there was work galore they would have to tackle first around the house.

Work? For Arnie? Everyone laughed. But an incredible transformation took place when Dad undertook to paint the house next day. Reacting to superior authority, backed up by superior strength, Arnie ran rings around Sonny in his effort to be helpful. He scrambled up and down ladders, scraped off the flaking paint, cleaned brushes, and encouraged all. In a couple of days, the dull-gray building took on a new, shiny-white countenance.

Dad turned next to repairing the frazzled fence around the chicken yard, securing the Jonathan more firmly to its moorings and replacing broken boards around the pigpen. And again there was a blur of action called Arnie, working with the gusto of a newly landed immigrant. And when the pigs bellowed with rage once at not being fed on time, he raced down to the riverside and, for the first time ever, cut down and brought back a big armload of horseweeds for them.

Then came the big job of laying in firewood for the Winter. For days Arnie sweated alongside Sonny and Dad, hauling heavy logs and driftwood up the steep bank from the bottomland and pulling, pulling on the big cross-cut saw across from Sonny...cutting everything down to foot-long chunks. This was followed by some lusty swinging of the double-bladed axe as the wood was split into stove-size pieces. Soon, a long wall of firewood was racked up, reaching all the way from the chopping block at the riverbank to the cistern near the kitchen door.

Finally, Dad took off for Huntington and his new job on the river....

• • •

The steamboat heralded its arrival with Dad's special signal from his railroading days. He let loose four blasts of its powerful steam whistle—two long, one short, one long—just like the mournful melodies that C&O trains sounded at grade crossings across the mighty Ohio on the West Virginia shore. It was the *James Philip* all right. And what a sight! A dozen barges piled high with coal, pushed by a towboat breathing smoke high into the air from twin stacks atop the raised wheelhouse—its huge stern paddlewheel splashing and foaming with gleaming white cascades of water as it sped downstream with the current toward Cincinnati.

And there was Dad just aft of the bridge, a megaphone in his hand.

"Hi, everyone!" he yelled as the boat drew abreast. And by everyone, he meant Sonny and the whole tribe, ranged on the riverbank and waving rags, weeds, sticks and whatever else came to hand. They screamed in return at the top of their lungs, though they knew that hardly anything could be heard out there on the noisy boat.

"Be back in a week!" Dad yelled again as the churning, chugging, smoke-belching vessel slipped on past and out of earshot.

That old feeling of aloneness once more hit Sonny after the brief, remote contact with his father. He had been so happy during the short visit with Dad, and he feared that this, too, would soon pass on, just like that riverboat.

Their last night together had been specially fun. After dinner was cleared from the table, Sonny asked where the Sebring family came from, and Dad joined Aunt Emma and Grampaw in coming up with answers. From what Grampaw had been told long ago, the Sebrings had crossed the Appalachians and settled in these parts during the Jefferson Administration. Grampaw himself was born in nearby Beaver Hollow in 1853 and still remembered the Civil War and armed bands fighting along the Ohio—especially downstream in Kentucky where there were plantations and slaves.

In those turbulent days this Tri-State area was largely free and pro-Union. Even so, a lot of local families had been torn asunder by the conflict, with individual members joining one side or the other and doing the absolutely unthinkable—fighting and killing each other. Then, when he was 12, Grampaw recalled hearing the terrible news of President Lincoln's assassination. This was followed shortly afterward by news of General Lee's surrender and the end of that dreadful war. And what welcome news that was!

Grampaw had eventually married a neighboring girl named Rachel Pemberton, and eight children had been born to them. Besides Dad and Aunt Emma, there were Joe, Jim, Charlie, Ben, Craton and Alice. The boys had grown up in their wooded holler as a brash, independent lot, with a well-earned reputation as hard workers and hard fighters—people you didn't mess around with, as Dad put it. Trouble-makers found that if one of the Sebring boys couldn't handle a situation, you might suddenly have five others on your back—not to mention their two-fisted pappy.

Now, all were scattered to the four winds. Charlie and Ben had settled in Pittsburgh. Craton had disappeared somewhere out west (Grampaw thought it was in Idaho). Alice had died some years back of pneumonia. And Joe and Jim now worked on riverboats out of Huntington— Jim aboard the spanking new, speedy *Erik Krogh*.

The strangest thing Sonny found out, though, was that when Grampaw was 10—Sonny's age when they first met—his own grandfather was then 85 and could still recall the Revolutionary War era. He had been born in 1778 and could tell his grandson he remembered well the great commotion over the adoption of this new nation's Constitution 10 years later. He also told that his own grandfather had been born in England in 1703 and had landed with his parents at Baltimore at age 8, in 1711.

Amazing! Sonny marveled at the idea that in the memories of just these two ancestors—Grampaw and his grandfather—you could go back to the very birth of the United States of America. Then, add in HIS grandfather and you'd find that in the lifetimes of just these three ancestors, you could go all the way back to the early settlements on this continent and the raw beginnings of America.

"Your roots are truly planted deep in America's soil," Dad said to all three children, adding pointedly: "And you better not forget what that means—or the duties and obligations that go with it."

Well, Sonny felt pretty good about hearing all this, but a smile broke over his face as he recalled that his absent Mom may have had the last word regarding the Sebrings. She had long maintained, first, that it didn't pay to look too closely at a person's family tree or you just might find some pretty odd characters hanging around in the outer branches. And when it came to the Sebrings, she joked that while everyone else went West and made a fortune, the Sebrings went nowhere and made trouble!

Mom's own family origins were veiled in the mists of unrecorded history. She knew only that one branch came from Scotland and another from Germany. But what she didn't know about family background was more than made up by her knowledge of Eastern Kentucky (also called Kaintuck in those parts). And what tales she told! Of backwoods life, tall trees and animals and the glories of nature, the horrors of coal mining, feuds among mountain clans, and wild days trying to teach wild kids at school. Then, just recently she had sent him a fantastic book which set all these wonders down onto paper. It was *Beyond Dark Hills*, by Jesse Stuart, a powerful writer who lived across the river near Greenup, Kentucky. Sonny treasured it beyond any other book he had—except, of course, for the *Holy Bible, McGuffey's Reader* and his *Boy Scout Handbook*.

A long week passed and, as predicted, the *James Philip* hove into view again, the air crackling with Dad's familiar whistle blast. And there he stood once more behind the wheelhouse, with Uncle Joe waving alongside.

"See you day after tomorrow!" he shouted as they chugged up-stream with a string of empties. And on they churned, to the tune of a lot more unintelligible shouting...until they slipped out of sight.

Far from feeling disappointed this time over Dad's all-too-brief appearance, though, Sonny was excited...for Sis had cooked up a bold action plan. She was certainly no less anxious than Sonny to see her idol again. So the two maneuvered past Aunt Emma and, out by the road under the big maple, they began to thumb a ride. Their destination: Lock 28. Their strategy: to get there before the *James Philip* arrived and greet Dad personally.

Sis looked curiously special today, Sonny thought. Then he saw why: She was wearing rouge over her freckles. And lipstick! Plus being dressed up. All, evidently, to show Dad how pretty she was getting. And she was, with the sun bringing out red tones in her straight blond hair. She looked fragile in her slenderness—but she was no such thing, Sonny knew. Working in the house had exposed her much more to Aunt Emma's haranguing; and if she could take that, he reasoned, she could hold her own in 'most any scrap.

Like the time she had tangled on his behalf with the

town bully, Larry Hearth....

• • •

It was washday and Aunt Emma had put Sonny to work hauling water, a ponderous bucket at a time, out to the big galvanized tub by the riverbank, where it was being heated over a wood fire. He would next haul the hot water back to the porch and empty it into the washing machine, then turn the crank for the wringer as his aunt toiled away on the scrubbingboard and rinsed the clothes.

Midway in the hauling, however, Larry came sauntering down the road with a B-B gun. Overgrown and overweight and equipped with a face as growly as a bulldog's, he took special delight in pushing small boys around. He had thus been labelled "Scary Larry."

At the sight of Sonny, he wiped his dirty hands off on his dirty overalls, let loose an Indian war-cry and waved the gun menacingly. Then, turning halfway around, he took aim at a sparrow on the powerline overhead. A shot rang out, and down fluttered the little bird. "This can't be happening!" a shocked Sonny moaned. He ran over to the sparrow and found the B-B had hit right behind the eye. The bird was dead.

"You're next, Sonnyboy!" Scary Larry called out, leveling the gun in his direction.

In even greater disbelief, Sonny dove behind a sweet potato ridge just as another shot rang out. He wasn't quite fast enough though. The B-B hit his rump right under the back pocket, stinging like a needle. He howled in pain.

By sheer accident, Sis was just then coming down the road from visiting the Sherlocks and got a full view of the unfolding situation. She took off like a shot from Scary Larry's gun and ran into him head-on, fists and fingernails a-flying. And over they bowled, Larry no doubt wondering what kind of wildcat had hit him. He began bawling.

Sis came up with the gun, went over to the big maple and swung it against the tree like a baseball bat. And swung it again and again...until the barrel curved upward like a banana.

"Here, you big bully, now you can go shoot yourself!" Sis shouted. "Take your ol' gun and git!"

And off Scary Larry went, stumbling across the field and boo-hooing brokenly, his bulldog face revealing profound shock. It was the first time anyone had ever called his bluff.

Sis had thus proven anew that she was really the best of all his friends. She was always considerate and helpful, never once asking for anything in return. Unless it was urging him to watch out for any stray "Modern Romance" or "True Story" he might run across. He considered these pretty dreadful reading but, for some reason he couldn't fathom, girls lapped them up. Stranger still, no one ever seemed to have the money to buy such magazines, yet the latest issues circulated around the community in one long stream.

In any case, today luck was with them regarding Sis's plan. J.P. himself came driving by, stopped the old pickup and said warmly, "Hop in!" He was on his way to Cheswick and said he'd be glad to drop them off at Lock 28.

"So your Pa's gone to work on the river, eh?" he opened up with a smile.

"Yeah, but it won't be for long," Sonny replied with a frown.

"Oh?"

"Nope. Company's layin' up his boat. Says the mills have to be closed down again and it's just not needed. All 'cause of the Depression."

"And that's because of the Jews," Sis added. "Least, that's what Mr. Alleck says. That's Smart's Pa."

"Oh?"

"Yessir. He says they're bleedin' off all the profit and stashin' the money away. Or sendin' it out of the country."

"Seems to know an awful lot, doesn't he?"

"Yes sir. And he says things are made even worse by all the furriners who've flooded into the country and taken our jobs. Calls them kikes, wops, hunkies, spics, pollocks—names I've never scarce heard since we left Pittsburgh. He also says the gov'ment is goin' bankrupt supportin' all those lazy niggers—people who won't work even if they have jobs...."

"No, NO!" J.P. abruptly exploded, slamming on the brakes and swerving off the road.

Screeching brakes simultaneously rent the air behind, as a close-following car swerved to miss J.P.'s.

"Hey, watch where you're goin', ya stupid country hick!" shouted a red-faced driver as he careened past.

"Stay off my tail or I'll throw ya' in jail!" J.P. yelled back. He pulled out a pencil and jotted down the license number. "For future reference," as he put it.

He got the pickup lurching forward again, turned to his well-shook-up passengers and said:

"Now, all those names you were using—can you think of any one of those folks who'd act worse than that s.o.b. going there?"

"Never!" Sis blurted out.

"And you noticed he's about as lily-white as they come, right?"

"But one rotten egg!" Sonny added

"And that word, 'nigger'—I hope I never hear you all say that again. Or talk that way about Jews and foreigners, either. That idiot Alleck is a sorehead. He's plumb full of condensed prunes. You'd come nearer the truth if you believed exactly the opposite of whatever he says."

"Yeah, it did sound pretty awful," an embarrassed Sis put in. Sonny grunted in agreement.

"The important thing you gotta remember is, we're everyone of us all Americans—regardless of where we come from, our color, our beliefs. And just because someone's different doesn't make him inferior. Might be just the opposite. Fact is, those very same diff'rences add a lot to our country—a real enrichment. Think how boring it would be if we were all alike!"

Sonny nodded vigorously in agreement, taking his boss' words as purest gospel. But Sis hung in there:

"Yeah, but a lot of them sure look funny! Act funny, too."

Surprisingly, J.P. didn't disagree: "Why sure…and they have different ideas about our schools, churches, politics, almost everything. You let in too many who are too different too soon, and they simply overwhelm our country's fabulous assimilation process—which is unlike anything anywhere in the whole world. But you don't have to worry about that—we got tough immigration laws to prevent that sort of thing."

The brakes went on again, more gently this time.

"Hey, here we are," J.P. called out. "See you later!"

And there at Lock 28 Sonny and Sis found themselves, just as Dad's steamboat and its tow were entering the downstream gates.

"Boy, will Dad ever be surprised!" Sis said as the ponderous gates swung together and water began raising the *James Philip* up to the river's higher level above the dam.

"Hey, there's Uncle Joe!" Sonny shouted, pointing to a rotund, pleasant-looking guy wearing dungarees and heavy work gloves and tending the lines up forward. They ran to meet him and got a big smile…followed by a deep frown.

"Bet you're here to see your Dad," he said hesitantly.

"Yeah, it's gonna be a BIG surprise!"

"Sorry, kids, but I'm afraid you can't. Not right now, anyway. He's...ah...tied up. I mean, he's...ah...under confinement. That is, he's very busy right now."

He looked around to see if anyone was listening in and added, hurriedly: "It's best you beat it back home, real fast. And tell Em to get over to our office in Huntington right away. It's important!"

Surprise and disappointment overcame Sonny and filled the children's faces.

"Hey, don't worry," Uncle Joe went on. "Your Dad's okay. Just get movin' and do like I say. Come on, now, scat!"

Sis was so distressed she began to cry, and Sonny tried to shore her up with half-felt reassurances. Trotting out through the lock's residential area, they managed to catch a ride home with an off-duty locktender. And soon, a completely dumbfounded Aunt Emma and Sonny were out on the road again, thumbing their way to Huntington.

Startling news met them at the Ohio River Coal Company's offices. Dad had been carted off the towboat by the police. He was in jail!

"Heavens above!" Aunt Emma blurted out. "Your Dad's become a jailbird! Which just goes to prove what I've said all along: Life, it ain't no joke!"

So off they hurried to the City Jail. Sonny was having a hard time absorbing all this and, as they hustled along, found himself sweating over a whole row of imagined disasters. At the jail, they got a sharp going-over from a burly police sergeant. They were then ushered into a cellblock, the heavy iron gates slamming behind them with a certain grim finality.

Sonny was getting more uneasy by the minute. What

had they done to Dad? he wondered. What were they going to do to THEM!

They finally came to a steel door, which creaked opened... and there stood a surprisingly whole and calm-looking Dad. The boy flew into his arms.

"There, there, Sonny," his father murmured between chuckles. "Things aren't exactly what they seem."

How in the world had he gotten there? asked Aunt Emma.

"Nothin' unusual, I just let the mate have it," he said with a laugh. "And, boy, did the big bum ever have it comin'!"

The set-to had taken place just after Dad's tow had passed by their homestead, he explained. He had leaned on the whistle extra hard, as he said they might have noted—and the mate had taken violent exception.

"You stupid, clod-hoppin' hillbilly," he bellowed, puffing himself up to his full size, which was a half-foot taller and a hundred pounds heavier than Dad, "you better watch yer step on this hyar boat, or else."

"Or else what?" Dad replied, not especially friendly-like.

"Or else I'm person'ly gonna throw you off!"

"Well, you'd better start throwing right now, you big ox—while you're still able," Dad said. And without further ado he landed a haymaker right on the mate's jaw!

That's when the action really got going. The mate bounced off the bulkhead and came back swinging...enormous roundhouse blows. If one had landed, Dad would certainly have wound up in the next county, as he said. But he ducked under them and drove a left into the mate's bloated stomach, all the way to the backbone. And as the mate coughed violently and doubled up in pain, another right crunched into his jaw. He sagged to the floor—out for the count this time.

"Not bad for an amateur, eh?" Dad laughed. "Just shows what

can happen to a guy when he doesn't know his opponent."

What the mate didn't know was that his new deckhand had been a champ boxer with the U.S. Army in France. So it was the big ox himself who turned out to be the stupid party—and he paid dearly for his ignorance.

The celldoor banged open and there stood the sergeant.

"Okay, buddy, you can pack up and go," he said. "You're a free man."

"Who says so?"

"Hey, you looking for another fight, mister? I said so, that's who! The company's dropped all charges. You're free. Now get out of here before I change my mind."

Well, it took mighty little time to clear that place, and soon they were home. There, they found a telephoned message of hearty congratulations from Uncle Joe, relayed through J.P. Evidently, he said, the firm's front office likewise felt the mate had it coming and wanted to avoid the publicity of a court hearing. Dad's paycheck—his first and last from Ohio River Coal—would shortly be in the mail. Or so they said.

Dad himself would shortly be hitting the road again, Sonny began to realize…and the thought wasn't sitting well with him at all. Dad's visit had had the effect of waving a magic wand over their home on the riverback. Grampaw had become less crotchety. Sis had begun to walk around like a regular lady. Arnie had shaped up and was now willingly helping out with the chores. Even Bowser was behaving more like a sir. Yet, it was Aunt Emma who had changed most of all. She was now downright cheerful, and was even occasionally heard humming tunes while she worked.

But what, Sonny wondered, would have happened if Mom had paid them a visit instead of Dad? Well, he feared he knew the answer to that one, all right. For Aunt Emma had made it pretty clear that his mother wasn't particulary welcome in these parts. And the children had long since decided to live with the situation as best they could.

Just thinking of all this renewed so many old disappointments that Sonny called Bowser and the two headed down toward their favorite place by the river. Here, Sonny stroked his pal and stared out over the silent water, which really and truly seemed to just keep rolling along, no matter what he, or anyone else, did or felt. He traced its rippling currents out from shore and far over to the hills on the other side. Well, he had to admit, it was beautiful! Even if he didn't feel much like appreciating it at the moment.

He began to think, here he was feeling sorry for himself and again looking at his glass as half-empty instead of half full…when nothing had actually changed except that Dad would soon be leaving after a grand visit. What was it J.P. had said on one of those really disastrous trips to market, when they had to sell their tomatoes at give-away prices?

"Don't worry about it, Sonny." he answered to his helper's moaning. "Despite what everyone hopes, it's far more normal for things to go wrong in life, than right. It's not what happens to you that counts. It's how you react and what you make of it: That's what counts!"

Thus, it was no coincidence that J.P. took that big gamble the next year and got his tomato plants in the ground long before anyone else. And, boy, did that ever pay off!

Right now, he didn't have his old home in Pittsburgh, that was for sure. But what was wrong with the present one? After all, here were Aunt Emma and Sis and Grampaw and Arnie and Bowser, their church and school and their many friends and neighbors—this whole realm of struggling, heroic people.

And didn't he also have this great silvery ribbon of river; this blessed land that gave them life; these erosion-scarred, coal-seamed, richly forested, emerald hills; this happy countryside with all its marvelous melodies?

What was it that old hymn said: "Count your many blessings—name them one by one…" Wasn't he silly to always be reaching out for something else when he had so much already? He got up and started up the riverbank, deciding, well, he wouldn't give up his dream of his family's reunion altogether; that wouldn't be fair to his memories of Mom. Nor would he stop looking forward to hearing her solution to the riddle of the ultimate secret of life, or stop searching for the real America. And what could reflect real America more than steamboating on the country's vast network of mighty inland rivers?

So, at least for the present, Sonny decided, he would consider these hills his home. Up to now, he had lived here, all right—but had always felt he belonged somewhere else. Now he resolved to look up to these hills, to his inner faith, and to this special life the Sebrings had carved out along the river, for the strength to endure—and prevail—in the years ahead.

Chapter 9
Crime and Punishment

"What do you consider the best way to live? I mean, the way to get the most out of life? And be the happiest?"

The questions, asked on the spur of the moment, seemed suddenly to stand out stark and lonely in mid-air in the high school class-room, surprising even Sonny himself, who had asked them.

Joe Raleigh, the teacher, paused in his talk and looked slowly around at the other Junior-class students. He had been going on and on about Emerson and Thoreau and their development of a mysterious-sounding philosophy called Transcendentalism. This seemed to emphasize individualism, reliance on intuition and communion with nature. So Sonny had seized the opportunity to pose his tie-in questions. The reason was the same as before: Without revealing his real motive, he wanted to see if he could dredge up some more clues about the ultimate secret of life.

"Well, what about it, class," Mr. Raleigh, who was Sonny's favorite teacher, came back, "any ideas?"

An even longer pause...until Clay Wilkes finally piped up: "Wine, women and song!"

"Or how 'bout getting rich?" another broke in. "Then you can have it all."

"Or become a hermit and get away from it all!"

"Hey, why not become a big sports star and get famous?"

This brought a rejoinder from the teacher: "Ah, but that takes inborn talent...and who do you know with that?"

"Arnie Sebring!" someone blurted out. To which Sonny modestly nodded his head—as though he was being honored, not his brother.

"Well, I'd like to become a nurse and take care of the sick," one of the more serious girls allowed.

"Say, what's the problem?" one of the more serious boys followed up. "Didn't Jesus give the real answer when he said, 'I am the way'? Why not take the less-traveled road?"

Now Jenny Lee Simms spoke up, ever so brightly: "Is there something wrong with having a devoted husband, children and a happy home?" Her gaze slid around the room, stopping ever so briefly on Sonny. He buried his face in his papers in feverish concentration.

The raucous sound of the hallway buzzer abruptly intervened, announcing a change of classes. Even so, Mr. Raleigh got in a few parting words:

"So there you have it, Sonny. The class's answer to your question is that there is no one answer. Everyone has his own. Or has to come up with his own. You and me, too."

Sonny nodded in heartfelt agreement, gathered up his books and headed for the gym. The discussion had given him still more to think about. Now, no less than in grade school, he was continuing his twin searches...always feeling that you never knew when a new clue or final answer would show up. Maybe even today!

In the locker room, he quickly changed into tennis shoes, shorts and T-shirt for the tumbling team's morning workout. As it turned out, this proved a stiff one...and soon Sonny sat with his teammates and Coach Hammer on some rickety benches alongside the football field, taking a deserved breather. It was a nice day in May of 1940, and the floor mats had been moved outside onto the grass to take advantage of the sunshine. Sonny, now 16, had a good feeling about the session; the coach had tossed him for a record high backflip…and he had landed, completely unexpectedly, squarely on his feet.

And who had been on hand to behold this feat? None other than Jenny Lee Simms herself! She had come outside during a free period and now moved over to sit near Sonny's group. A Junior like him, she had grown taller and was lovelier than ever. The dark braids were still there, but were now wrapped around her head, making her look older and more sophisticated. Sonny felt kind of overwhelmed by her presence, especially when they studied together at examination time. Boy, did he have a hard time concentrating on his books! Yet he hardly dared tell her that.

Meanwhile, Clay warned that unless he "straightened himself up" and moved in on her fast, someone else would steal her right out from under his nose. "And it'll serve you right, souphead!" he had added. Indeed, Arnie and each of The Boys, at one time or another, had made a big play for her—only to get a very cold shoulder.

Suddenly, the quiet was broken as six big boys came whooping across the field from the school building, right toward them. That was odd enough, since class hours were still in effect. Odder still was what were they carrying in their hands: Brown paper bags!

The whooping abruptly stopped, and the runners veered off to the right and disappeared over the riverbank. But not before Sonny and the others recognized Smart Alleck in the lead, with Arnie and the rest of The Boys close behind.

"Oh, no," Sonny thought, "they gotta be up to no good."

The coach just shook his head and looked disgusted. Returning to the gym to shower and change clothes in time for lunch, Sonny and the other tumblers found the place in an uproar. A whole mess of lunches had been stolen! Their would-be eaters were now prowling the hallways, along with teachers and a highly upset principal, Mrs. Barker, searching in vain for either the lunch bags or the thieves who had taken them.

Well, it didn't take long to clear things up. Hammer gave Mrs. Barker an eye-witness account of their sightings out on the playing field—and, soon, the six well-fed culprits were being hauled into the principal's office. Sadly enough, Sonny was also hauled in as a live witness, though a most unwilling one, along with Jenny Lee. As it turned out, he didn't have to give a single word of testimony.

"Yeah, it was us," Arnie volunteered straight-out.

"Yeah! What kind of language is that?" demanded Mrs. Barker, sticking out her square jaw.

"Yes, ma'm! Yes, ma'm, it was us."

"Us? Us! After four years of high school, you can't do any better than that?"

"We! Yes, ma'm, it was we! We done it."

"Oh I give up!" exclaimed Mrs. Barker, turning slightly livid and raising her hefty frame out of her chair. "No wonder you boys are always getting into trouble. But this time, I assure you, YOU'VE...GONE...TOO...FAR. Theft is a terrible thing. So is tramping on the rights of others. And you're going to pay the penalty."

A sorrowful look came over her face:

"I simply cannot understand why you people would pull such pranks. God's given you something he's bestowed on no other creature, and that's the human brain. It's a thing of pure magic!

"There is absolutely no end to the knowledge a human brain can absorb. Or the problems it can solve. Or the wonders it can imagine...and create. And it never once stops working for you. It's always probing, seeking, reaching out...and, yes, pulling in. It's a fabulous force for good—a force you can direct into any channel you choose. So in what direction will you direct this wondrous force? Toward what personal goals?"

Her face looked even more disgusted than Hammer's as she declaimed: "Toward stealing lunches! Here, you're grabbing for some dumb momentary thrill and throwing away all the good you should be achieving. For yourselves, I might add."

She struck her most commanding pose and declared sternly, "In two weeks, all of you boys were supposed to graduate and receive your diplomas. That..." she fairly spit out the word, "is NOT going to happen. You are all suspended from further attendance at this school—beginning right now."

She sat back down, cleared her throat noisily, patted her iron-gray hair and turned her back on the gathering.

What in the world does she mean by "suspended"? wondered Sonny, completely puzzled. Were The Boys being kicked out? Expelled? Terminated?

The culprits themselves fidgeted around, obviously asking the same questions and uncertain of what to do next.

After what seemed a very long time, Mrs. Barker spun around in her chair again:

"What! Still here? Didn't I say you were suspended? That, you bunch of thieves, means you're washed up here.

Done, as one of you said. Go home...or wherever else you hang out. Dismissed!"

With that, some very contrite characters shuffled out into the hall and down to their home-room to collect their belongings. Arnie put his hand on Sonny's shoulder as they were leaving.

"Darn it all," he whispered, "we hadn't figured on your whole tumbling team being out there on the field this morning."

Word had spread and Sis came running up, blinking her eyes to hold back the tears.

"Isn't this terrible? Oh, it's awful! I can't graduate without you, Arnie. What will we do?"

"Darned if I know! Sure looks like you ain't a-gonna graduate with me. Anyway, right now, we're off to the Langleys. We gotta talk this thing over."

As the others took off, Jenny Lee came up and took Sonny's hand. She pressed it and said she was really sorry over the mess Arnie had gotten into. And could she help in any way?

Well, Sonny was so surprised—and so taken up with Arnie's situation—that he managed nothing more than to grunt out, "No thanks." And walked away! Just like the souphead Clay said he was.

The uproar now moved from the schoolroom to the livingroom, where six very unhappy families pondered their sons' fate. Some took the position that The Boys had gotten their just desserts. Others felt the punishment was much too severe for the crime and began to pound on the principal's door, seeking leniency. At the same time, as so often happens, virtually no one gave much thought to the victims, who had to finish that fateful day with some very empty stomachs.

Sonny experienced mixed feelings over Arnie's plight. His

older brother had bedeviled and tormented him all his life, that was for sure. And one side of his personality was surprisingly finding outright pleasure at Arnie's stiff comeuppance. But the other side went to war against this errant feeling, condemning it as evil and in conflict with everything he had learned and tried to practice about brotherly love, etc. So now he shoved such thinking angrily away every time it came a-sneaking into his brain.

Reverend Smith told Sonny once that he should always try "to walk in the other guy's moccasins." Accordingly, Sonny asked Arnie what he would do if he were in Mrs. Barker's position.

"Why, that's easy. I'd make each of us bring another lunch to school—to replace those we took." (The Boys had stopped using the incriminating word "steal.")

"And you think that would square things up?"

"Abs'lutely!"

Mrs. Barker, sad to relate, didn't seem to agree.

At home, Arnie moped around, the wind knocked completely out of his sails. Expelled from school! What kind of recommendation was that to take out into the world?

But hadn't he only been suspended? came Sonny's answer.

Yeah, but what did that mean? Was there any real difference? And hadn't the principal said we were all washed up?

No one knew the answer to that riddle. And despite all the knocking on her door, Mrs. Barker evidently could not be moved to clarify her position. Not to mention to consider changing it.

Even Aunt Emma showed unaccustomed sympathy for Arnie, though she didn't hesitate to announce: "Without that diploma, son, you ain't a-goin' nowhere. Or ever get a decent job. 'Cept, maybe, as a ditchdigger."

And Grampaw added unhelpfully: "Course, you can always join Al Capone's mob and become a real thief."

Clearly, Arnie had neither end in mind. Baseball was his greatest passion, and he had been hoping to get a try-out with the Pittsburgh Pirates after graduation. And he needed Coach Hammer's continuing help on that as an absolute prerequisite. He had established a unique reputation throughout the area as a top-drawer ballplayer. Arnie played shortstop with real flash and dash, ran the bases like a sprinter and batted like Ty Cobb. And he had sparked the Cheswick High team to one victory after another over other teams throughout the Tri-State region.

Of course, other players had pitched in, too, since it did take at least nine to make a team. But Arnie got the lion's share of the credit. And he wore the mantle of sports hero like a champ.

He loved it—and so did the girls. Which, naturally, made him love it even more.

As it happened, though, the big event that had really secured Arnie's place in local sports annals came not on the diamond but on the gridiron. It took place last Fall at the county seat, Ironton. Cheswick's small but determined team, intensively trained and skillfully directed by Hammer, had managed to battle its way to the All-County Play-Offs, where it then faced Ironton's much bigger, tougher team. It turned out to be a slugging match, with Cheswick's thin ranks sustaining one injury on top of another and getting thinner with each play. Still, The Boys hung on, with Arnie's passes connecting repeatedly with lanky Clem Langley. Then, in the closing minutes of the fourth quarter, with Ironton leading 17-14, Coach Hammer signaled in his trickiest play.

Cheswick lined up with Arnie in the backfield on the far

right. At the snap of the ball, he swept around to the left, taking the ball on a hand-off from the quarterback. Meanwhile, Clem, at left end, took off down the field and crossed over toward the right. Far to the left and back of the line of scrimmage, Arnie stopped in his tracks, whirled around...and threw the longest pass of his career. Above and beyond both teams it soared. While everyone held his breath, Clem, outrunning Ironton's surprised secondary, gathered in the pigskin on a dead run...and romped over for a touchdown.

And that's the way the big game ended, with Cheswick coming out on top 20-17. It was a play and a game that Sonny and the whole school would never forget.

But as everyone knows, it takes more than just athletic prowess to get through school. When it came to classwork, Arnie showed the same disdain in high school that he had in grade school. It was only through the grace of God—or, more accurately, through much help from his fellow classmate, Sis—that he had been able to get in the required study papers and make it this far. Sis, for her part, got consistently good marks; she had luckily received the same love of books and reading from Mom as Sonny had.

Meanwhile, the suspension crisis rolled on....

Five days before graduation day, Mrs. Barker surprised everyone by calling Arnie and The Boys, plus the eye-witnesses, back into her office. By now the culprits had lost their last traces of bravado and were a very worried and apologetic lot. But somewhat hopeful, too. Was the principal going to relent after all?

Sonny boarded the school bus that morning with Sis and a nervous Arnie for the five-mile run through Shirlington and Cheswick to the school—a two-story rectangle of faded yellow brick, with the gym-auditorium tacked on behind. As usual, Constable Flint was following close behind in J.P.'s police car. And, sure enough, right by the Shirlington church, a car came sailing by in the opposite direction—right past the stopped bus with its flashing red lights. Sonny saw Flint's arm shoot out. The wayward driver screeched to a halt, was scathingly dressed down by the constable, and the two cars shortly sped off toward J.P.'s office.

There, Sonny knew from wide-eyed earlier observation, swift and decisive justice would be meted out in the form of a fine of $8. Speeding, naturally, got tougher treatment. A few yards down the road from the Appletons, in an area astutely avoided by the locals, speed-limit signs had been cunningly arranged to nose-dive from 50 MPH to 25 MPH. And countless drivers never quite made the transition. At least not quickly enough. As a result, there was no end of lawbreakers being snared in the speed trap...and no end to law enforcing being done. Not only was the community thus well protected by J.P. and his trusty right arm, Flint, but the fines they collected several times daily also supported them well.

Now, though, another kind of justice was about to be meted out, and the whole school bus buzzed with talk about the various possibilities. Just as the whole area did. In fact, people almost came to blows over the alternatives. The matter had been taken up by the Langleys with the Board of Education in Ironton. To no avail, apparently. One kind soul even offered the revolutionary proposal that the government provide all students with a free lunch, so that no one would ever be tempted to steal.

Arnie simply held his peace and stared out the school bus window.

"Relax!" Coach Hammer had told him privately. "It could

be that the top cat is only playing with you mice. All for your own good, though, of course."

Relax? Arnie found it wasn't all that easy. And certainly not when they gathered once again in the principal's office, reluctant witnesses and all. Sonny saw Mrs. Barker's eyes narrow and her jaw jut out even more than usual as she lined up the visibly apprehensive boys. For their final execution? he wondered.

"I'm going to make this short and..." the principal stopped for a very long moment and looked each quaking boy in the eye, "...sweet."

"The suspension is over! You boys are now seniors again. And in a few days you'll be allowed to graduate."

Cheers broke out on all sides, and Sonny felt a great surge of relief...probably second only to Arnie. However, that died out quickly as Mrs. Barker held up her hand and said with an ominous undertone, "BUT...."

"But, students, you have to earn your way back to grace, and your diploma. In three days, I want each one of you to deliver to this office and hand over to me...personally...three hand-written copies of the Declaration of Independence and the United States Constitution. And please include its Bill of Rights and all other amendments. And I mean in your own handwriting...."

A rumble of groans, grunts and sighs greeted the assignment.

"Ah, perhaps you don't know about these great documents? Maybe never heard of them? Well, I'll give you a clue: One begins with the stirring words, 'When in the course of human events....' And the other with 'We the People of the United States....'

"Now it just happens that you lucky devils are among those people. And we're going to make you better citizens whether you like it or not!"

Mrs. Barker now began to pace slowly up and down along the line of boys, her brow furrowed and her eyes focused on something deep within. Sonny got the distinct impression she was settling in for a long session. Yet, her concentration and earnestness compelled everyone's utmost attention.

"By doing this little assignment, you lads might...just might...yet learn the meaning of law and justice and the rights of others.

"Now, I know you consider your own rights a glorious thing, don't you? But you'd better start giving some serious thought to others' rights, as well. And I mean starting today! Because rights are indivisible—just as indivisible as our nation of 48 states. And if you don't respect and honor the rights of others, there'll come a day when you'll lose yours, too.

"You live in a great country—one truly blessed—blessed with freedom. But what a misunderstood word that is! Freedom isn't a license to steal lunches or tramp on others or behave in just any way you choose. That's anarchy. Freedom carries with it great responsibilities—to other people, to your community, to America, to God. In fact, your own freedom can be enjoyed only to the extent you control yourself and your own excesses...and direct your energies toward promoting everyone's good—the common good."

Mrs. Barker stopped pacing, turned and looked earnestly at The Boys, and said, "Let me sum all of this up in one thought, which I urge you to remember the rest of your life: Strive always to consider and protect other people's rights and freedoms...and you'll never have to worry about your own."

She then twisted the knife. "But if you can't control yourself, then you'll find to your regret that the state, the police, the military will do it for you. And I can guarantee you, you won't like the results. Or I myself will…as you've just seen. And I don't imagine you liked that much either.

"Now, I know there's a lot of the swashbuckler and gambler in each of you boys. It's a part of our heritage. And I'm not asking you to get rid of that. But you do have to keep it under reasonable restraint. And THAT I'm not asking; I'm demanding! At least as long as you're under my jurisdiction."

She faced The Boys and smiled broadly—something no one could ever remember seeing before—and said, "Look, lads, you've had a bad time. We all know that. But you've also learned a valuable lesson—perhaps the most valuable lesson this school will ever teach you. But do us all a big favor: Please don't forget it!"

Once again she looked each boy in the eye to make sure her words were sinking in. Then she spoke with sharp finality: "Dismissed!"

Six boys lunged for the door, almost trampling each other in the stampede toward freedom. Outside, Arnie, showing some of his old bravado again, turned to his brother:

"You know, Sonny, this here school stuff may not be so bad after all!"

Oh, if Mom could only have been present to hear such a revelation! Sonny thought. Certainly, she would soon be reading about it in his letters to her. For one and all had just been tried in a fiery furnace and come out somewhat scorched but still surprisingly whole. And even though Sonny was apparently the only one aware of it, they had also been treated to an extra-special, true-to-life lesson about the real America.

Chapter 10
The Circle Narrows

One of the foremost evils that the Reverend Smith railed against during church services was gambling. He tarred it as a "devil that deprives families of money for the basic necessities of life—a devil as evil as alcohol or drugs." Which, too often, he added, was accompanied by both.

Trouble was, like most of the minister's sermons, it seemed to Sonny that few in the congregation really listened. And of those who did, few remembered. And of those who remembered, few acted on the message. Sonny considered himself at least a partial exception to this discouraging rule...mainly because he was eager to see if the pastor would reveal more clues regarding the ultimate secret of life. Which he often did.

Topping the list among the sermon non-listeners were The Boys—IF you were lucky enough to get them into the church building. Thus, a week later, their unsettling experience and narrow escape with Mrs. Barker shoved into the background, The Boys became involved in a dubious bet. They put in a dollar each and came up with a kitty of five dollars to back up a wager that Arnie couldn't swim the Ohio River. Now, since the river was less than a half-mile wide here, this shouldn't have been all that difficult. But the bettors threw in a few tough conditions. Arnie was to swim straight across, proceed to swim a mile upstream, cross back again, then swim back to homebase. A reluctant Sonny was to hold the pot, including the matching five dollars that Arnie had to put up.

Course, Arnie normally had no money whatsoever, but Aunt Emma had done the absolutely unbelievable and presented both him and Sis with a crisp $100 bill each as a graduation gift. ONE HUNDRED DOLLARS! This was intended "to help you get started out in the cold, hard, cruel world," as she put it.

And where had she gotten the money? From pinching nickels and dimes from the family's funds over many years—funds which Sonny's own hard work had contributed to handsomely. They had all gone a little hungrier as a result. But, as Arnie put it so well in response to Sonny's grumbling, "who's gonna quibble over such minor details on the day the big C-Notes are handed out?"

Aunt Emma protested heatedly against Arnie risking any part of his new wealth in such a "frivolous" manner. "A fool and his money are soon parted," she said.

Arnie, however, argued that the bet would only expand his holdings. "Natchrally, I'm gonna win," he assured her.

Sonny wished he could be half as sure. He had given up using his wishbone for such occasions; somehow, it just didn't fit in with his advanced age, he felt. But, of course, there was nothing wrong in wishing Arnie well despite his doubts.

The two words, "straight across," formed the key to the bet. As Sonny had seen before, others had swum the river but drifted with the current and wound up on the other shore far downstream toward the mouth of the Big Sandy. The Boys' special requirement meant that Arnie not only had to cross the river but, to stay on a straight course, had to fight the current all the way. Then, he had to buck the current head-on almost to Lock 28 and do the same thing again to get back to the starting point. It wore Sonny out just thinking about it.

Grampaw also got involved in his own way: Giving free advice. Which Arnie considered just about as valuable as what he had paid for it.

"He who swims 'gainst the current gets farthest in life," he intoned in the quaking voice he reserved for special sermons based on experience.

"That's a lot of bull," Arnie muttered to Sonny. "Why, I can swim downstream four times as fast as up."

"Yeah, but I think he means something else."

"Like what?"

That ended the conversation. For both knew that Grampaw became as silent as a sphinx when it came to explaining his sweeping statements.

Arnie had cooked up the big bet as a bit of farewell grandstanding with his pals. With Coach Hammer's fine-tuned help, the coveted try-out with the Pirates had finally been arranged, and Arnie was to leave for Pittsburgh the following week. Sonny felt a keen sadness that, somehow, a grand era was ending for the both of them. But could something even grander be ahead?

Decision day came, along with high heat and humidity. The whole Sebring family gathered at the river's edge in bathing suits, along with Bowser, and watched as Clem Langley and another of The Boys came rowing rhythmically downstream in the johnboat they would use to accompany Arnie on the big test. For Grampaw, it was a rare occasion; now 87, his joints getting stiffer by the day, he seldom ventured down to the river because of the steep climb back.

On the way down the riverbank, Sonny had offered his shoulder for Grampaw to lean on with one hand—his trusty old cane in the other. Even so, by the time they reached the willows at the riverside, the old timer was pretty well tuckered out. They stopped alongside an old log, a twisted survivor of innumerable floods, so he could sit a spell and catch his breath.

"How you doin', Grampaw?"

"Ah, good 'nough. Least for someone who's been playin' tag all day."

"Tag?" Sonny asked in surprise.

"Yup, hide and go seek. Every day I hide…and that ol' devil, Death, comes a-seekin'. This li'l game began when I turned 85. And by cracky," he grinned mischievously, "I bin winnin' every day since!"

The grin slowly gave 'way to a frown.

"Course," he added wistfully, "we both know who's gonna win bye and bye."

Jarred by the tone of Grampaw's voice even more than by what he was saying, Sonny looked searchingly at the oldtimer, seeing him clearly for the first time in ages. Yes, he was getting older—thinner, the shoulders sagging, the lines in his face deeper, the eyes watery, the voice shaky, the hearing failing. And as his senses slipped, Grampaw was losing contact with the people and happenings around him and withdrawing more and more into his own inner world.

Sonny felt a pang of deep sorrow. What a cruel joke life plays on us!, he thought. Here, Grampaw has spent a whole long lifetime developing his mind and body, his knowledge and abilities—and now it was all fading away right before his eyes. And wouldn't Sonny himself, who was growing tall and wiry just like Grampaw, have to go through the same roller-coaster rise-and-fall process in his own lifetime?

Well, that very question had been taken up by Reverend Smith in a recent sermon...and he had impressed Sonny with the position that rather than hang your head in self-pity over the tragedy of the natural course nature was taking, you ought to be darn glad for the chance to experience life at all. And live deeply and fully while you could and develop yourself and contribute your utmost to the world around you. Yet, while Sonny felt that reasoning was okay for him, it did not lessen the sadness he now felt for Grampaw's decline.

At the riverside, they found Arnie taking his good old time getting ready for the plunge, smearing himself first thoroughly with vaseline. And as he worked it in, the muscles rippled across his shoulders and chest and gleamed in the sun.

"What in hell you puttin' that stuff on for?" Clem called out. "And in this ungodly heat!"

"The water's cold, knothead. Besides, we gotta approach this professional-like."

"Okay, Big Shot, but let's stop the stallin' tactics," came the response. "We got urgent uses for all that money Sonny's holding."

"Sorry, buster, I've already promised Grampaw it would go to buy him a new cane."

"Ha, ha, ha! Well, he's gonna find out your promises ain't worth a nickel—let alone five dollars!"

"You'll see, you'll see...."

And with those final words Arnie slipped into the stream and struck out straight across with long, even strokes for the far shore, the oars of Clem's rowboat dipping and creaking behind. The family let out a big cheer, and Sonny surveyed the scene with new wonder. The bright sun sparkled on the lazy ripples stirred up by the boat and swimmer; the river's shiny surface reflected a scattering of fluffy white clouds in a vast blue sky. And framing the whole scene were both the faraway hills and the nearby willows, flood-bent and battered and struggling like time-twisted old men to stand erect. The river—the mighty Ohio—had never looked so beautiful.

Sonny watched until the group was far out in the stream. The river, he mused, seemed to lead a unique life of its own, oblivious to all the strivings of people along its shores. It could be angry and destructive, as it was during the Great Flood. Or, like today, it could be a playground, placid and serene, at least on the surface. It was timeless, too— its waters flowing past this point since long before the arrival of man. It was endless in its reaches across the vast American continent and down to the Gulf and beyond to the world. It was raw, powerful, unyielding, uncompromising, potentially deadly.

Aunt Emma gave a final wave to the group, said "Oh it's hot!" and splashed into the water—Sonny and Sis following hard behind. Even Grampaw took off his shoes and waded in, leaning heavily on his cane as he lumbered unsteadily over the wet stones.

Unlike Aunt Emma, Sonny and Sis had long since become good swimmers, and now they circled around her like Indians besieging a wagon-train, laughing and throwing water—all to the accompaniment of Bowser's joyful barking along the shore.

But then, without warning of any kind, Aunt Emma stepped into a hole, cried out and disappeared under the surface. She came up splashing water wildly and shouted:

"Big hole…gurg, glug!…can't swim…gurg!…HELP!"

Sonny rocketed over as she went down again, dove under the water and caught hold of her arm and tried to haul her back. But the water was over his head, too. Aunt Emma thrashed and fought so that he almost lost his grip.

"Help, Sis! Help, Grampaw!" he screamed. They both went under again, the current carrying them on.

Sis splashed downstream while Grampaw stumbled toward them along the shore. Breathing heavily, his stiff legs nearly breaking with each step, he drew alongside the struggling pair, waded in up to his waist, and reached out his gnarled cane. Sonny desperately threw his arm around the curved handgrip and held on. Grampaw slipped and faltered and almost went under as the full load hit.

"Damn and tarnation!" he bellowed.

Just then Sis came splashing up and threw her arms around his waist for support. He gasped for air, regained his balance and began pulling the drowning pair in—Aunt Emma still struggling wildly, scared out of her wits. Slowly, slowly, the chain worked its way shoreward—Sis holding Grampaw, Grampaw holding Sonny with his cane, Sonny hanging on to Aunt Emma.

"Jesus, help us!" moaned Sonny. "This is like my baptism all over again, only worse!"

And it was worse. Snorting, coughing, crying, Aunt Emma was finally dragged ashore and, while all eyes were on her, Grampaw crumbled into a heap behind them. Sonny heard an abrupt change in Bowser's barking, then a long, soft sigh, like air escaping from a tire. He turned around...and there Grampaw lay on the hard shore-side stones, looking strangely relaxed.

Sonny bent down and raised his head. It felt oddly heavy and inert.

"Grampaw!" he cried.

Aunt Emma stopped carrying on and, helped by Sis, turned to Grampaw. She felt for his pulse, listened to the heart. Her face blanched.

"Run, Sonny, run. Run and get help!" she shouted. "Run and get J.P. Hurry!"

And Sonny ran, dripping water from his bathing trunks along the trail. Grampaw had saved his life at least once, he kept thinking...and maybe, if he ran fast enough, maybe he could save Grampaw in return. But even as he and Bowser scrambled up the steep riverbank and ran along the lush tomato patch toward the Appletons'—his heart beating so hard he thought it might jump right out of his chest—

something told him it would do no good. He feared that Death had finally won that grim game Grampaw had mentioned—that the river had claimed one of its own.

And that's the conclusion J.P. reached when Sonny led him and Constable Flint back to the river.

"Heart attack, I would say," he declared. "Your Grampaw was one tough hombre, me boy...but not tough enough to take all that extra strain. And certainly not at his age."

"And, Em," he said, turning to her, "you've got to admit that he died for one mighty good purpose!"

He noted Sonny's distressed look and patted his old helper on the back: "You don't have to feel all that bad either, me boy. Your Grampaw lived a long and full life. And I'd say he checked out at just about the right time. Unlike a lot of people who simply go on and on, living way too long—slowly, sadly and painfully wasting away. And all the time becoming a big burden on both themselves and everyone around them. Pretty clever, that old gent!"

J.P. and Flint fashioned a crude stretcher out of their shirts and a couple willow poles and carried Grampaw up to the house. There they laid him, for the last time, on his bed in the small bedroom, in his small house. A stray thought hit Sonny as he looked at the oldtimer lying pale and gaunt on his back, his nose oddly standing out leaner and longer than ever: Funny, the house will never again shake and tremble from all that lusty snoring through that great trumpet.

Once the others had left, Sonny sat down heavily on a chair beside the bed—Bowser stretching out at his feet, his sad brown eyes the very soul of mourning. Sonny had meant to come in and say a final, private good-bye, but he was abruptly struck by the awful contrast between being alive and being dead. Grampaw's spirit—everything that Venton Sebring was—had somehow left, mysteriously and completely, and now only the hollow shell of his body remained. It was as though a once-bright and shining light had been switched off, leaving a dull and useless bulb behind.

A sudden chill shot through Sonny, making his skin crawl. He looked uneasily at Grampaw, then around the small room, half expecting to be seized by the Angel of Death or some other horrible spector. It was eerie to be alone in the presence of the dead. Scary! He felt like running for his life.

But Sonny, said a distant voice within, why are you afraid? Don't you remember what to do? *Just reach up and take My hand!* He did. And relaxed.

Time had run out for Grampaw. Yet, as J.P. had remarked on one of their drives to market, "time is our most precious possession of all—one that, unfortunately, runs through your fingers as fast as that ol' river out there at flood stage."

"You're young, me boy," he had added, "and the years stretch before you in a long and seemingly endless procession. But one day you suddenly find your hair turning gray, like mine, and you sit there wondering 'what in the world did I do with my life?' So see that you use your time wisely. Do the things you really want to do in this one life you're given. And make those coming years count."

Well, Grampaw certainly hadn't seemed concerned about such things, as Sonny knew. Like most people in the area, he had simply worked hard and taken care of his family's needs and lived from day to day, without any apparent thought of either getting the most out of this life or preparing for the next.

The next? Had Grampaw or his spirit gone on to heaven?

Sonny wondered. Aunt Emma, who had turned strangely silent since losing her old sparring partner, would have maintained earlier that he had gone the other direction. But would she say so now? Well, God alone could know the answer to that one, Sonny told himself.

But what kind of heaven was there to go to?

Having heard endless disputes at church on that point, Sonny had long since decided to leave that answer to God, too. He was sure that something as singular and precious as the human spirit had to go on to some special place after death, but he wasn't at all sure it was like anything here on earth. In fact, he thought heaven might be as different from our earthly surroundings as the spirit is from the body that houses it.

In any event, he felt there was little point in pondering about eternity, that making the most of this life was the important thing, not worrying about the next. Besides, he had concluded that the truly remarkable aspect of it all was that if you really tried hard to live up to high ideals here on earth, that would be the best guarantee of admission into whatever heaven might come later.

At the same time, he had come to recognize the great comfort and joy that a deep belief in a rewarding afterlife could bring. This was shown vividly one Thursday evening the previous Winter when their church group had gathered at the Langleys' on the other side of town. While Clem had never evidenced any particular belief in anything, at least not so's you could notice it, his grandmother was fervently religious. She was very frail and very old—some said over a hundred.

That night she sat in an old rocking chair beside the fireplace. And on her face glowed the most peaceful and serene look Sonny had ever seen. Everyone had joined in softly singing those beautiful hymns, "Rock of Ages" and "Abide with Me" and, in a more spirited tempo, "Give Me That Oldtime Religion." The songs proved to be everyone's farewell to Mrs. Langley. She died quietly in her sleep that night.

This left Sonny wondering whether the ultimate secret of life might surely lie in developing just this kind of deep and abiding faith. But how many people can overcome the normal questions and doubts and achieve such a tranquility of spirit? In Mrs. Langley's case, it seemed almost as though she had spent most of this life preparing for the next. But was that any way to live? Or was it THE way? A thoroughly baffled Sonny simply shook his head.

Memories of life with Grampaw now came crowding in for Sonny: Their days of hoeing corn and pitching hay together under the Summer sun, Grampaw showing him how to saw and chop wood and whittle with a knife, that time he killed the snake in the berry patch and their talk by his special shrine in the ravine. Sonny had discovered his grandfather to be a loner—a man of very few words. He didn't bother others and he darn well didn't tolerate others bothering him. Even so, Sonny felt they had built up a special camaraderie, these two. And he would carry that with him always. In a way, Grampaw represented all of his yesterdays, including those his forefathers had lived before he was born. And he, in turn, represented all of Grampaw's tomorrows—at least those here on earth. He decided he would try hard to live up to that special responsibility.

Hilarious shouting erupted outside just then. Arnie and The Boys were returning from the big test, and Arnie came bursting through the door. He had won the bet hands down!

he proudly announced. So where was Sonny? he demanded to know. And where was the big jackpot?

His brother came out from Grampaw's resting-place and nodded back toward the bedroom. Seeing the long faces and sensing the hushed silence, Arnie gathered immediately what was wrong.

"Oh, damn it all!" he blurted out, almost crying. "I really was going to buy Grampaw a new cane."

Sonny felt that old empty depression returning in his stomach. Grampaw was now gone—and Arnie, too, would soon be leaving. The family circle was getting smaller and smaller. He closed his eyes and prayed to God on behalf of Grampaw and his spirit.

The funeral arrangements went by in a blur. Dad flew in from Detroit and handled everything, setting burial for his father at the old cemetery on the hill overlooking the Ohio River, with West Virginia on the far shore.

Sonny found it wasn't easy to deal with the blunt, naked reality of death...despite having his faith to hold onto as an anchor against the storms of life. However, at their white-steepled Shirlington church, two things happened that lifted his spirits:

Their church choir sang the hymn that he wanted so much to hear—"In the Garden."

And Reverend Smith read the 121st Psalm, with its endearing memories of that peaceful shrine in the deep woods:

"I will lift up mine eyes unto the hills, from whence cometh my help....

The Lord shall preserve thee from all evil: He shall preserve thy soul...from this time forth, and even for evermore."

From this time forth, Sonny repeated to himself. And even for evermore.

As Sonny prayed for Grampaw that night, a wondrous thing happened. The beloved image of Jesus appeared before him, as it did so often in his prayers...and he heard again those comforting words: "I am with you always...."

Then, surprisingly, the image slowly faded away, and Grampaw himself appeared in its place, emerging sharp and clear from the measureless reaches of eternity, and saying exactly the same words that Jesus had uttered:

I am with you always, even unto the end of the world.

The effect was stunning. Sonny sat bolt upright in his bed, feeling as though a heavy load had been lifted from his shoulders. He now sensed that Grampaw, though lost physically, would always be with him in spirit. Always! That, like all loved ones who die, he would be enshrined in Sonny's soul.

• • •

One question that Grampaw innocently raised continued to bother Sonny—so much so that he went to see Reverend Smith again one day "to thrash it out." It had been some three years since his last visit to the church's well-cluttered little office, and that's exactly how it still appeared—except maybe even more cluttered. The minister's smile hadn't changed, though. It was as heart-warming as ever, encouraging Sonny to plow right into his problem:

"You know, Pastor Smith, Grampaw used to say that people are actually animals. That is, if you press the right button, they plumb forget they're s'posed to be civilized and go right back to actin' like wild beasts. Yet Aunt Emma says we're really spiritual beings. Anyway, after hearing them...er, discussing this point so long, I just don't know who or what to believe."

The minister stifled a laugh on hearing again about Shirlington's notorious former combatants.

"Sonny," he said, "the fact is, they're both right. For a change! Actually, man is an animal in that God gave us all the internal needs and drives that animals have. But he also gave us two absolutely crucial elements that no animal has. He put into man the spirit of an angel—your conscience—so that we would know right from wrong and how to control our animal drives. And he gave us willpower...to enforce that control."

"But which is the most important? Which really drives people?"

"Ah, that's THE question! Certainly, our animal drives are the most forceful—and forcing. And to the extent we give in to them, we do, indeed, act like animals. Yet it's the human spirit that counts above all. It's the spirit that raises us above our low animal nature and makes us truly human."

Apparently encouraged by Sonny's rapt expression, Reverend Smith dug deeper into the subject:

"Now, no one says it's easy, this awesome job of controlling our animal nature. And you've really got to admire those who manage to do so. Look at how short a time man's been civilized—if you can call it that. It's only a little over 5,000 years since the first civilizations were established in ancient Mesopotamia, Egypt, and the Orient. Just compare that with the millions of years it took for man to emerge from the cave and the jungle. Why, it's like comparing a fraction of an inch to a whole yardstick! And it's only a few centuries since Western man climbed out of the Dark Ages. So, if people continue to give in to their animal drives, well, that's deplorable...but it's also understandable. That means we just have to fight harder to achieve control."

The minister paused and caught his breath, along with Sonny...and changed expression:

"Now, I don't want to knock bodily pleasures, either. Nature made sure they can be pretty grand. Trouble is, they disappear almost the moment we experience them. And nothing is so futile as chasing after more and more. Fact is, the more you squeeze that turnip, the drier it gets. On the other hand, whatever you do to nurture and develop your spirit lasts as long as life itself—and probably longer."

"Think Grampaw would've agreed with all this?" Sonny asked.

Evidently taken aback by the request to interpret another person's views, Reverend Smith responded hesitantly, "Well, I think so. But certainly, in his own way—in his own unique way. As you know, he wasn't much for going to church. Yet, he heartily agreed with me once when I said that churches are our frontline fighter for civilization. Just think of a world without churches! Without their constant civilizing pressure! Why, man would soon return to acting exactly like those wild beasts your Grampaw talked about. With our next stop the cave!"

"So you think he also believed in God?"

"No doubt about it. Don't you think so, too?"

"Yessir! Always have...."

"But haven't you noticed how hard it is for people to agree on the nature of God? So we have almost as many versions as there are people. Everyone obviously interprets

God to meet his own special needs. Yet, the grand thing, the glorious thing, is that God is everywhere—all around us, all the time. He doesn't impose Himself on people, though. Oh no! You have to reach out and take Him in, and make Him a central part of your life. And the more you honor Him and His teachings, the more He will honor and bless you. Then you'll feel the difference. Then you'll KNOW the difference! For your spirit will have joined and become one with its Creator—with God Almighty!"

Pastor Smith abruptly threw up his hands and looked embarrassed. "Oh, please forgive me! I got carried away. Forgot completely I was preaching to the converted...."

Sonny, much awed, a little nervous, looked anxiously around the room. "You mean God is right here? Right now?"

"Absolutely!"

Well, Sonny didn't know quite whether to react to this news with joy or fright. He thought that, sure, one would be bound to feel more protected, more secure with God present. But having Him as a constant companion also seemed kind of intimidating. So he was glad when Pastor Smith looked up at his wall map of the United States, pointed out the window for emphasis, and spoke again:

"Everything our society out there does—everything WE do—should be judged in terms of its impact on the human spirit. Nowadays, however, that seems to be the LAST thing that's considered. Indeed, on this score, you have to say that modern society is failing miserably. How? In our near-total obsession with money, material goods, sex, and entertainment. These are the new opiates of the people. NOT religion, as Karl Marx so glibly alleged. Now, top this off with what I call the four P's, and you get the impression we're all going to hell on one fast track...."

"The Four P's?" a puzzled Sonny asked.

"Yes, the Four P's. Remember how you youngsters used to say that 'sticks and stones may break my bones...but words, they cannot hurt me'? Well, that's not true, either. Just look at how the German Nazis and Soviet Communists have turned propaganda into a fine art form. Yet, I've got to say they're pikers compared with some of the shoddy stuff coming out of both Hollywood and the media. Out of Washington, too. I'm referring again to the Four P's—permissiveness, pornography, perversion and promiscuity. And to their horrible handmaidens—drugs and drinking, gambling and prostitution, crime and violence. The Four P's are the deadly new Four Horsemen of the Apocalypse. Yet they're so insidiously camouflaged that only one person in a million recognizes their impact. So they go on tramping down our values, corrupting our youth, and tearing our society apart. They're destroying our very soul!"

The big P-words hit Sonny like a club. He wasn't sure what they meant, but they sure sounded evil. Particularly promiscuity. He tried to comprehend the kind of world described by Pastor Smith. But it seemed as mysterious and remote from his grasp and their farm community as the Planet Pluto. It struck him as scary...yet also somehow intriguing.

The minister rose, came around the desk and put his hand on the boy's shoulder.

"Worst of all," he continued, "is the impact of the Four P's on youngsters like you, Sonny. Young people badly need to have models to imitate—adults setting solid personal examples of behavior. They need firm guidance on what's right and wrong. They need to be taught the highest moral and ethical standards. Without this essential preparation for life, they're like a ship floundering around on the ocean, without charts or compass...or even a rudder. If they don't capsize at sea under the first waves that come along, they'll sooner or later pile up on the reefs of life. Many parents don't seem to realize this. They're taken in by people preaching permissiveness and free choice—often with ulterior motives. Parents wouldn't think of exposing their kids to wild beasts. Yet, abandoning children to the modern media message madhouse is like throwing them to the wolves. Their future, too—as well as everyone else's. For the young ARE the future."

"But why on earth would parents even think of doing such a thing? To their own kids!" Sonny asked angrily, completely upset by what he was hearing.

"A lot of reasons. There's ignorance, as I indicated before. Most simply don't know what's going on in this area...or its devastating impact. Laziness is another reason. It takes real effort to screen out society's communications garbage and steer kids into the right channels. Next, you find that many parents want above all to be buddies with their children, so they give in to their pleadings even when they know its wrong. This leads to the ridiculous situation where unaware children are calling the shots instead of supposedly informed adults. Finally, there's the sorriest spectacle of all: Parents who abandon tried-and-true approaches to child-raising in favor of new methods just so they can appear modern in their thinking."

A look of deep sorrow came over the minister's face.

"Saddest of all, Sonny, is that, in the public's herd-like stampede after the dangerous lures of the Four P's, our spirit—the angel within us—is getting shorter and shorter shrift. Yet, in order to survive and thrive, it needs constant nourishment and care. And if we give it that...if we strive continuously for a true nobility of spirit, we'll live a full, rich and rewarding life."

Dear Lord, he almost said it! Sonny nearly shouted straight out. Was he really on the road to unraveling the riddle of the ultimate secret of life? Dwelling on the minister's revelations, he startled so visibly that Reverend Smith asked if something was wrong.

"No, not wrong at all!" Sonny replied on the instant. "No... it's just that you're so right!"

And with that he bolted out the door, again muttering, "Thank you...thank you!" Leaving in his wake a very surprised, wide-eyed and perplexed Reverend Smith.

Chapter 11
Love Thy Neighbor!

The weird aspect of Grampaw's passing was the sudden stillness around the house. But even weirder for Sonny was his empty rocking chair on the front porch. There it now sat, forlorn and empty. No one quite dared to sit in it, sensing it just might be haunted by Grampaw's ghost. However, one of Arnie's pals came by one day and, in total ignorance of the situation, plunked himself right down in its welcoming embrace. Well, everyone thought he would die right then and there!

Grieving over Grampaw couldn't last long, though, for there was simply too much work to be done. And as Aunt Emma tirelessly pointed out, "somebody"—now meaning Sonny alone—had to earn some money. This led to another major development in Sonny's life, involving a favorite neighbor—a development that would make the Summer of 1940 stand out forever.

This favorite neighbor was pretty and had flowing blond hair—so much so that Sonny came to call her "Blond Boss" (though never to her face). And her pay scale was extraordinary!

As a matter of fact, it simply didn't make sense. Here was Mrs. Deere paying him twice as much as most others in the area—and for half as much work. Crazy! It made Sonny wonder vaguely if the riddle were somehow connected to his so-far-unresolved search for the ultimate secret of life.

When school let out that Summer, Sonny began to work every day for neighboring farmers and home-owners. And that meant bringing more and more "bacon" home to Aunt Emma, who, in turn, smiled more and more. The contribution wasn't much, actually, even though it made a big difference in their skinny household budget: $1.50 a day here, $1.75 there, $2.00 elsewhere. But in this one extra-special case, a whopping $3.00!

The person behind this unbelievable generosity bore the fancy name of Mrs. Donaldson D. Deere—otherwise known more simply in church circles as Grace. Sonny mowed the lawn and handled other assorted chores around her house every Tuesday.

The work schedule Grace Deere set was as surprising as her big pay-out. He showed up at 8 a.m. and worked five hours, signing off at 1 p.m. She then whipped up a lunch for him of soup and sandwiches, topped off by a big slab of her own delicious home-made dessert, like apple pie. Then, at 2:p.m., instead of sending him back to work, she set him down with a carefully selected book or for a long chat about the most far-fetched subjects. He was finally turned loose before 5 o'clock.

Why the two or three hours of pure loafing?

"Well, Sonny," she said, "if I send you home to your aunt, she'll just put you to work around the house. And while that might be great for your family, it's not fair to you. I can think of a dozen better uses for your time." And she did!

Thus, for some five hours of actual work, he collected three big bucks. And while it didn't make much sense, he wasn't about to kick such a golden gift horse in the teeth. He liked Mrs. Deere. And he felt she liked him, too.

Grace Deere did things differently because she was different. In fact, she hardly belonged in these parts. She and her husband, Don, came from the Pacific Northwest. A place which, to Sonny, seemed as remote and exotic as paradise.

Don was a civil engineer, and Grace a librarian and sometimes teacher. They had moved into a house on the riverbank near Woodworth's grocery some two years before. Don was said to be working on a big construction project in the hills back of Huntington. He was gone five, sometimes six days a week, so was seldom seen around the neighborhood.

Grace, meanwhile, worked a couple days a week in the Marshall College library across the river in Huntington, and had simultaneously been overseeing Sonny's labors around her house every Tuesday since they moved in. When he wasn't in school, that is. And even then, he would at least mow the lawn after school let out. As he had, indeed, been doing all this year since the first cutting in April.

From their first encounter, he had found Grace Deere fascinating, and never more so than this year. Tall and in her mid-30s, she had honey-colored hair framing a round face with enormous blue, intent eyes that looked at you with a startling openness and honesty. She was pretty in a different way, too—in an unpretentious, non-flashy sort of way. But, oh! when she smiled! Then came a brilliant, dimpled smile that lit up her whole countenance…and made her the most beautiful woman Sonny had ever seen.

Grace Deere had a weight problem, though. And this led to her being put down by church gossips, who got their licks in at her at every Sunday service, which she attended…well…religiously. As reported from the scene by Aunt Emma, the gossips, all of whom were real heavyweights, meowed mightily that Grace "was grazin' too much." The little dear, they said, had thus become a big

Deere. And so they began to call her Grazing Grace—well behind her back, of course.

But all this was now past tense. This Spring a new Grace had emerged from a Winter of travel, dieting and hard physical work-outs. When she appeared at church the last Sunday of March, the excess pounds had vanished. And in their place was a trimmed-down silhouette that could only be described as a knock-out. Her face had changed, too. As cheeks returned to their old contours, high cheekbones and a wider, fuller mouth emerged. To Sonny's wondering eyes, she had now become beautiful, period—whether smiling or not.

Especially when she came walking down the church aisle that first day with her eyes level, shoulders back and chest out—really out. She was wearing a loose suit evidently designed to hide her charms...and failing to do so one hundred per cent. The gossips, deprived of an easy prey, were outraged. The men, sneaking furtive glances so as not to enrage their wives, were delighted. Grazing Grace was on the way to becoming known as Amazing Grace.

Nor was anyone more amazed than Sonny. When Grace seated herself and looked around, she spied Sonny on the other side of the church and flashed that brilliant smile over the heads of the congregation. Sonny gulped and gawked like a dumb ox, so stunned he couldn't even smile back.

Arnie was plenty impressed by the new Grace, too. So much so that he tried to horn in on mowing her lawn. Arnie mowing lawns? Unheard of! Anyway, Grace would have nothing to do with such a shift-over, so Arnie was spared the toil and trouble.

That first springtime Tuesday of working together renewed the grand pattern that Sonny had come to like so much. He mowed and trimmed the grass, then tended the Deeres' vegetable plot while Grace worked nearby on her flower garden—a riot of roses whose sweet scents surrounded her like a cloud. He could hardly keep his mind on his hoeing. However hard he tried not to, he kept peeking as Blond Boss bent, crouched, twisted and turned in her work.

Because of the heat, she had pinned her dark-gold hair up on top of her head. This made her look more sophisticated, which struck Sonny as both more alluring and vaguely out of place in the garden. Then, as the temperature rose toward noon, she took off her smock, and her light dress began to stick to her body here and there. Sonny's eyes bulged right out of their sockets.

Promptly at one o'clock Grace straightened up, stretched her arms to the sky and called a halt. Each then washed up separately, Grace using the indoor bath that had hot and cold running water. Seems engineer Don had scrapped the old cistern system, had a well drilled down to the underground water table, rigged up an electric pump, storage tank and water heater, and piped in water to the kitchen and baths. Ingenious! thought Sonny.

As they sat down for lunch in the kitchen, Grace smiled and said: "You've changed, haven't you, Sonny?"

"Yeah, I s'pose. How do you mean?"

"Grown taller. Now even more than me. And you look stronger. Bet you don't have an ounce of fat on you."

" 'Cept between the ears!" he hooted, a bit too loud.

"How old are you now?"

"Sixteen. In March."

"Oh, what a lovely age!" she laughed. "Like to change places?"

"Ah, heck, you're not much older, are you?"

"Well...." Her voice trailed off. Then, getting back on track:

"Won't you be a senior next year?"

"Yep, Mrs. Deere. And I'm really lookin' forward to graduatin'...and maybe even going on to college."

"Oh, come on, Sonny, what's this missus all about? Didn't you say I'm not much older than you? You've got to call me Grace."

She reached over and squeezed his hand briefly to emphasize her point. Sonny felt sparks flying.

"No, let's go one better," she continued. "Did you know I have a middle name? It's Ann. Back home my real friends call me Grace Ann. Couldn't you, too?"

"Yes, ma'm," he mumbled. "I mean, yes, Grace Ann."

He found the name as pretty as she was. Her hair had been let down, and now it tumbled in long, soft waves onto her shoulders. She sat to his right at the white enamelled kitchen table, so close he found it hard to speak. She herself had changed so much.

"Today I've got a surprise," she announced gaily. "See this big book? It's filled with reproductions of the finest paintings in the world. Like to go through it with me?"

"Uh-huh!" he fairly shouted, relieved to have something to concentrate on other than his beautiful boss.

Grace cleared the table and pulled her chair around beside him, setting off more sparks. And for the next couple of hours, they leafed through the art of the ages—Grace providing an enthusiastic running commentary.

Ancient Egypt, Greece, and Rome came first. For, as Grace said, "You've got to know the roots of our civilization. Else, you have no depth and no real grip on the ground. And without knowledge of our common culture, you have no breadth. And you don't want to be a one-dimensional person, do you, Sonny?"

In time they also came to Leonardo da Vinci's striking painting of Mona Lisa, with her enigmatic smile.

"Can you guess what she's smiling about?" asked Grace.

Sonny stared and thought a while, then announced triumphantly: "Sure, she's in love!"

"Like you and me?" Grace laughed merrily.

Sonny blushed and gurgled out some words that died a-borning in his throat. His boss had touched a very sensitive nerve: He was developing an overwhelming crush on her…and felt he was doing a miserable job of trying not to show it.

"You know, Sonny, you can't really appreciate what da Vinci achieved with this masterpiece until you've seen Mona Lisa alongside contemporary paintings in Paris."

"You've been to Paris?" he asked in awe.

"Yes…and there she hangs in a long hall in the great museum, the Louvre, surrounded by paintings from the same era. But what a difference! The rest are all flat and two-dimensional. Almost caricatures of people. But then you see Mona Lisa, with shadows and perspective and depth—a real human being!"

"But why such a funny smile?"

"Ah, so now you think I know everything! Well, only da Vinci and Mona Lisa herself knew the answer to that riddle…and they didn't bother to tell anyone."

Next came Michelangelo's powerful paintings in the Sistine Chapel in Rome and the richly hued works of Titian and Raphael. Many peopled by what Sonny considered very well-fed women. With many in the nude!

"Why all those…er, heavyweights?" he ventured to ask.

Grace laughed, thought a moment, and then turned the book all the way to the late 1800s, to Renoir's rosy-cheeked, plump young French women.

"It's hard to believe today, but that kind of shape was then thought to be the ultimate in female beauty. It's only recently that women were expected to be thin...like movie stars or those poor emaciated models you see in magazine ads."

She paused and passed a hand over her breastline: "Course, we're also expected to achieve the impossible and at the same time be buxom up here."

Sonny followed her gesture and looked...and looked flustered. He was also feeling plenty uncomfortable among all those nude pictures. He further concluded that if Grace could walk straight into any of those paintings, she would make all the others look pretty sad by comparison.

"Why do you think I went to all the effort to lose that surplus weight last Winter?" she continued. "I did it because people had begun to think of me as middle-aged. At 34! I also felt it was downright sinful to take this marvelous body God gave us—the only one we'll ever have—and misuse and abuse it. By overeating and underdoing. As though we could readily trade it in for a replacement—like a used car! So I decided to shape up. And now I feel YOUNG again!"

On sudden impulse she threw her arm around her companion and hugged him: "And you, Sonny...you make me feel even younger!"

Now he really gurgled.

Getting back on track, Grace then talked about the great Rembrandt as she showed off his paintings of dark backgrounds and contrasting golden light.

"You almost think there's a real light source in these pictures. Yet the light comes from sheer wizardry. It's created wholly by the artist juxtaposing light areas against adjoining dark ones. Perhaps life itself is like that, too...don't you think,

Sonny? That you can't really appreciate plenty until you first know want. That you can't know the lightness of happiness unless you also experience the darkness of sorrow?"

More gurgling was heard. Sonny found himself so involved in this new world that he hardly knew what to think at the moment.

Grace showed the sweeping cloudscapes of Constable and then returned to the French Impressionists, which she said she loved most of all. Especially the works of Monet, over which they lingered long. For here was sun and watery reflections and shimmering movement. She finally stopped at the emotion-charged, red-splashed paintings of Norway's Edvard Munch.

"I'm extra interested in Munch because both of my parents came from Scandinavia. Which you may have guessed. But tell me, Sonny, what do you think of 'The Scream'?"

He looked at the twisted, tormented face against its eerily twisted background and exclaimed: "Boy, it's scary!"

"Okay, now what do you think of his 'Madonna'?"

"Oh, she's beautiful!"

"You really FEEL the difference?" Obviously pleased with his reaction, she continued, "It's sad, Sonny, but beauty is mostly wasted on the young. Most are in an awful rush to get who-knows-where. So few seem able to see beauty even when it's right in front of their eyes...and fewer still seem to appreciate it."

She sighed deeply. "Anyway, you'd hardly think these two paintings were by the same artist, right? Which proves that the mood an artist brings to a concept is everything."

Grace turned and waved her arm around the room:

"And think of the different moods that architects bring to designing buildings. That can be great art, too...as well as great engineering. Think of the Greek temples, India's Taj Mahal, a Gothic cathedral, our own National Capitol, a Frank Lloyd Wright house integrated with its setting or a skyscraper. Harmony in stone and steel!"

Grace caught her breath and said, "Ah, but all this is a subject for future exploration." She looked directly at Sonny and asked, "Have you ever thought of painting?"

"Well, I draw a little. Sure...but I'd never, ever be able to do anything like this!"

"Maybe not, but you never know what you're really capable of doing until you try. Course, you would need a good model."

She smiled and asked, almost shyly: "Could I be your model, Sonny?"

This kicked off a prolonged coughing spell.

Grace closed the book and placed it in Sonny's hands "on loan till next Tuesday." This had happened with all the other books they had gone over during the past two years. First, he had been put to reading them one by one, then the following Tuesday came discussion time. This left his head spinning, like today, with new and often inspiring experiences.

So Sonny went home this latest Tuesday walking a bit on air, the big art book under his arm. And as he glided along the river's edge, he found himself looking at his surroundings with a strange new intensity. Now he saw pictures everywhere. Trees were no longer plain green...but myriad shades of green and shadows. Clouds were no longer just white...but rose-tinted and all shades of gray, topped by snowy fluff. And the sky! It ranged from the lightest blue at the horizon to pure sapphire overhead. The young man's vision—his perception—had truly changed. And

Grace was the magician who had made it happen. Just thinking of her made him catch his breath.

• • •

Sonny recalled vividly how their reading adventures had been launched, for they began with a startling statement.

"What you read is what you'll become," Grace declared.

That day she appeared on the kitchen study scene with her hair swept straight back and tied into a clump in back. It was what Sonny came to understand was her "classroom look". She wore horn-rimmed reading glasses which magnified her wide-set blue eyes and made them doubly expressive. She thus somehow managed to look to her enamored pupil both more severe and more attractive, at the same time.

Sonny worked over her revolutionary statement a while, then asked: "Does that mean that if I read a lot about animals, I might become one?"

"You are already!" she laughed, adding, "at least partly. No...I meant that if you read trash, you'll absorb it...and eventually become trashy. The same if you listen to trashy music. Or see trashy movies. Or associate with trashy people. The trash will rub off on you!"

"So how do I get rid of it?"

"You don't have to—you avoid it. You go for the best. You expose yourself continually to the best. And then, by the grace of God, you'll become the best!"

Grace shook her head, looking almost angry. "People today seem to be caught up in a perverse Gresham's Law, where the social good is being driven out of circulation by the bad. Or reverse alchemy, where gold is being turned into lead. Mass marketing, mass communications, mass entertainment, mass politicking—they're all aimed at the lowest common denominator of people's tastes and feelings. The result is they're gradually degrading and debasing our common culture. What we're witnessing today is nothing less than the vulgarization of America."

"Gosh, is it really that bad?" Sonny thought of what J.P. had said about politics and of Pastor Smith's comments about the deadly Four P's. It all seemed as threatening as a scenario right out of a frightening book he had recently read—Aldous Huxley's *Brave New World*.

"That bad?" Grace answered. "Yes, and it may be even worse. America—as well as Western civilization as a whole—could well be committing cultural suicide."

Sonny frowned, inside as well as out. His teachers maintained that man was constantly improving through the centuries, steadily distancing himself from the jungle. In technology, of course...but also in cultural awareness and human understanding. Now, though, what he was hearing was just the opposite. He got the uncomfortable feeling that, unless things changed radically, everyone would shortly be going back to swinging through the treetops.

Noting his forlorn look, Grace brightened visibly and said, "Hey, there, Sonny...cheer up! You don't have to be taken in by these efforts to turn America into a cultural trashpile. Nor me, either. And we won't!"

"You know, Grace Ann, you sound a lot like Pastor Smith. J.P., too."

"Oh?" she replied. "Well, maybe so...but with a big difference. J.P., you've noticed, is interested mainly in the broader world we live in—the EX-ternal. I'm more concerned with what happens inside people—with the IN-ternal."

"And Pastor Smith?"

"Morals, the spiritual—the E-ternal!"

Putting her literary prescription into practical form, they proceeded to take up a whole row of books, starting with novels. This, Grace said, was meant "to add more fun to the first steps."

Sonny thus soon found himself struggling through the sewers of Paris with Jean Valjean in Victor Hugo's *Les Miserables*.

He fought with and against Indians in James Fenimore Cooper's *The Last of the Mohicans*.

He hunted Arctic gold with the great dog Buck in Jack London's *Call of the Wild*.

He went through tortuous growing-up pains with Somerset Maugham in *Of Human Bondage*.

He slogged through trench warfare horrors with Erich Maria Remarque in *All Quiet on the Western Front*.

He agonized over the fate of the fallen in Thornton Wilder's *The Bridge of San Luis Rey*.

He rebelled against Captain Bligh's iron rule in Nordhoff and Hall's *Mutiny on the Bounty*.

He trembled with fright with Robert Louis Stevenson in *The Strange Case of Dr. Jekyll and Mr. Hyde*, with Mary Shelley in *Frankenstein* and with Oscar Wilde in *The Picture of Dorian Gray*.

He joined the Okies and Arkies in fleeing the dustbowl for a hostile California in a disturbing new book—John Steinbeck's *The Grapes of Wrath*.

They also covered many other modern writers, among them Dreiser, Dos Passos, Hemingway, O'Neill, Ibsen, Faulkner, Fitzgerald. Plus Grace's favorite—Thomas Wolfe—who, she said, "wrote prose like poetry."

For his own all-time favorite, Sonny had to go back to the 1800s, to Herman Melville's *Moby Dick*. He loved the gripping story of Captain Ahab's crazed search for the great white whale that had been responsible for the loss of his leg—even though the search ended in utter disaster.

"Readers get so caught up in this story that they miss the moral," Grace cautioned. "And that's simply that you've got to beware of the obsessed and extremists of the world. And don't waste your time seeking revenge and digging graves for others. You just might fall in yourself!"

Next came the plays of Shakespeare, which seemed as dense as mud at first, but cleared up amazingly under Grace's magic touch.

"Literature is filled with allusions to both the Bible and Shakespeare," she pointed out. "You already know the Bible, Sonny, but you also have to know the great Bard. For no one depicted better our human foibles—greed, lust, jealousy, deceit, power madness."

So they went over many plays line by line, with special attention being paid to "Hamlet", "Julius Ceasar" and "Anthony and Cleopatra". Sonny could thus now quote verbatim "Hamlet's" to be or not to be" musings and the aging Polonius' advice to his departing son, Laertus, including the classic "this above all" conclusion.

"This ending has got to be one of the most precious pieces of guidance ever given anyone," Grace said, again reading it out loud:

> This above all, to thine own self be true;
> And it must follow, as the night the day,
> Thou canst not then be false to any man.

"This wonder contains a basic flaw, though," she went on. "Can you name it, Sonny?"

"Nope. Sounds fine to me."

"It's simply that it assumes you have the right stuff—the solid, quality stuff inside—to be true to. And that's exactly what you and I are working on now."

Grace also picked out as among Shakespeare's finest lines those uttered by Hamlet's friend, Horatio, as the dead prince's body is carried out after his fatal duel:

"Good night, sweet prince; and flights of angels sing thee to thy rest!"

"Note, Sonny, it's 'good night', not good-bye—as though Hamlet may awaken in the morning. And it's 'flights' of angels—not just a flock, group or a bunch. And they 'sing' Hamlet away—not take or carry. And he goes to 'rest'—not to his death or a cold grave. Inspiring!"

"So angels can sing as well as play the harp?"

"You said it! And I can tell you the melody they sing by, too. It's the Andante Movement from Beethoven's great Ninth Symphony. I'll play it for you one day. It's the loveliest music this side of heaven. And maybe in heaven, too."

From "Julius Ceasar" Sonny learned to quote the lines which the plotter Cassius (he of the "lean and hungry look") said to Brutus ("the noblest Roman of them all") as they discussed their great leader (who "doth bestride the narrow world like a Colossus"):

"The fault, dear Brutus, is not in our stars, but in ourselves, that we are underlings."

"There you have the hard truth, Sonny," Grace interjected. "If you fail to get anywhere in life, you can't blame anyone but you-know-who!"

"Not you?'

"Not any more!"

She also lingered over a passage from "Anthony and Cleopatra" where a Roman army officer is describing the ravishing queen of Egypt in these words:

"Age cannot wither her, nor custom stale her infinite variety."

She laughed and apologized "for not quite measuring up to Cleopatra," then added: "But I'm closer now than last Summer!" To which Sonny could only breathe a silent amen.

In parting that day, Grace summed up their reading adventures by saying, "Befriend good books, Sonny, and you'll never be lonely. For right within reach of the nearest bookshelf or library, you'll find a dozen close companions—a dozen really unusual companions. People who can inform, inspire, excite, scare, sooth. And they ask nothing in return except your interest. What a deal!"

• • •

The following Tuesday turned out to be the hottest day of the year. Heat and high humidity lay like a blanket across the river valley, unrelieved by even the slightest breeze. Even so, Sonny was greeted as he arrived at the Deeres by the happy blare of trumpets. The whole house was jumping...and so was Grace as she came to meet him at the backporch door.

"Isn't it fantastic!" she shouted above the din. "It's the victory march from Aida—the grandest of grand operas. You know, the one Verdi wrote for the opening of the Suez Canal...."

Needless to say, Sonny didn't know at all, but that didn't mean it didn't sound just as fantastic as Grace said.

"The wonder-world of music—that's the next item on our agenda, Sonny."

And with that she dispatched him to mow the lawn. Done with that by 11 o'clock, and sweating profusely, he tackled the vegetable garden. And here Grace also soon appeared, looking fresh as her roses. However, after a half-hour of working with her flowers, she began to look as wilted as Sonny. Whereupon she announced she was giving up.

"This is impossible! It's like taking a sauna—a steam bath. Let's go inside. We can find better things to do than this."

Sonny didn't protest at all. So Grace gave him a terry-cloth robe and told him to get out of his wet clothes, hang them on the porch line, and cool off in the outdoor shower. They would then have an early lunch.

Refreshed, skin tingling, he finally sat down in the cool kitchen with his boss, who had also showered and now looked as fresh as her roses again. He plowed through a ham-and-tomato sandwich ("no soup today!"), then waded into a big slice of yellow cake topped with chocolate icing. Grace, eating almost nothing, watched him enviously.

"You're an odd duck, Sonny," she said, noting his newly acquired robe. "Here you go around in a frazzled shirt and worn over-alls, working yourself ragged. Yet, you've got the manners of an aristocrat. So tell me your secret: What makes Sonny work?"

"Shucks, ev'ryone works here'bouts. If you wanna eat, you gotta work. And I like to eat!"

"But that's not true everywhere. I see lots of young people just hanging around, sponging off others. They seem to feel that the world owes them a living…while they owe nothing to anyone. They're loafers, regular parasites. And before you know it, they've become troublemakers…and worse."

"Gee, they wouldn't last long 'round here."

"Thank goodness! But tell me, why do you work so hard?"

"Guess I just like physical effort—usin' your muscles. If I wasn't workin', I'd be runnin' or playin' ball. And the harder, the better. It feels so good when you stop!"

"It also sounds like the three keys to success. Which is effort, effort and more effort. Ever heard of the law of psychic equivalents? No? Well, it says simply that you can't get more out of anything than you put in. So the loafers are missing out on a lot, while you're getting in on a lot. You see, it pays to have to struggle!"

"So why am I always broke?"

"Ah, now you've become as bad as those money-mooching parasites! Sonny, you've got to get yourself a wholly different measuring stick for value in life. And money is NOT it…despite all the wonderful things money can buy. Did you know?…some of the unhappiest people anywhere are also the richest."

"Don't think Aunt Emma would agree with that!"

"Yes…she's probably suffered too much from its lack. You, though…you can still be salvaged."

Grace cleared the dishes off the table, came back and ran her hands through his hair on the way to her seat. "And look here what you've also got: Wavy hair! Most people would give their big toe for that."

Sonny reddened and brushed his hair back from his eyes while he looked closely at Blond Boss. Her own hair was now piled up on top again in what she called her "concert look." By any name it would have looked great—her, too—he thought.

"Bet you have a lot of girl friends," Grace continued.

"Nope. Don't have time."

"But isn't there at least one you really like?"

"Well, there's Jenny Lee Simms…but…ah…." Sonny didn't know quite how to finish the sentence.

Grace nodded approvingly. "Good taste! Is she the prettiest girl you know?"

"No, Grace Ann. There's one other who beats them all." Sonny paused, gulped, blushed, then charged on: "It's YOU! You're the most beautiful girl I've ever known!"

Grace threw her head back and laughed so the whole room danced. "Why, Sonny, that's the nicest thing anyone has ever said to me! I could kiss you for that. In fact, I will!"

She jumped up and came over to Sonny's chair and gave him a soft peck on the cheek. Then he felt a sharp change come over her. She kissed him full on the mouth. And kissed and kept kissing—eyes, cheek, neck. She pulled him to his feet and embraced him. His own arms, sprung like a triggered trap, locked around her—a warm, writhing bundle of exquisite softness.

Then, as suddenly as it started, it stopped.

Grace pulled away abruptly, covered her face with her hands and moaned: "Oh, Sonny, I'm so sorry…so, so sorry! I don't know what made me do that. It was wrong. Terribly wrong. Forgive me!"

Well, Sonny hardly knew what she was talking about. Wrong? Sorry? His head spun from the sheer wonder of her embrace, her very presence. His insides felt like the time he picked up a short-circuited fan and found he couldn't remove his hands…while electricity coursed through his body. Until someone came running and pulled the plug. And now, like then, he found himself completely charged up. But this time by Grace. It was glorious!

"Let's get out of here and go swimming," Grace suggested, a bit breathless. "We can take our books along. And go through them down by the river."

So Sonny got outfitted with Don's swimtrunks, which fit him like oversized bloomers. Grace, meanwhile, changed into a two-piece suit, topped by a light smock. And down to the river they ran, like two kids on a lark…through the sweltering bottomland to the cool waterside willows. Where they placed their things on a fallen tree trunk.

Clearing a smooth sitting place in the sand, Sonny looked up just as Grace began taking off her smock. There she stood against the shimmering stream, raising the garment up over her head, high, to full arm's length, revealing her body with all its streamed lines and fluid curves: Long legs, narrow hips, narrower waist and a magnificent bustline. She dropped her right arm holding the smock; tossed her head back—her sun-kissed hair cascading toward the ground; rose on tiptoes, and reached higher and higher with her left hand—reaching toward the clouds, the sky, the unseen stars, heaven itself.

Sonny stared as though hypnotized as something clicked inside his brain. It was his mental camera. Nothing…nothing he had ever seen before—not all the pictures in her art book—could compare with Grace's living, breathing, moving reality. And he wanted to record and remember this moment forever.

"How am I doing, Sonny?" she said, bouncing back to earth and coming closer. "What do you think of the new Grace Ann?"

No answer. Sonny was so intoxicated he had ceased to think.

She sat beside him on the cool ground, enveloped in a heady fragrance. "You're not afraid of me, are you, Sonny?"

"Afraid? No, Grace Ann. Gee, no! Can you be afraid of someone you like so much?"

"I really like you, too, Sonny. You're the one close friend I have in this whole community. I'd do anything for you. But… but…but…." She sputtered down like a sleek racing car running out of gas.

She threw a hopeful look at Sonny. "You've forgiven me for getting carried away a while ago?"

"Heck, I never blamed you."

"Okay...then see if you can beat me into the river!"

And so they ran headlong into the cool water and raced each other far from shore, Grace finally splashing water and yelling "you win!" They paddled back slowly and, dripping water across the hot stones, sank against the tree trunk, catching their breath.

"What a grand place this is!" she exclaimed. Then, turning serious, "You know, people are a lot like our river."

"They're all wet?"

"No! Well, maybe that, too. But I was really thinking that what you see is a glittering surface. The real life is underneath. It's that way with me, too."

"Are women that much different from men?"

"Oh, men are such clowns!" she burst out. "And I don't mean you, Sonny. At least you're not one yet. But men see a cute face and a nice figure and hardly bother to look further. They just think of how heavenly they're going to have it in bed. The great awakening, all too often, comes later...once they're married."

"But how do you avoid making such a mess of things?"

"Well, first of all you have to think of life as one big masquerade. Most people are just filled with pretense and posturing. They can play as many roles as Broadway actors...and wear as many false faces as kids at Halloween. Yet underneath it all is this person you'll have to live with—maybe for the rest of your life. So you've simply got to pry off that mask and find out who that person really is. And I mean BEFORE you marry!"

"But doing...ah...that sort of thing before marriage," Sonny blushed and stammered, completely misunderstanding, "isn't that...isn't that a sure way to go to hell?"

Grace laughed. "Sure, but there's an even faster way to get there—and that's through promiscuity."

Wow, there's that word again! Sonny thought. It sounded even worse this time. He wrestled with it a while and finally decided to try it out on his pal Clay Wilkes rather than show how dumb he was right there before Grace. Then he dredged up the question he had always wanted to ask someone but never quite dared, until now when he felt he had a most willing oracle:

"The Bible, Grace Ann...doesn't the Bible forbid adultery? It says you cannot covet your neighbor's wife. It warns again and again against...well, you know...."

"But Sonny, dear Sonny, I go to church, too, remember? And I can assure you that you can't do something you know is wrong, and hope to get away with it. Love is the greatest gift God has given us. The awful sin—the unforgivable sin—is to rob it of its spiritual quality and beauty and make it coarse and ugly."

"But what about your husband? Just being together like now—isn't that pretty bad, for him?"

"Donaldson, you mean?" she laughed again. "You don't have to worry about him. We're apart so much, we have wonderful reunions. Absence really does make the heart grow fonder!"

"But the Bible says...."

"Sure, Sonny, the Bible contains more wisdom than we poor souls can ever know. And the ancients knew one thing well: That sex involves our strongest emotions. It's pure dynamite. And that man has an unlimited capacity to take even the purest and loveliest thing and turn it into raw dirt. That's why pornography is so terrible. It robs sex of all spiritual content and drives people down to the lowest, rawest animal state—if not beyond. So sex is turned into lust, perversion, rape, prostitution, drugs, crime, violence. Madness! Man-made madness! So our spiritual forefathers tried to wall in this precious gift and contain it within the one institution that can hope to handle it—marriage."

"So shouldn't we be married before being together so much?"

Grace sat up. "You're not proposing to me, are you?"

"Could I?"

"And how do you think Don would feel about THAT!"

She slid back onto her back and took her companion's hand. "Someday, Sonny, you'll find the right girl and get married. So let me tell you something very important. Do you know what'll make that girl want to marry you?"

"Love?" Then he fairly howled with laughter: "Or because I'm so handsome?"

"You don't deserve that girl, you rascal!" Grace teased.

"No," she continued, "you can put her in that mood by courting her. Wooing her. Playing up to her. But now comes the big blunder almost everyone makes. They think courtship ends the day they get married. Golly, that's when it should begin! And go on every day for the rest of your life."

"But, Grace Ann, how will you know when it's true love?"

"Well, not when you're thinking only of what your partner can do for you. You'll know it's true love when you find yourself thinking mainly of what you can do for her. That's unconditional love—the rarest of all. And I can guarantee you one thing, Sonny," she added with extra emphasis: "The happier you make your wife, the happier she's going to make you!"

Sonny chewed on that a long while, decided it was something he wanted to remember, then asked, "So is there any special formula for creatin' a happy home?"

"What do you think it takes?"

Another pause...then, recalling Aunt Emma and Grampaw's shenanigans, he almost yelled: "Cooperation! Respect for each other!"

Grace nodded vigorously. "People getting married have to get rid of a lot of illusions and recognize that even the best marriages are filled with friction. And then they've got to commit themselves to make a go of things regardless. To work out disagreements and difficulties together. That's what the wedding vows are all about, right? But now, compare that with the loose arrangements you see so often today. Where's the commitment, the partnership? The first time someone frowns, the other bolts out the door!"

"Then comes divorce?"

"That should never happen IF couples planning to marry check out their 'Marital A.P.' first."

"A.P.? Associated Press?"

"No, silly! A.P. stands for After Passion. Newlyweds inevitably find to their sorrow that after some weeks, months or years, their initial desire, their passion ebbs away. Then, they look at each other and find there's nothing left to fall back on. No shared interests, no camaraderie, no mutual respect—nothing left to hold them together. That's when the real trouble begins."

Grace paused over some vagrant thought, then continued: "You know, Sonny, marriage is probably the most important decision you'll ever make. The great irony, though, is that most people make it when they're young, uninformed, inexperienced and least able to do so. They don't realize that marriage is probably the shakiest of human creations."

"Shakiest! Why's that?"

"Because it's basically lopsided, unbalanced. It probably

suits the family's security needs more than the man's biological drives. This means the man has to work harder to make the marriage work…while the woman has to work harder to make their lovelife work. Does that make sense?"

"No…."

"Well, it will some day." This was followed by a lilting laugh: "Maybe for me, too!"

"But aren't a lot of men pretty rough with their wives? Even brutal or…er…ah…."

"Tyrannical?"

"Yeah, that's the word!"

"And you think men have a monopoly on tyranny?"

"Well…."

"Not so, Sonnyboy! Want to get in on the world's worst-kept secret? It's that women beat men hands down as natural-born tyrants. Course, they have their own ways, their more subtle ways. But the worst part is, the more men buckle under to their special ways of tyrannizing, the more tyrannical they become."

"So how can the two create a marriage of equals—one where neither one tyrannizes the other? And live together in peace?"

Grace shook her head, laughed and said, "Class dismissed!"

"Why…on what grounds?"

"Student asks questions without answers!"

An impish look came over her face. "Want to get in on another secret?"

"Think I can take it?"

"You'll like this one. You know how men are criticized for being obsessed with running after money and power. But who is it that prods them on? Women! While men chase after money and power, women chase after men WITH money and power. And who knows that better than anyone? Men!"

"Are women really that difficult?"

"Not really. They're just...well, they're just women."

"Huh?"

"Well, it's like this, Sonny. God so loved man that He made and gave him that most exotic of creations—woman. And man's been trying ever since to find a way to live with that glorious gift!"

"Oh-h-h..." Sonny felt he was treading on some very treacherous ground, but raced on.

"Can I squeeze in just one more question? Didn't you say that men just think of er...ah...you know what I mean...when they think of gettin' married?"

"Yes, which just shows that people almost always focus on the wrong things in life. Remember that piece of cake you had for lunch? Well, sex is like the icing on that cake. It's grand! But if you eat just icing, you'll soon get plenty sick of it. Or sick, period. So you've got to focus on the cake itself—your relationship. Do things together. Have fun together. Season everything with a good sense of humor. Build a good relationship and you'll find that your Love life will take care of itself."

Grace, now looking more serious than ever, leaned over as though she wanted to stress a special point. "Above all, Sonny, keep the tenderness in your relationship. The world is becoming so cold and harsh—so impersonal and dehumanized. Civility, decency, consideration for others—so much that is important to making life worthwhile—are disappearing from modern life. So hold on to these at home with all your might. Make your marriage, your home, your family a refuge. Keep caring for each other. Keep supporting each other. Keep the tenderness!"

That afternoon as he headed home, Sonny felt he was beginning to develop a new understanding of some very complex human problems out of these revelations from his beautiful boss. But some deeper feelings were developing, too. His heart full of Grace, full of love, he went into such trances the next week that Aunt Emma thought for sure he was "comin' down with the Summer flu."

• • •

More music greeted Sonny when he reported for duty the following Tuesday. It was a soprano singing the loveliest song he had ever heard, and he said so with no little awe in his voice.

"It's 'O mio babbino caro'," Grace replied, adding at his bewildered look, 'O my beloved father.' It's from a beautiful one-act opera by the Italian composer, Puccini…called 'Gianni Schicchi'."

"Please play it again, Grace Ann," he pleaded, thinking, gee, what a world of difference that is from "She'll Be Comin' 'Round the Mountain" or 'Old Shep'." Or even Stephen Foster's grand songs.

"You really like it, Sonny?" Grace asked happily. "Okay, then, for that we'll turn the day upside down: Music now, work later!"

She took Sonny into the livingroom, had him sit before the finest record-player he had seen…and selected a record from an astonishing collection. She placed it on the turntable and stepped back: "Try this one…."

Now came a tenor singing what she said was Rudolfo's role from "La Boheme", together with a soprano singing "They Call Me Mimi." It was fantastic! Sonny found his spirits soaring, and showed it.

Grace clapped her hands with a little girl's unbounded glee. "Oh, I'm so glad you like it! You know, not everyone likes opera. You have to develop a taste for it over a long time. But once you get hooked, you love it. It's inspiring. It's a call to greatness! Here, let me show you."

A tenor with a big voice now came on singing "Nessun Dorma"—"None Shall Sleep"—from Puccini's opera set in China, "Turandot". Sonny felt carried away on musical wings.

Grace next played something she said was different and "very special"—a tenor from Norway singing a moving song called "Naar Fjordene Blaaner" (When the Fjords Turn Blue). "It's Erling Krogh," she said, "one of the greatest of them all. Great because his voice has vitality, power and resonance...and he puts tremendous enthusiasm into his singing. Hear it? People in Scandinavia love him!"

Grace paused, a happy, far-away look on her face, while she sorted through more records.

"Okay, now you've had a taste of arias," she went on, "particularly those by tenors, who always seem to get the best numbers and the most applause. And one day we'll take up Richard Wagner and his sweeping 'Ring'—four grand operas based on German/Norse mythology. That takes a more developed taste, though. So right now.... Remember the 'Victory March' from Aida? Well, let's return to Verdi and play something a little different—a piece that really shows his artistry."

And with that she played that marvel in harmony, the Quartet from "Rigoletto". All four singers seemed to be coming right into the room, surrounding them with stirring sound.

"Think you could compose something like that, Sonny?"

"Oh, no...gee, NO! I'm too young and...."

"But what if I told you about a composer who was writing complicated musical scores by his tenth birthday? Incredible!

It was Mozart. We owe much of our finest music to him—especially piano concertos. Here, let me play the one I like best—Number 21—the Andante Movement."

Sonny listened...and said nothing. What could you say in the face of such wonder?

"Remember that other Andante Movement I mentioned? The one from Beethoven's Ninth Symphony? See if I'm right in saying it's the sweetest music this side of heaven."

It was! Sonny decided. He felt that the operatic arias picked you up, all the way to the mountain top. But what he heard now vibrated along the innermost heart strings and brought visions of golden meadows, rippling waters, drifting clouds, rainbows and starry nights. The emotional touch of pure magic!

"You still play the recorder, Sonny? Okay, then here's a piece I know you'll want to learn by heart. It's the 'Intermezzo' from Mascagna's opera 'Cavalleria Rusticana'."

Sonny sank deeper into the room's big wing-tip chair he had been occupying while dreaming away to the tune of Grace's stellar performance. He was brought back to reality when his boss suddenly whirled into a graceful pirouette right in front of him.

"There's so much more wonderful music I want you to hear. For instance, there's Tchaikovsky's 'Violin Concerto' and Edvard Grieg's 'Peer Gynt Suite.' And we haven't even touched on Gershwin, Cole Porter, Irving Berlin and the other American composers and their Broadway musicals. There's simply no end to the sheer joy music can bring you!"

She pulled him to his feet. "Now I want you to hear something that's totally different—something just for you and me."

She put on a French love song and, with mock gravity, asked her partner for a dance. Which it wasn't. Or at least it wasn't like the stiff-armed, one-two-step exercises he had tried but never quite mastered at school events. They simply held each other and swayed to the haunting refrain of Paris and springtime and soft breezes along the Seine and the wonder of love. The "Paris Shuffle," she called it.

Grace put her right arm around his neck, pressing her soft cheek against his. Her voice dropped to a whisper. "Tell me, Sonny, have you ever had a 19-year-old girl friend?"

"Oh, no, Grace Ann…you know I never…," he stuttered as electricity surged through him, setting off more sparks.

"Well, you have now! You've chopped 15 years off my age. Oh, Sonny, you make me feel so FREE!" She kissed him on the cheek and he almost collapsed with rapture.

At lunch they sat closer than usual…and time and again Grace flashed that brilliant, contagious smile. He had never seen her so carefree, so happy.

"Is this what music does to you, Grace Ann?"

"No, it's what you do!"

She rose slowly from the table: "It's amazing how warm it's gotten here. Think we'd better go swimming."

At the river they lounged in the shade, talked about the lives of great composers, went swimming and lounged still more.

"Gosh, Grace Ann," Sonny murmured, letting his eyes wander among the shadowed willows along the sun-streaked shoreline, then back at her, "heaven couldn't possibly be better than this!"

"No, I don't think so, either…except for one big difference: Heaven is forever."

Sonny felt a blast of cold wind come out of nowhere—the same kind he had felt too often before—but then surrendered once more to the languorous setting and his amazing Grace.

She rose on her elbow, looked directly at him and asked: "Why do you think we're doing all this, Sonny? I mean the music, our books, the visual arts...."

"Because you love the arts?"

"And want you to love them, too. All the seven classical arts. Can you name them?"

Sonny tried but soon gave up as Grace went on. "And you make it fun, too. You absorb everything like a sponge, digest it and make it your own."

She caught her breath. "What we're doing, Sonny, is something you won't learn in school. Even though it's more important than almost anything. Why? Because the arts touch your soul and contribute like nothing else to the art of living."

This got Sonny's attention in a big way. Was Grace getting to the ultimate secret of life? He decided she had to be getting close...because what she was teaching him was so special and stirred him so deeply. Her remarks triggered a key question:

"J.P. says that if you can get hold of both knowledge and religious faith, you'll really score in life. But now, you're sayin' somethin' else...or are you?"

"Yes, indeed! J.P.'s right—as far as he goes. Yet, there's another major dimension to personal development that he probably didn't get around to mentioning. One that can keep you from being as flat as those cut-out dolls your sister clips from magazines. Or those phony Western towns Hollywood sometimes builds—with propped-up store fronts and nothing in back. Just length and height but no depth, like a square. You don't want to be a square, do you, Sonny?"

"Gosh, no," he said, frowning. Then, brightening up: "So how do I add some depth—like, say, a cube?"

Grace broke out another big smile, then frowned. "Let's say you simply want to become a complete person. Most people, I'm afraid, have few, if any, intellectual or cultural interests, with the result that they're almost totally dependent on outside stimulation. They're more like hollow widgets, stamped out and steered by a promotion-saturated, materialistic society...and desperately trying to fill their emptiness with goods and good times. All in vain! Most just plod their way through life, shuffling along on an endless treadmill between their work, their kitchen, bathroom and bedroom, and the nearest shops. Or they get so wrapped up in earning a living and riding the maddening modern money-go-round that they completely forget to live!

"What I'm really saying Sonny is this: Unless you develop a strong inner world, you fall easy victim to the crass outer world, and wind up pushed around like a leaf in a windstorm."

Sonny blanched. It all sounded like the bells at their church tolling for a funeral.

"Young people owe it to themselves to do better than that. Much better! You've got to go beyond developing your mind and job capabilities, important as that is, and work on your soul."

"Soul?" Sonny perked up. That word brought back a lot of old, unanswered questions. What really is the soul? Where's it located? How does it differ from the spirit, or even the heart?

Finally, he came up with an answer:

"Ah, that's what you've got, Grace Ann. You've got soul! How can I get what you've got?"

"Well, I'm hanging on to mine...so that means you've got to develop your own! Soul, Sonny, is what you really are. It's your character, your personality, your attitudes and behavior, your human warmth, your treatment of others. It's something you have to earn. And you earn it by putting your life into it."

Her face took on a carried-away look. "You have to develop a sensitivity for the beauty that's all around us—in nature, in design and handicrafts, in man's great cultural achievements over the centuries. I mean a deep appreciation for art and culture. For those very things we've been talking about right along —the literary classics, the creative arts, the performing arts. And of them all, opera is the grandest...because it combines so gloriously all the other arts. It is pretty grand, don't you think so, too?"

"Sure...and it's you who've made it so!" Sonny exclaimed.

Grace's voice dropped as she looked at him intently. "How would you like to have a love affair?"

"Oh? OH!" Sonny blushed, totally speechless.

"Not that kind! I'm referring to the lovingest affair of all—one with nature. Nature provides rich food for the soul. Man came out of nature and needs to return regularly to his origins. He needs to escape the workaday, tension-filled world and immerse himself in nature's wondrous, soothing, healing powers. Then he can return again—a new, whole being."

Sonny grunted in hearty agreement. Along the river, he hadn't found it necessary to reach out for nature. Here, nature surrounded, covered and embraced you. And Sonny loved it. So it was, in fact, a real, personal love affair. One that had started the day he arrived from Smoky City.

Something about art was bothering him, though, so he brought it right out: "You know, a lot of art looks pretty funny. Strange! How do you know what's really good?"

The question straightened Grace up. "Ha...another impossible question from Socrates himself! So now you think I'm an art expert, too? Anyway, the answer the art world would give is that art is what the artists say it is. Which is hogwash. Insider arrogance! The actual answer is that there's a lot of junk out there parading around as art. Which you've got to expect. Artists are almost desperate to create something new and different, something provocative and attention-getting.

Unfortunately, they rarely succeed in producing things of lasting quality. Yet, if the average guy has the nerve to question this non-art and say, hey, what's this! he gets clobbered. The whole art colony rises and ridicules him as an art ignoramus—as someone who 'simply doesn't understand.'"

"So do you just give in and shut up?"

"Never! These are pure intimidation tactics. Just go on and develop your own conclusions as to what's good. And bad. Then, assuming you work at it hard enough, chances are you'll be as right as anyone else."

Sonny nodded, then found himself also wrestling with Grace's earlier remarks about culture as one of three dimensions—alongside learning and religion. "Is there a fourth dimension?" he asked.

"A fourth dimension!"

Grace started visibly and threw Sonny a penetrating look—the kind Captain Kidd might have fastened on someone finding the map for his long-lost secret treasure. Their eyes locked together so long he began to wonder if he had said something wrong.

"Yes-s-s, there is," she said slowly, thoughtfully. "But if I tell you, you'll just forget it. So go and find out yourself, and then it'll stick."

"Not even a clue?"

"Okay, here's one. The three dimensions we've discussed so far deal with self. With looking inward. With a person's development of his own capacities, of himself as a human being. But people don't just live alone, do they? We're all part of a family, a community, a nation...the world. So what kind of relationship will you develop with all these others who live with you and around you...and are affected by you?"

"So that's the final dimension?"

"The last! Find that one, Sonny, and you'll not only discover the fourth dimension. More important, if you live that role, along with the first three, you'll become a rounded, developed, civilized human being. And by that I mean that you'll not only enjoy life to the fullest, but others will enjoy having you around, too!"

Great! he thought. Just one more step, now, and I'm finally onto the ultimate secret of life!

Arriving home that afternoon after what struck him as one of the most revealing days he had lived, Sonny was met by a very worried Aunt Emma: "You're sure lookin' a bit peaked."

"Yeah, she really worked my tail off today...."

And that's the most far-fetched tale I've ever told, he felt like adding.

• • •

After a seemingly endless week of reliving every moment of his day with Grace, Sonny returned to the Deeres with great expectations. He was met by a crescendo of sound…from a full orchestra and massed chorus. Yet this recording was different—and so was Grace. Her face bore a look of sadness.

"Know what that music is, Sonny?"

"N-n-no," he stuttered, taken aback.

"It's another part of Beethoven's Ninth Symphony—his fantastic adaptation of Friedrich Schiller's inspiring poem, 'Ode to Joy.' He composed it when he was stone deaf…so many consider it a gift from God Himself. It was Beethoven's supreme tribute to mankind—a call to real human greatness."

Sonny was bewildered. "But…but…but what's that got to do with us?"

"It's tough, Sonny, but we've got to heed that call, too, whether we want to or not. So, to begin with, today's got to be a regular workday."

Well, Sonny didn't know what that meant, either. But he went to work...and worked as though Satan himself was chasing him. He ran the handmower over the lawn so fast that he was soon covered with grass clippings. In the same way, he roared through the vegetable plot, hoeing down some prized bean plants in the process. Next, he splashed whitewash over the picket fence surrounding the house so aimlessly that he came to look like a ghost. He then raced over the first-floor windows until they gleamed as seldom before.

Winding up, he felt Grace's hand on his shoulder...and almost jumped with joy. When he turned around, however, she backed away.

"Come on into the kitchen, Sonny, it's time for lunch," she said in a strange, flat voice.

He washed up, sat down, and stared at his food, unable to eat.

"What's wrong, Grace Ann," he choked out. "You know how I feel about you. I...I love you!"

She placed her hand on his arm. "That's exactly what's wrong, Sonny. We're becoming too close. I no longer know how to treat you—or how to behave. Whether like the boss I'm supposed to be. Or a teacher or a mother...or a sweetheart. Which is all wrong! The truth is, I'm too young to be your mother, and you're too young to be my sweetheart—even if I were available, which I'm not. Even worse, I'm now finding I would rather talk with you than my own husband. And what a recipe for disaster that is! Think of the field day the yellow journalists would have under this headline:

"34-Year-Old Woman
"Leaves Husband of 11 Years
"For 16-Year-Old Boy."

"Yellow journalists? You mean the Chinese?"

"Sonny!" she exploded in exasperation. Then added, with her old tenderness, "That's what I love about you—you're so open and innocent. No, I meant the scandal-mongering press. Remember? The first New York newspaper that really went in for muckraking was printed on yellow paper...."

"I don't care what they say!" he cut in. "I love you!"

"Yes, dear Sonny...but remember when we talked about playing with dynamite? I thought we could be close friends...but now we're becoming emotionally involved. And I can't hurt you more than I have already. Or my husband. Or myself. We've got to pull back."

She ended with a plea: "Let's go back to being just good pals, okay, Sonny?"

Sonny's head bent lower and lower as Grace spoke...and as he tried to hide the tears in his eyes. But now they broke loose in a flood. Grace, her own eyes swimming, put her arms around him and held him in silence for a long time.

"Gee, what a stupid little cry-baby I've become!" he blubbered at last. "Next, you'll be giving me a bottle."

They laughed hesitantly, then laughed some more.

"Okay, Grace Ann. Just friends again. But I can tell you, I'll never stop loving you in my heart."

The rest of the afternoon was devoted to more music. The one thing that stood out for him was the opera "Carmen", written by the Frenchman, Bizet, and set in Spain. Especially its rollicking "Torreador" melody and the touching "Flower Song."

Despite her lovely singing, Carmen was no classic heroine, Grace assured Sonny. She was a gypsy vixen who used her sexual charms to ensnare men. Then, when she tired of their presence, discarded them. Yet, there was one who refused to be discarded. Driven to distraction, he kills her.

Grace fastened big eyes and a mischievous grin on Sonny and asked: "You don't consider me a vixen, too, do you, Sonny?"

"Do vixens have the face of an angel?"

"Like who?"

"Like you!"

"Whoa there, Sonnyboy!" she burst out laughing. "You're learning a little too fast. Why, those angel-like types are the most dangerous kind of all. You'll meet them all through life. Or worse, they'll arrange to meet you. Watch out!"

"Oh, I can take care of myself," he grumbled.

"You don't say!" She turned and leaned softly against him: "Remember that time I kissed you so wildly? What if I did that again right now. Think you could resist that?"

"For you I'd go to hell and back!"

"Trouble is," she rejoined, "you might never return."

She paused and asked a puzzling question, "Will you remember me, Sonny?"

"Gosh, I don't have to. You're right here!"

"But what if Don had to move on to another project one day? And I, of course, went along?"

"Me forget YOU, Grace Ann? How could I? Ever!"

"Then how will you remember me? In what one way?"

Now it was Sonny's time to turn thoughtful. This lasted only a second as he answered with a playful grin, "You mean, besides your heart-warming smile?"

"Is that the one way?"

"Or besides your glorious kisses?"

"Now you're cheating!"

"Or besides the worlds of art and music and books you've pried open for me?"

"You're a regular little demon!" she cried out, clamping a hand over his mouth. She vowed not to let go until he promised to stick to her rules. Eyes dancing with laughter, he finally forced out "uncle!" and said:

"Okay, one way. And that's gotta be the time we went swimming and you took off your smock and rose on your toes…and reached higher and higher upward. There and then, you turned into the most beautiful creature God ever made! If I ever became a painter or sculptor, I would work forever to reproduce that image of you…and that magic moment."

"And what would you call it?"

"Oof, that's easy: Grace."

"Is that a name, harmonious movement or a spiritual quality?"

"In your case, all three!"

"There you go again!" she scolded, immediately brightening up. "But how 'bout a name that tells exactly what I was doing at that moment. How 'bout 'Reaching'? Frankly, I don't even know what I was reaching for. Was it for meaning? For understanding? For beauty? For love? For life itself? Somehow, Sonny, you yourself have been involved in all those things. Innocently, yes…but in a very important way for me."

It was time to go. At the backdoor, Grace, her eyes suddenly moist, hugged him and said, "You're a true believer, Sonny. You believe in the Bible, the Boy Scout law, America, people…so believe also in us. You've given me the chance to relive some of the most precious things I ever learned. We've had a world of fun. And think how beautiful we've kept our relationship. That's what I'll remember you for…always!"

A warm, lingering kiss…and he was on the way home, his head swimming and his heart overflowing more than ever.

• • •

Sonny worked from sunup to sundown the next two days

in J.P.'s tomato patch, sweating rivers in the July heat. When he came home Thursday afternoon and was washing up on the backporch, he overheard Aunt Emma talking to a neighbor:

"Did you see that big truck up at the Deeres?"

"Yep, looked like a movin' van."

His heart skipped several beats as he horned in and choked out: "Wha...you mean...is it still there?"

"Nope, left quite a spell back."

He heard no more. He dropped his towel and ran wildly out of the house, to the others' amazement.

At the Deeres, he found the fence gate open—open!—and stormed into the backyard, then through an unlatched screendoor. Looking in through the windows, he saw only emptiness. Everything—everything!—had been moved out. He felt like screaming. He looked aimlessly around. Then, there in the innermost corner of the porch, where Grace had often set him to reading, he saw a stack of three big books and a box, topped by a piece of paper. It read "For Sonny Sebring."

Picking the books up one by one, he saw that the first was entitled, *Literature, Now and Then*. Another, *The Wonderworld of Music*. And the third, *Art through the Ages*. Each bore this inside inscription in Grace's familiar handwriting:

To Sonny,
To help in your search.
Remembering....
Grace Ann Deere.

And the box! He ripped off the wrapping and found inside a set of oil paints and brushes. "Oh, Grace Ann!" he cried out...and collapsed onto the floor in a torrent of tears and wracking sobs.

Finally getting to his feet, he picked up Grace's farewell gifts and stumbled blindly down to the river, tore off his clothes and dived in…swimming with all his might upstream. His fists beat the water, his feet kicked wildly, his heart almost burst from the frenzied effort. Nearing total exhaustion, he thought he heard his mother's voice coming out of the past: "Play for time, Sonny…don't do anything dumb."

"I hear you, Mom," he answered to the wind, "I won't…I won't."

His arms turned leaden, he flopped over onto his back and floated back to his starting point, gasping in lungsful of air until his strength returned. There, he dragged himself onto the shoreside rocks and lay face down for a very long time. The tears were gone—for good, he resolved. The break in his heart, however, was another story.

Back home he went to bed without eating, to everyone's shock. Aunt Emma, however, wasn't so shocked that she couldn't snoop out his new books and note the inscriptions. The next morning she "harrumped" a couple times and said, "Hm-m-m, I didn't know Grace Deere had a middle name. And what's she mean here by this 'remembering'?"

"Oh that?" Sonny replied. "I guess she just wanted me to try to remember all the things in those books."

"And what on earth is this 'search' all 'bout?"

"Yeah, that was a little joke we had." Sonny said, at the same time wondering how Grace had gotten onto his secret mission. He guessed she had simply assumed it from all his questions. "Yep, seems there're some silly people who go 'round searching for the ultimate secret of life…or some such thing. Guess she thought I would get a laugh out of that one."

"Well, I do!" Aunt Emma chortled. "There's no mystery there, I can jolly well assure you. The big secret—

ultimate or whatever—is MONEY. The more, the merrier!"

"You think money can really make people happier?"

"You bet! Them that has it are sure as shootin' happier than us poor, miserable creatures that don't."

And with that she banged out the screendoor to hang up the day's washing, leaving Sonny looking distantly out the window, chewing over Aunt Emma's remarks. Certainly, he didn't have any money...but in all his life, even when the going got toughest, he had never felt poor. And what with all his work and study and other interests, never once miserable. Then Grace had opened up still wider, more intriguing worlds. And now she took over his every thought—her image as magnificent as ever, her approach to life equally compelling.

Unlike anyone else he had ever met, Sonny concluded, she walks in beauty, she lives for beauty. She keeps her thoughts and spirit beautiful. She surrounds herself with beauty. She filters out every impulse from the outside world except those that contribute to beauty. So she became beautiful—and would have become so even if she had been as homely as a mud fence. And she had shared that beauty wholeheartedly with him...gloriously...in a way that still made his skin crawl.

Had she also bared for him the ultimate secret of life? He shook his head, too upset at the moment to be sure of anything. Certainly, she had brought him closer to his goal than anything or anyone so far. But he couldn't be certain that even her answer was enough. Hadn't the Reverend Smith and J.P. put forward their own—different—answers?

But was it also possible that the ultimate secret lay in all of these answers put together? In that case, though, shouldn't there be a connecting thread—a kind of glue that joined them all into a unified whole? No answers occurred to him...so Sonny decided he had to go on with the search, even as Grace had urged him to do in her book inscriptions.

That Christmas season the postman delivered a letter postmarked Seattle and addressed to "The Sebrings."

"Cain't understand who'd be sendin' us this," Aunt Emma said as she slit open the envelope. But Sonny knew...and his heart almost stopped. Inside was a plain card written in a well-remembered, beloved script:

"Love God.
"Love your family.
"Love thy neighbor.
"Love the memories of your dearest friends.
"Love Grace Ann
"(& Don) Deere."

"My, my! Didn't know she felt all that close to us'ns," Aunt Emma humphed. "And looky here! She's s'posed to be so high-fallutin' edgycaited...but she didn't know 'nough to put a comma after 'love'."

Well, Sonny knew that was no accident. He felt his whole being would burst with sheer joy. Here she was asking for his love, as well as his forgiveness for her leaving without saying good-bye. But there was nothing to forgive; he had understood immediately. He excused himself and headed outside...and let the cold north wind blow over his face.

Dear Grace Ann, he breathed, you remember, too!

He looked up into the night sky, found the Big Dipper and followed its end-pointers to the North Star, turned to the left and looked searchingly far off beyond the northwest horizon...and vowed that some day, somehow, somewhere they would meet again.

Chapter 12
Crossing the River

As his last year of high school resumed after the Holidays, Sonny began putting together a secret plan to pull up stakes after graduation and head west. He simply couldn't shake thoughts of Grace from his mind. However, as the days marched by into Spring and past his 17th birthday, he began to have some second, much more sober thoughts. What in the world would Grace do with a lovesick calf hanging around making goo-goo eyes at her? And, even more ominous, what would her husband do?

So Sonny eventually scrapped his plan and decided, instead, to concentrate on graduating. Even though he would hold onto, with all his might, his dream of seeing Grace again.

The time soon came for his last day at Cheswick High and his first, dreaded public speech—his Valedictory address. Sonny hadn't been so frightened since the Great Flood nearly five years before. He felt his heart pounding, throat choking, stomach churning, hands trembling, head aching. He vowed that if he ever got through this ordeal in one piece, he would never, ever give another speech again in his whole life.

He sat sweating beneath a black robe and square hat in the front row of the Cheswick High School graduating class of 1941, on a raised stage facing an auditorium jam-packed with people. It was the same place that, at other times, had echoed with the joyful sounds of basketball games and other sports events. But for Sonny there was no joy in Cheswick this day.

Now he looked out over a large crowd where everyone was gaily dressed in Summer colors. They looked friendly enough, he had to admit. It should also have helped that his old buddies, Sis and Aunt Emma, were right out there in front, lending him precious moral support.

Mom should have been sitting right beside them, too. This time for sure, she had written, she really wanted to be on hand. But then it turned out that she had to attend graduation exercises at her own school instead. In any event, she sent a touching note of congratulations and best wishes, writing a PS at the end:

"I assume you're winding up work on your search for the real America. And how's it going with the ultimate secret of life? Will be looking forward to discussing both with you real soon."

Well, he could have added, so was he!

Sonny had been experiencing all kinds of qualms all morning over the upcoming chore he had to perform, and this added immeasurably to his present internal uproar. So now he looked out and saw all eyes boring straight into him...and felt that everyone was ready to pounce at his slightest move. He tried mightily to bury himself in his hard folding chair.

"Darn it all!" he said angrily to himself, "why are my nerves always getting in the way of what I'm trying to do?"

He had asked the class home-room teacher, Jack Raleigh, the same question earlier in rehearsing his talk and got a pretty pointed answer:

"The problem, Sonny, is you're straining too hard to make a good impression. Sure, you don't want to make a fool out of yourself when you speak. But the great irony is that the more you fear looking foolish, the more likely it is that you will. You've got to relax and dare to make some mistakes. And even have people laugh at them. Or at yourself. It's like the first time you tried to speak Spanish here at school. Remember? You used the wrong words in the wrong way and mispronounced everything. But it was only when you dared to do this...in spite of the hilarious giggles it set off...that you began making real progress."

Principal Barker, apparently not bothered by anything like Sonny's qualms, was now speaking at considerable length about the glories of education and graduation. Yet Sonny, completely pre-occupied with his own problems, hardly heard a word.

He should never have allowed this to happen! Today, Jenny Lee Simms might well have stood here giving the Valedictory (which Aunt Emma kept calling the vale-victory). But Jenny was now lucky enough to be sitting in the row behind him. Which led Sonny to conclude that this simply showed how much smarter she was.

Course, he would have done just about anything for Jenny Lee, anyway. The other night at the graduation dance, she had danced with him several times, and mighty close to boot. He had shown her the "Paris shuffle" that Grace had taught him. And she had loved it! Then, at the end of the last dance, she had kissed him on the cheek. Well, he had almost fallen right down on the floor.

Clay, who now sat alongside him on the stage, maintained that Jenny Lee was only setting Sonny up for the slaughter, which was now at hand. He really didn't want to believe that, but his suspicions were growing.

In his inner pocket was the short, typed-out speech he was

supposed to give—one that Mr. Raleigh had worked up for him. His main problem was that he didn't like it. It just didn't sound like him. In fact, it sounded like all the fluff Mrs. Barker was now orating. He decided he just had to try to come up with his own comments, instead—preferably something mercifully short and to the point.

Oh, oh! Sonny noted with alarm that the principal was now winding up at the podium. But no, he was saved! Temporarily, that is. Mr. Raleigh was stepping forward to talk about the class itself. Sonny let loose a quaking sigh of relief.

Clay, seeing his pal's agitation, whispered that the best way to deal with stage-fright was to focus on something else. Okay, Sonny murmured, he would…hard….

• • •

These past four years of high school had passed like a dream. Classes in English, science, algebra and geometry, geography, Latin and Spanish had marched by in a fascinating progression, and he had gotten top grades in almost all subjects. Not that he considered himself that smart. But he had arrived in this farm community seven years before with one unusual advantage over his fellow students. Growing up on city streets and playing and fighting with every race and nationality, religion and creed, had given him a special perspective. No one had to tell him the world was round. From the hard knocks of personal experience, he already knew it.

The strange thing about such a radical change-over, though, was that he sometimes felt as if he had been caught up in an eerie Time Machine and magically projected from modern-day urban life all the way back into the last century. He had long and fervently hoped for a reverse projection, but Mom's ongoing absence had put a stop to that. And lately, by contrast, he had found himself hoping just as fervently that his present wonderful world could go on and on.

Then, there was his inherited love of reading and search for knowledge—which, as J.P. Appleton had predicted, was actually proving itself a great adventure. Sad to say, though, there were some school subjects, like Phys Ed, typing and public speaking, where he hadn't scored so well. But Jenny Lee did well in these classes, and that was why the two of them had been running a neck-and-neck race in the overall class standings. He hadn't really minded the prospect of her winning, though, since as special punishment for her efforts, she would have to give the dreaded Valedictory speech. But now, incredibly, the tables had been turned...and he had become the goat! The final grade ratings gave him the nod by an eyelash.

He moaned out loud, almost kicking himself right there in public for his stupidity. Why, he could have lain back just a little in almost any subject and Jenny Lee would have won. But wasn't he obliged to do his best...always, as J.P. had so pointedly urged him back in their tomato patch discussions?

Thinking back to his first days along the *Ohio*, he recalled how he had found four guiding stars: *The Holy Bible*, *McGuffey's Reader*, the *Boy Scout Handbook* and his frayed American history text, with its great documents on mankind in a free society. These books had given him perspective and a sense of stability, a secure frame of reference against which he could judge the value of almost everything.

They had also finally guided him to the deeper meaning of the real America which he had spent the past seven years exploring. He had discovered that this special, more human America was dedicated first and foremost to hard work, home and family, strict "raisin'," tough schooling, a deep spiritual commitment, community involvement and love of country. Yet, there were specific aspects that still eluded him. So, overwhelmed by the sheer volume of all his discoveries and reports to Mom, he recently went to the wisest person he knew—J.P.—and laid his cards on the table. What was the practical significance behind his findings?

This kicked off a lot of hard thinking, particularly on J.P.'s part, and much back-and-forth talk. Finally, it was settled that these books and way of life taught....

...People to work, to build, to produce, to achieve, to excel.

...Civility and decency, tolerance and a spirit of compromise and cooperation—the basic building blocks of any civilization worthy of the name.

...What America, liberty, democracy, human rights and self-governing are all about, as well as the true nature of their brutal and oppressive opposites—communism, fascism and all the other forms of tyranny that exact obedience at the point of a gun and seek to crush the human spirit.

...That freedom without individual responsibility and self-discipline leads to anarchy—that freedom gives you the priceless chance to control yourself rather than have the state do it for you, and truly develop as a human being.

...Orderliness and basic hygiene, respect for our elders, and reverence for those most fragile parents of us all: Mother Nature and the environment.

...That there's a spiritual world beyond the realms of reason and the senses, which can enrich our lives, ennoble the soul and provide ultimate meaning for existence.

So Sonny felt that his long, eventful search for the real America had finally reached the goals Mom had set and was now finished. And one day, he decided, he would retrieve all the letters he had written and put them together into a book so that every other boy and girl could share in his discovery.

As for his search for the ultimate secret of life, though, he had to admit he was now roundly confused by all the various clues to this mystery. So much so that he had set the whole matter aside until he could talk to Mom. Hadn't she said that the fog would lift one day and there would appear the answer?

Sonny breathed an audible "yes" and nodded his head.

"Hey, man, now you're day-dreaming," Clay whispered. "You're supposed to focus on something tangible!"

Sonny nodded and decided to try the future....

• • •

Surprisingly, the Cheswick Women's Club had selected him to receive its special award for scholarship—a year's tuition at Marshall College. He suspected, but couldn't prove it, that this had come about through some backstage pushing from Mrs. Appleton, who was active in the group. So J.P., he concluded, had apparently taken a hand in providing some of the means toward his goal of attending college.

College! It was amazing, Sonny thought: It had taken eight generations in America but, finally, the Sebrings had turned up someone to attend college. And what was he going to do with this unexpected opportunity? Well, he had resolved all those questions J.P. raised during their old tomato patch talk by deciding to begin with Pre-Med studies...and otherwise postpone any refinements on this decision into the future.

The guy now speaking had a lot to do with that decision. Mr. Raleigh taught General Science. But he maintained that he was a teacher not of Biology or Physics or Chemistry or

Astronomy, but of Wonder. Everything in this world, he told his classes, had a fascinating story to tell, from the tiniest grain of sand to the glories of the universe, from the lowest worm to the human anatomy, from man's inventions to the mystery of life itself. From him, Sonny had learned to look at the world around him with a sense of awe, of respect...yes, of wonder. And wasn't human existence the greatest wonder of all? So medical study it was going to be.

Arnie, meanwhile, steadfastly maintaining his unblemished record of avoiding studies—past, present and future—had hit it off with the Pirates and was now "farmed out" as a shortstop with their Oil City farm club. Sis had landed a job as a typist with *The Huntington Advertiser* and was staying with Uncle Joe temporarily while going to secretarial school at night.

Then came the shocker: As family members drifted away, Aunt Emma, who had proven to be a real pal and supporter, announced she would sell their house and move to Huntington, where Sonny would attend college. It was a rough blow, for losing the memory-packed little farm was like losing part of his soul. He could hardly blame her, though. For years she had almost single-handedly pulled the family pieces together and made their little place on the riverbank a real home.

Moving into the city had one big advantage, however: Mom could now visit with him without colliding with Aunt Emma. And soon, she said, she would catch a bus and do just that.

It had taken time, but Sonny had also finally figured out why Aunt Emma complained so loud and long about money problems. Since no one he knew seemed particularly anxious to take in and raise another couple's three children, Dad had apparently inveigled his sister into doing so by promising to send her considerable sums regularly. But this had proven impossible under Depression-era employment conditions. Even so, Aunt Emma felt both sandbagged and short-changed...and vented her feelings accordingly. For her, as she had both feared and stated so often, life was no joke at all.

Making the best of his own impoverished situation, Sonny had managed to get a clerk's job at the Marshall College Library. Aunt Emma, meanwhile, was out looking for an apartment for her, Sonny and his Sister, plus Bowser. She reasoned: "The family is ev'rything; if we don't hang together, we'll darn well hang separate."

Thinking of Bowser brought a smile. The little dog had proven himself such a warm and wonderful pal that they had actually knighted him. No more names like mongrel or mutt, just as Arnie could no longer call his brother a runt or shrimp. As Sis had suggested that night the river had washed Bowser up ages ago, their dog had now become SIR Bowser!

Strange, when Sonny wrote his father that he would be going to college, Dad had written back, "Forget all that college nonsense! Come on up to Detroit and I'll get you a good job and...."

Well, that reaction left him puzzled...and hurt, too. He had discussed the situation with J.P. and Mr. Raleigh, and finally decided after some soul-searching that he would simply have to go against his father's wishes and follow his own star, regardless of where that might lead.

And who could be sure these days what the future might hold? The news reports from overseas were terrible. Europe was on fire, just like their old scout meetinghouse, with one country after the other falling before Hitler's seemingly invincible legions. And nothing but trouble was reported with the Japanese in the Pacific.

The worst personal aspect of all this was that Sonny was now 17 and Arnie, 20. If America was drawn into the war, which J.P. said was bound to happen, they would be the first to go, whether they had to or not. Arnie, he knew, would do so simply because he was Arnie.

And Sonny? Well, he had asked himself that same question many times, and the same answer now came back again. He had found that some things were more important than life itself—or than his own life, in any event. There was love of God and this blessed country; devotion to family, friends and neighbors; and an unbreakable commitment to the principles and values he had grown up with and believed in.

Most important, if he had to go to war, he would not go alone. He would go with and have at his side a very special friend, supporter and protector. He could hear His voice once more, sharp and clear...just as he had heard it that night along the river long ago:

I am with you always—even unto the end of the world. Just reach up and take my hand.

This brought back another memory—this one of that long-past poetry recital in the Shirlington grade school. This led Sonny to recall wistfully the last lines of the last poem in McGuffey's Reader, "My Mother's Bible":

"The mines of earth no treasures give
   That could this volume buy;
In teaching me the way to live,
   It taught me how to die."

A clapping noise broke into his thoughts, jarring him into realizing how far away he had traveled. And...oh, no! It was for him! In fact, Mr. Raleigh had just finished introducing him.

For one crazy moment, he thought of bolting out the side door and running for his life. Instead, he gathered his dark robe around and marched unsteadily to the podium, only half conscious of his surroundings. Now, he feared, would come the final horror: He would open his mouth and nothing, NOTHING, would come out.

He gripped the podium hard and lifted his eyes toward the audience...and a strange thing happened. He looked at Aunt Emma and saw on her face such a strained expression of concern on his behalf that he nearly laughed out loud.

"Hey, Aunt Emma," he felt like calling, "I'm the one who should be worried!"

He smiled at her. She smiled back...and Sonny began to speak. It was heavy going at first. Haltingly, he thanked his teacher for the introduction, then allowed as how he had in his pocket the real valedictory speech—but wanted, instead, to make a few personal remarks.

Well, he thought the audience looked downright relieved at that comment. But not Mr. Raleigh, whose face bore an expression of concern bordering on alarm.

Numerous "ers" and "ahs" followed...until, finally getting over the hump, Sonny began to hit stride:

"On behalf of all my classmates—all these lucky people you see up here today—I would like to make this a very special Thanksgiving Day...even though it's mid-June."

He took a long, deep breath and gripped the podium harder.

"As I look around this familiar old room, I can't help but think of what these four years here have meant to me...and to my classmates. We graduate today and enter a very uncertain, a very dangerous world. And I suspect we'll shortly forget some of what we learned here. But there's one thing we can

NEVER forget and that's the experience of it all. It's been fun. It's been rewarding. It's been FANTASTIC!"

Oh, my, Sonny thought, I'm beginning to sound like Preacher Johnson. But maybe, just maybe, I might yet live through this ordeal.

"You out there—our families—have made that experience possible. And you up here—our teachers—GAVE it to us… sometimes in no uncertain terms!"

Gee, was that laughter he was hearing? he wondered.

"So I want to single out the REAL people we should be honoring today. And I would like to ask all my classmates to join in a great big cheer…not for us but for all our TEACHERS."

Sonny turned to the rooting section behind him and called out, "Okay, gang, let's give it to THEM!"

And the auditorium shook with the booming release of pent-up emotions from the whole graduating class. Sonny noticed that their teachers—even Mr. Raleigh—were laughing at the sudden turn of events and unexpected public acclaim. But they were also shifting around a bit in their chairs, not quite sure of what to make of it all. Nor was he!

He waited a moment, then held up his hand:

"And now I would like to ask everyone—EVERYONE—to join in a big cheer for our families—for all of you out there who made all of this possible for all of us up here."

And an even bigger cheer went up from teachers, students, the whole assembly. It rocked the building, and kept going on and on.

Sonny waved to the noisemakers and to Aunt Emma and Sis, said a completely inaudible "Thank you!"…and now bolted out the sidedoor. Outside, he leaned up against the cool brick wall and gulped down several deep breaths.

He had survived!

The noise was subsiding, and he started to go back. But as he turned around, he found himself looking out through a break in the trees on the riverbank and beyond the playing field. And there across the broad Ohio he saw the silhouetted jumble of city buildings and Marshall College on the far shore. It was a different world—a VERY different world—a difficult and deeply challenging world.

"Tomorrow," he said to no one in particular, "tomorrow I will cross the river."

A sudden wave of apprehension swept over him as he realized the enormity of coming changes in his life. He caught his breath, dropped his head in uncertainty and fear and closed his eyes hard. Regaining his composure after a second, he returned to the auditorium, meeting with a flurry of cheers and laughs.

The diplomas were handed out and the ceremony concluded. This was followed by a lot of milling around, with friends and neighbors congratulating the new crop of graduates and everyone saying so-long—some tearfully, some joyfully. Sonny, who a few minutes earlier had been walking on air, came down to earth as the family left early and caught a ride home with a Shirlington neighbor.

Back at the old house on the riverbank, Sis and Aunt Emma got together on the frontporch for a talk. But Sonny felt a need to be alone, so he excused himself and walked toward the back. Tomorrow, finally, he would indeed cross the river...and he didn't like it. He looked around wistfully at all the things he had come to know and love. There was the chicken shed that had housed old Jerry with his rousing wake-up call, the Jonathan that had survived the Great Flood, Jack and Jill's pigpen, the cistern and the garden and the chopping block.

He walked on, down to the river to the spot where Grampaw died. It was now a hallowed place where they had set up a small white cross. The next flood, he knew, would sweep it away. But not the memory. In fact, the place now seemed kind of spooky. So Sonny wandered on upriver, to the fallen willow where he and Grace had sat and talked so many times. And what memories that brought back!

Sonny sat down in exactly the same spot as during those inspiring sessions and looked out over the river's glistening surface. He turned his head to the right, toward the far-off Kentucky hills, to Mom's old stomping grounds. Just thinking of her made him feel vaguely irritated.

How...he wondered, how could Mom have sent him on such a wild goose chase as searching for the ultimate secret of life? What could she possibly have meant by handing him such an impossible assignment? Was there something in her instructions that he had somehow missed?

Sonny knew his mother well enough to know that she wouldn't ask him to do something without the most serious intent. But what, he pressed himself to answer, could that be?

Sis, being a couple years older and no little wiser, maintained that Mom had put Sonny onto these twin missions so that he would have plenty to think about and not feel too homesick for their old place in Pittsburgh. For his part, however, he felt something much more was involved.

"Maybe life itself is a wild goose chase." he declared aloud in disgust. He sensed deeply Grace's presence and wished she were here to talk to again. SHE would know the answer, he felt.

Yes, it was there, right before his eyes, that she had stood and reached toward the heavens. For what? For meaning? she herself had asked. Or understanding? Or life itself? "Reaching" was the name she had given that beautiful, singular posture.

REACHING!

Suddenly, a lot of those old clues began to flash inside Sonny's head, like lights coming on in a ballpark for a night game. J.P. had once shocked him by maintaining that striving and struggling to reach goals was more important even than attaining those goals. That the road itself was the goal, not the destination.

And what had Mom said when she first told him to search for the ultimate secret of life? That searching is the key. And when, completely bewildered, he had written asking for clarification of his assignment, what answer came back? "Keep searching!"

That had seemed as enigmatic then as a pronouncement from the Oracle of Delphi. But what if his mother wasn't urging him to keep searching, but was actually providing THE answer? That searching, striving, reaching for answers…that THIS is the ultimate secret of life?

Sonny leaped to his feet, filled with excitement. Yes, that had to be the answer! All along, his eyes had probably been fixed like glue on the wrong target. It now struck him that it was probably a total waste of time searching FOR the ultimate secret of life. Searching IS the ultimate secret of life!

Thinking further over his old clues, he found that from J.P. and his teachers he had learned to search for knowledge and ultimate truth, however elusive.

From Grace Deere, he had learned to explore the world of art and culture and search for beauty.

From Pastor Smith, he had learned to search for the greatest personal prize of all—a nobility of spirit—that wondrous quality that brings us closest to the Creator, to the All-Mighty, the Eternal.

Finally, from his own family, as well as everyone he had encountered in life, he had learned something crucial, too: To break out of the shell of self-absorption, search for human understanding and develop a pervading concern for others.

In fact, Sonny concluded, this HAD to be the Fourth Dimension Grace had hinted at—the final piece in the make-up of the complete person she said he should strive to become. For wasn't this what Jesus had taught during His short time on earth? And what Scouting had taught, too? And wasn't caring for and helping others also fundamental to the spirit of the real America he had spent so much time exploring?

This key dimension isn't merely a matter of doing good, either—important as that is, he decided. For, as Pastor Smith had said, unless people can really begin to care for others, could there ever be peace in our homes? Our neighborhoods? Or among nations?

The ideal of the 4-Dimensional Human struck him as closely connected to America, too. For wasn't this the grand human model that our forefathers had striven so mightily to attain, even when our continent was still virtually a wilderness? Thomas Jefferson had to be a foremost example. Countless others had come close through the years, too, with many scoring high in one or two areas, and some in three—but few, very few in all four.

Nor was learning and cultural awareness all that decisive in this final human equation, Sonny decided. Some of the finest people he knew didn't have much formal education, but they ranked A-1 in spiritual depth and concern for others. They had character!

And weren't J.P., Pastor Smith and Grace Ann just as impressive examples in their own way? They, too, went on searching through life—through personal contacts, books and the arts, religion and philosophy, travel and daily experience. And oh, how lucky he had been to have these guiding stars!

Yet, Sonny now began to realize that in all the vital areas of life they had covered—knowledge, cultural awareness, spiritual values and human understanding—he would probably never find any absolute answers. Solving life's mysteries looked as difficult as chasing a rainbow. Yet, wasn't man compelled to go on striving, reaching, searching?

He also began to realize what a grand and glorious thing life could be as long as one kept up the search, the quest for those elusive answers. And if you did, wouldn't you always remain young in spirit, regardless of age?

Perhaps this was even man's ultimate glory: To never, never give up the searching, the upward striving...despite the difficulties, the disappointments, the defeats. And that, Sonny now decided, had to be what his mother intended for him to discover—on his own, if possible—when she put him onto this fantastic mission.

Sonny's conclusions triggered a great sigh of relief. He felt as though he had long been banging his head against a closed door. And suddenly this door had opened, revealing the way to an appealing, deeply experienced, fulfilling life. The same kind of exaltation swept over him that Grace must have felt as she reached toward the clouds, the sky, the stars—toward heaven itself.

Instead of looking upward now, however, he bowed his head for a long, thoughtful moment...and only gradually became aware he was looking at his hands. They rested in his lap, folded and sun-darkened, the long fingers blunted and the palms calloused by wielding a thousand hoes, pitchforks, spades, axes, shovels, picks, and sledgehammers. And there on the back of his left hand, etched against the tan, stood a small, jagged white cross—an indelible reminder of that nearly disastrous encounter which he and Grampaw had with the rattler long ago.

All at once an image came out of nowhere and stuck in Sonny's mind. He saw again a tall, straight, weather-scarred old-timer wearing faded over-alls and a floppy straw hat. There he stood, smiling and waiting, swinging a big bucket in his hand. And right alongside, no higher than his shoulder, came an admiring boy, clad in the same outfit. Side by side, they walked slowly across the fog-shrouded meadow...finally disappearing into the far-away hills.

Author's Afterword

One night during a raging storm at sea in early 1946, the *S.S. Byron Darnton*—one of those workhorse American Liberty ships of World War II whose tub-like silhouette earned them the name of "the ugly ducklings of the seven seas"—piled up on a reef off the coast of Scotland, broke in two, and sank. An unusual circumstance emerged from this maritime disaster: Aboard were seven young Norwegian women bound for American colleges under the first postwar scholarship exchange program. Luckily, all were rescued. After a week of recovery in Glasgow, they set sail for the New World on another U.S. Liberty ship, the *S.S. William B. Travis*.

One of the engineering officers aboard the *Travis*, winding up 3 1/2 years of wartime service with the U.S. Merchant Marine, just happened to be the author of this book. And that's how I came to meet my future wife—Inger Krogh, of Oslo, daughter of Norway's beloved opera and folk singer, the late Erling Krogh.

To say that this chance meeting on the high seas changed my life would be putting it mildly. For the fair Inger turned out to be much more than this wartime seaman had bargained for. As this newcomer's sympathetic yet intrinsically honest and objective gaze took in the immensely varied, often chaotic American scene, she came to ask a million probing questions about this new land. None were easy to answer for a thoroughly indoctrinated ("culturalized") native-born son. Many were irritating. Some infuriating.

In forcing me to take off my blinders and see America as others see it, she also made me begin to think—yes, actually think—of what it is that makes an American. Are there unique ingredients in our culture and upbringing that make us significantly different from other peoples? And what are their impact and significance?

Intimate involvement in subsequent years with my wife's foreign society served to sharpen these questions. So did a year's research the two of us undertook into government policies across Europe and the Mideast and into the Soviet Union in the early 1960s under a prized Eisenhower Exchange Fellowship.

Now, take a long leap forward to the 1980s....

After an eventful career in Washington news reporting, public affairs and government, I was asked by the American Legion to overhaul the organization's 8,000,000-reader general-interest publication, *The American Legion Magazine*. Working with staff to reshape graphics and editorial focus, we decided among other things to launch a series of articles by national leaders that would reach back into their childhoods and develop the theme, "This Is My America." Easier planned than done! People we contacted seemed either unable to put it all together or didn't have the time to do so. I then concluded I would have to fall back on my own childhood as offering precisely the elements the series was seeking to bring out. Yet, I also felt that the telling of this story would require more than an article's format. The result of all this, after many delays, is what you've just read: **AMERICA: The Search and the Secret.**

James N. Sites

I'm sure that even the most casual reader will have concluded by now that Sonny Sebring, the boy, must surely have grown up to become Jim Sites the man. And you're right, up to a point. My brother and sister and I were "farmed out" from our native Pittsburgh during the rough years of the Great Depression, and I grew up in precisely this story's setting, living through similar experiences. It's also worth noting that the name of Sebring wasn't just pulled out of a hat; it's the family name of my mother's mother.

So this story is as true to this basic segment of American life as you can get. It was put into the form of an autobiographical novel, with name changes, to allow for free expression. This form was chosen to make the story more vivid for the reader. Besides, as life proves every day, there's much nonfiction in fiction, and a great deal of fiction in nonfiction.

It may not have been necessary to novelize Sonny's story "in order to protect the innocent," as publishers sometimes put it. Oceans of water have flowed down the Ohio in the hectic half-century since he lived alongside that great river, and almost all those whom Sonny knew, learned from, and loved have been scattered over the earth or passed on beyond. Even the locale is hardly recognizable. Grampaw's little white house on the riverbank has long since made way for modern ranchtypes. A superhighway has been gouged through the pastureland at the base of the hill where

Sonny discovered his spring and peaceful ravine. And the river has been altered; high dams built at enormous public expense to provide "low cost" transportation for riverside industry have raised the water level and obliterated the rock-strewn shore, the gnarled willows and much of the fertile bottomland that provided the setting for this story.

And yet that former world lives on today, as fresh and vital as though the events of the foregoing 12 chapters had happened only yesterday. Their memories have been sustained by the deepest attachment—the kind a child feels for his mother—an attachment born of awareness.

An interesting word, AWARENESS. Most people live lives of unquestioning acceptance of the "naturalness," if not the superiority, of their surroundings and customs. So did Sonny, for the first decade of his life. Then he found himself uprooted from the steep streets of his city and transplanted to a wholly new, rural environment. And while he remembers almost nothing of his first 10 years, he recalls almost everything of the next 7. For awareness had hit, as hard as a sledgehammer. Just as awareness also hit this writer when he married a foreigner and came to see America and its unique qualities through the searching eyes of a newcomer.

(Speaking of newcomers, it's worth noting that wife Inger never gave up on the primary mission that brought her to America. Eleven years, three schools, two sons, several jobs and a U.S. citizenship later, she received her Master's Degree from Catholic University and went on to become a librarian, foreign-language tour guide and teacher of Norwegian at the U.S. State Department's Foreign Service Institute. Inger and her own discoveries of America—ah, but that's *another* story!)

As the one who lived Sonny's story, it is my fondest

hope that the main beneficiaries of this unadorned, unabashed, unapologetic reaffirmation of faith in America and its traditional values might be the newest generation of our young people. For these are values that emphasize home and family, tough schooling, spiritual commitment, community involvement and love of country. Values from a very special yesterday that the American centuries have shown to work...and which can serve as building blocks for tomorrow. For it is the young who, like Sonny, must go through the often-rending process of growing up and learning about living—about good and evil, handling joy and sorrow and coping with tragedy, getting along with others and getting educated and laying a solid personal foundation for the future. And seldom with adequate guidance from their elders...or from the past.

This is what gives added importance to the second, more personal aspect of this story. For in Sonny's discovery of the Four Dimensional Human lies a vision of a grand alternative development goal for young people over the narrow, job-related objectives of our technology-driven, commercialized age. Obviously, people have to learn enough to earn a living; but learning to live is equally imperative. Thus this inspiring vision of the intensively developed, contributing being that anyone can strive to become—in his own interest as well as that of everyone he encounters.

This book, therefore, is essentially a celebration of not only America's traditional values but also of the vast, though seldom realized, potentials for human development. Reaching these, however, would require that parents, educators, and public leaders, first, expand their vision of what a person CAN become and, second, fight head-on against the debasing effects of an increasingly de-personalized, money-possessed, entertainment-obsessed society.

Not easy! Especially when the main models of achievement and success seem to be jet-setting movie, rock and media stars, Midas-touched sports figures, smooth talkers and big spenders. Yet, the results of this tough, challenging, 4-D approach can be remarkable: Less emptiness and aimlessness among the young, plus the rewarding feeling one gets from putting real effort into fulfilling one's inborn capabilities and promises.

Personal experience tells me that today's young people are much smarter than their elders give them credit for being. They ask as many questions as Sonny did while searching for the real America and the ultimate secret of life. And they deserve realistic answers, just as Sonny got in this chronicle of exploration, discovery and hope. They're also smart enough to realize that there's something fundamentally wrong with any society or way of life that sinks into a let-it-all-hang out, anything-goes approach: They soon find that nothing goes.

There's another lesson in Sonny's story that today's hardpressed young people and their harassed parents might take note of, as well—especially those who have missed out on America's amazing postwar affluence: Hard times at home and menial work outside are no barriers whatever to advancement in life. The real keys are developing positive attitudes, acquiring knowledge and putting forth the hard effort it takes.

It can be done! ***AMERICA: The Search and the Secret*** proves that.

James N. Sites